LEBANON PUBLIC LIBRARY
W9-CFB-229

The Heart's Progress

Also by Claudia Bepko

The Responsibility Trap
(co-author)

Too Good for Her Own Good
(co-author)

Singing at the Top of Our Lungs: Women, Love, and Creativity
(co-author)

Feminism and Addiction
(editor)

The Heart's Progress

A LESBIAN MEMOIR

Claudia Bepko

VIKING

VIKING
Published by the Penguin Group
Penguin Books USA Inc., 375 Hudson Street,
New York, New York 10014, U.S.A.
Penguin Books Ltd, 27 Wrights Lane,
London W8 5TZ, England
Penguin Books Australia Ltd, Ringwood,
Victoria, Australia
Penguin Books Canada Ltd, 10 Alcorn Avenue,
Toronto, Ontario, Canada M4V 3B2
Penguin Books (N.Z.) Ltd, 182–190 Wairau Road,
Auckland 10, New Zealand

Penguin Books Ltd, Registered Offices:
Harmondsworth, Middlesex, England

First published in 1997 by Viking Penguin,
a division of Penguin Books USA Inc.

10 9 8 7 6 5 4 3 2 1

LIBRARY OF CONGRESS CATALOGING IN PUBLICATION DATA
Bepko, Claudia.
The heart's progress / Claudia Bepko.
p. cm.
ISBN 0-670-85921-4
1. Bepko, Claudia. 2. Lesbians—United States—Biography.
3. Family therapists—United States—Biography. I. Title.
HQ75.4.B47A3 1997
307.76'63'092—dc20
[B] 96-32570

This book is printed on acid-free paper.
♾

Printed in the United States of America
Set in New Aster

This book is dedicated to
the memory of Barbara Schnurr,
whose leaving I was privileged to witness,
and to Molly, for coming back.

Acknowledgments

Many people helped in the process of writing this book, with both editorial suggestions and emotional support. Jane Sloven, Ellen Fox, and Jenny Hanson each read early versions of the manuscript. A dear friend who wishes not to be named read tirelessly, edited, discussed, and in general bolstered me through many rewrites. Betsey Alden, Barb Schnurr, Ann Hartman, and Joan Laird kept me afloat emotionally in many important ways. My agent, Joy Harris, and her late husband were instrumental in shaping the early proposal. My editor, Jane von Mehren, was patient, persistent, and gentle in her work with my writing. Harriet Lerner, as always, gave generous amounts of time, support, and encouragement. Pat Peard and the Authors Guild offered excellent legal counsel. I am deeply grateful to them all.

The lives of many people connected to me are described in this narrative. To be as respectful of their privacy as possible, I have altered characteristics, changed names, fictionalized certain minor details and events, and changed much identifying data.

Contents

Prologue

I don't recall how I heard about the woman or how I knew where to look for her. What I do remember is the bleached, medicinal smell of the hallways and labs of the chemistry building on the campus of the university where I found her.

She propped herself up to sit on one of the lab stools, and, taking my cue from her, I did the same. Classes were over for the day. It was getting dark out; the lights inside were dim.

It was in this redolent, dusky silence that I first confessed to a total stranger that I thought I was a lesbian. Someone had told me that she talked to people about such things and might be able to help. She looked at me for a long while, seeming to mix and weigh and measure me as she might some chemical compound. Finally she said, "You may not be strong enough to be gay." Her pronouncement lodged itself permanently in my mind, and it may be that my life since then has been dedicated to proving her wrong.

To her, I must have seemed wide-eyed and vulnerable—heterosexual, even, since I was married then. Indeed, I was not strong enough to be gay, if being gay meant putting on the mantle one is vested with by society—the cloak of deviance and isolation, the shroud of "otherness." I was capable only of knowing whom I loved. And I was beginning to acknowledge the truth that love and pain would forever be connected for me and that my life would be hard. Not that this is not a truth for all of us, but I didn't know that then.

That night, I was my usual polite self. I slid down off the lab stool, thanked the woman, and found my way out onto the campus knowing no more than when I had gone in. The man I had married waited for me at home. I still looked the part of a "normal" woman. I made love with a man and worried about birth control. I cooked gourmet meals for our church get-togethers. I enjoyed all the social privileges of my married state. When it was expedient, I could call myself "Mrs." How responsible and upstanding it made me feel! How well it let me off the hook!

Underneath, however, none of it was true; the role was a false one. The truth was that when he and I made love, it would be satisfying enough and companionable, but afterward I would cry because I longed to be with a woman. The feeling rarely left me; it haunted my days and nights, my body. My journals were filled with tormented passages questioning myself, wondering how this could be. He tried to be understanding, listened to my obsessions much more than he should have. But deep down he thought it was only a phase I was going through, and that sooner or later I would get it out of my system.

I never have, and I don't expect I ever will. Occasionally I think that if we really do live many lives, I would still prefer to love a woman in a next one. I simply cannot conceive of life without the intensely erotic passion I feel for women. I cannot conceive of a life without being myself. Men interest me, but women compel. With men I don't ever quite feel myself; with women, I am most fully who I am.

I learned very little from the meeting in the chemistry building; it was a dead end in my quest to know how to be a lesbian. I remember thinking that I found the woman unapproachable and hard, somewhat dour and without warmth. Is this what "real" lesbians are like? I thought. There was more anguish and self-doubt because I was a prisoner of stereotype. "They" are all alike. If I am not like the one self-proclaimed lesbian I have met, then I must not be one. So who am I, and why do I have this passion? The questions kept glancing like blows off the already pained surface of my mind. There being nothing else to do, I went back home, cooked dinner, and waited another day for my real life to begin.

I was a woman on the verge. As insignificant as my encounter in the lab might seem, it was a declaration—one step toward a coming out to myself. I was unraveling a great mystery. There had been signs and signals along the way, but until that point I had denied that my emotional experience of life could mean I was a lesbian. I had never even used the word.

Now I see that the longing for a woman was always there. It brought me to my knees, this feeling; it was inevitable, uncompromising. It didn't matter that I acquired a cloak of deviance and that some people despised me. I loved who I loved, and that reality was powerful enough to fight for.

I think of my lesbianism as the wildness in me. It is the single most continuous current of energy in my life. My love for women is the root of my passion; it is what animates and drives me; it is the source of all peace. It is my spiritual path. It has not been an easy one, but no authentic path ever is. That's what a path is—something that teaches, hones, and shapes you, that fires you in the kiln of exposure. I didn't choose this path; it chose me. All these years I have just followed it, being led where I seemed meant to go.

This is a story about the way the path unfolded. It is a story about love and about the absence of love, about the darkness and the brilliance that together make life whole. It is my reflection on the truth of authentic passion and the dangers of avoiding it, though sometimes the detours teach as much as the destinations.

One day we all will accept the primacy of love and passion in our lives. We won't need to confer our mantles of distinction and disgrace any longer. For now, the different among us tell our stories, because we are all only human and so much need a witness to the truth.

PART ONE

1.
Family Values

My father was beating the dog and the dog was cowering, flinching with every blow of the strap. My sisters and I watched with horror; my heart was racing. My mother shook her head. "Tony, that's enough."

"Shut up, goddamnit. I'm sick of this bastard. He's going to stop this, or I'll keep this up every day until he does."

"Go lay down," he yelled.

The dog, a big, formidable-looking brown boxer with a black mug, raced to his mat by the door and threw himself down, submissive now, panting. His collar was so twisted by his trying to get away that it was choking him.

We all sat down to eat our dinner of pork chops and mashed potatoes and green beans, and nobody said a word. My mother put the food on the table while I poured milk into my sisters' glasses. I didn't even know what the dog had done.

This scene would be repeated often. It wasn't only the dog who got the strap. My sister Ann, five years younger than I, somehow managed to be as unruly and defiant as the dog. There was the evening my father called Ann home from the neighbor's. When she walked in some fifteen minutes later, he glared at her, unhooked his belt, pulled it from around his waist, and started slapping it against the back of her legs, cursing her: "You come when you're called, you little shit."

The bottle of whiskey and the shot glass sat in their usual spot on the counter. My father poured himself another glass of beer and he sat down to eat. Every time he walked into the kitchen for the rest of the night, he took a swig of the whiskey. My mother cleaned the stove for hours, polishing the rim of each burner until it shone; the rest of us went off to our rooms to do our homework and waited for my father to fall asleep.

My father never beat me and I'm not sure why. Somehow I knew he wouldn't dare. When I wanted to defy him, I simply withdrew to my room and stopped talking. Therese, the youngest, was too young, too frail for beatings. It was only Ann who would take him on. Strangely, she was his favorite. When he beat her she stood and laughed at him—she had made up her mind early on that she wouldn't let him make her cry.

My father always said to us, "When I hit you it hurts me more than it hurts you. It's for your own good." Every time he said it, it made less sense to me. Sometimes I thought of fighting back, of challenging this strange premise of his. But when I tried to be rational, to argue back, my mother called me a Philadelphia lawyer. She would say, mocking me, "Oh, you're so abused," and my father would decide that I needed to be punished. I never knew what was hate and what was love in this family; I was always trying to figure it out.

My two sisters and I were raised in New England in a blue-collar town known for its Catholicism, its municipal corruption, and its painstaking replica of the Holy Land built on the highest hill in the area. My early life was dominated by my father, by alcohol, and by the image of the Holy Land's aluminum cross towering over the crumbling factories that had once been the city's economic foundation. The cross's colors were changed depending on the liturgical season, and whenever my family rode through town, our major distraction was to check on its color—not out of devotion to the changing seasons of the church, but because there was nothing else to do.

If there were any other lesbians in that city, I never knew them; but, then again, I never thought to look. Although my sisters and I were all raised in the same family, by the same parents, only I am gay. From the time I was barely five, and clung adoringly to the skirts of an older cousin who visited often on Sundays with my aunt and uncle, I was emotionally drawn to women.

My family was Italian and, of course, Catholic. Both of my parents and numbers of grandparents, aunts, and uncles were alcoholic. My mother was an only child, the daughter of an alcoholic father. She had a wildness in her that was tamed by hardship. She was defeated before she started—shy, dependent on my grandmother, hated by her father. She said she married my father because he was the first of her suitors to come home from the war. She had wanted to be a nurse but married instead. When I was born she was overwhelmed. Then she was left alone with me when my father was called back to the Navy to serve in Korea. She never crooned the delights of having babies. She said I looked like a plucked chicken and that I was sick from the day I was born. The other story she told about my birth was that my father was so certain I would be a boy, he went out and bought a train set. When I turned out to be a girl, the trains were put away. I discovered them years later in a closet. I never much used them, and when I did, it was always with the knowledge that they hadn't been meant for me.

My mother couldn't be warm emotionally except when I was sick. Once, when my fever spiked to 104 or 105, as it often did, and I cried with the pain of an ear infection, I remember her rubbing me with alcohol, stroking my forehead, looking at me with what must have been tenderness, and saying, "I would take the pain for you if I could." I believed her. I never forgot that moment.

In the early days, my mother comforted herself by retreating to what she called the "den." The den was an eight-by-ten room in our little three-bedroom house. A cabinet with glass doors that her father had built stored her books and records. The only other furniture in the room was an aluminum chaise longue chair with a green cushion on it, our toy box, and the record player.

My mother would finish cleaning the kitchen, go to the den, and close the door, and soon we would hear strains of Tchaikovsky and Rimsky-Korsakov bellowing from the room. Or sometimes it was Gershwin or Leroy Anderson. We were not invited in. We knew Mother needed her escape, but sometimes we would push open the door and see her sitting on the floor in front of the record player, her head lowered, totally lost in the music.

Most of her record collection had been given to her by her bachelor uncle Andy. When we were older, we came to understand that Uncle Andy was gay. We learned that as a teenager my mother would visit Uncle Andy at his lover's house and they would listen for hours together to his classical-music collection. Uncle Andy came with his lover to all family functions. Ira was accepted and well loved, but nobody ever named their relationship. Only after I came out did my parents and I talk about Uncle Andy. I was surprised to learn that, accepted as Ira was, nobody understood or liked the fact that he and Andy were gay.

Between the births of Ann and Therese, when I was eleven, my mother lost a baby. One night I woke to sounds of her crying and my father, still dressed from work, talking on the phone. I went to the door of their bedroom. She lay there looking at me; all I could feel was the terror of not knowing what was wrong. "I have to go to the hospital," she said. I was trembling. Finally, I couldn't contain the fear anymore and I raced to her and she held me. It was the only time she ever held me, comforting me while I cried, but nothing more was said. When she came home from the hospital I somehow thought we would be closer, that I would have a real mother. I followed her around the house, looking to her expectantly, waiting for her to become responsive and warm again. But she was as distant as ever, as if nothing had happened. And she mourned because she felt certain that the baby she lost had been a boy—the son she wanted to give my father.

In the emotional absence of my mother, my sister Ann and my grandmother became the central connections in my life. Since I was five years older than Ann, I taught her everything I knew. I played teacher and she played student. We went to my grandmother's house often after school. She gave us little books of scrap paper that she brought home from work, and I would sit at the desk in her den and instruct Ann in her letters and numbers. Ann would write her letters laboriously in the little books. I progressed through the alphabet, giving her homilies that I had heard from some teacher along the way. By the time Ann went to school she already knew her letters and numbers and she was beginning to read. I taught her to play baseball with a Wiffle bat and ball, and she quickly surpassed me in skill. This was the beginning of a fierce competitiveness between us. My father was not the only object of Ann's defiance. Soon she became determined to best me at everything, and she was certainly determined to fight my authority as an older sister. But when we were not fighting, we had wonderful times together. We sang constantly. We would put records on the record player and sing for hours. We learned duets that we performed for my mother and father and anyone else in the family who would listen.

Perhaps it was in the early bonds of sisterhood that I learned the satisfaction of sharing life with a female, because this companionship, this sharing of the good of life, the playfulness, the creativity, was such an important part of my experience. I learned that with females I could be myself, but with males there was always trouble. Even the little boys I played with, Ray-Ray and Howard, who lived on the street behind our house, couldn't be trusted. One day I was an esteemed member of their little band of marauding cowboys who roamed wildly through the neighborhood chasing imaginary bad guys; the next, Ray-Ray's garage door would be resolutely slammed in my face and I would be excluded from this privileged group because I was a girl.

Gradually my mother spent less time in the den with her records and gradually the room came to mean as much to me as it had to her. My father joined me here in the evenings when I pulled out my accordion to practice my lessons. This instrument had been bought with the meager amount of money left after his mother's death. He missed his mother desperately. He would stretch out on the green chaise longue and smile benevolently at me. "Play this" or "play that," he would cajole. "Yes, okay, that's better. Hey, you're getting good." Sometimes he would get his harmonica and join me. Every week he took me for my music lesson. He took pride in me and enjoyed his role. I played for every family picnic and party. My aunts and uncles tolerated me; my father was happy.

One day when I was nine or ten, my mother took me into the den and pulled out her old high school English book. She opened to her favorite poem, Wordsworth's "The Daffodils," and told me to read it. She talked briefly, wistfully, of how she had loved to read. She said I could have the book. From that time on, she begged what little money she could from my father—she had none of her own—to buy a set of children's classics. Once a month a book would come in the mail, and once a month my father would complain about the bill.

Out of these few resources, I built an inner life. I read and read. I created a world in my mind. School and learning became my life. The more bookish I became, the more my father turned away from me. I was becoming more like my mother, and he was angry with her all the time.

And it was in the den that my mother taught me what it meant to be a woman. It was an evening not too long after she had given me the book with the Wordsworth poem. She said, "It's time for us to have a talk." I sat down on the rickety lawn furniture. She stood leaning against the wall, her arms bent behind her back, looking uncomfortable and uneasy. My sister Ann rattled around outside the door, knowing by the look on my mother's face that something serious was happening. My mother never made a point of talking to any of us so deliberately.

As if she were lecturing to a class, she began. "One day soon, you will start to have bleeding once a month. You've seen that it happens to me. I've never tried to hide it from you. This doesn't mean you are sick. It means you have become a woman. And what that means is that you will be able to have babies. You only have babies when you are married and really love a man, but your body will be capable of it and so you must always be very careful with boys about how you behave. I don't think you need to know now how it happens that two people create a baby, but that's what your period means. When it happens I'll show you what you need to do. You must keep yourself very clean. Some people think this is something very negative and they have very bad reactions, but it's not, there's nothing wrong, it's all very normal. It's a special time, it means you are a woman."

This was the end of the talk—she opened the door and left the room. I wandered out into the hall to face giggles from my little sister, and I felt awkward, embarrassed, and alone.

This was all I ever learned directly from my mother about what it meant to be a woman, and this was the last time she ever mentioned sex. This was the mother of the stern reprimands to "keep your hands out from under the covers," who washed our genitals until it hurt when we were small, and who reacted with disgust when she found us playing doctor. I don't know what she thought about sexual feeling, but she never alluded to it.

When I was twelve we moved to a new house. Now I had my own room. Ann and I became more separate, and Therese was born. My father's drinking got worse, and now, slowly, my mother started to drink wine and beer in the evenings while she cleaned the stove. Somehow I felt more lonely. When I wasn't in my room reading, I combed the woods that surrounded the house. It was a neighborhood yet to be developed, and there was space—ragged paths through seemingly endless woods. I began to discover the joys of solitude in the out-of-doors. About a half mile from home, far up in a hilly part of the woods, I found a huge outcropping of rock surrounded by strawberry and laurel bushes. From here I could look out for miles over woods. This became my private retreat. I would go here to meditate, to be alone, to enjoy the beauty of the changing seasons.

The woods around the house blanketed us with a peacefulness that was comforting. In the summers, Ann and I would sit in the kitchen with the lights out and the windows wide open, with only the blue glow of the TV lighting the night, watching old movies and eating popcorn. We would turn off the television and just listen in the dark. The noises of the woods were so deep and insistent, Ann used to say it seemed like we lived in the tropics, or what she knew of the tropics from TV. There were nights we would hear sounds of animals crashing through the brush, and we'd joke that it was a good thing my mother was asleep because she'd be convinced there was danger out there, evil people ready to disturb the safety of our lives.

Like my mother, I was dreamy, a ruminator with a vivid imagination. When I was eleven or twelve, I had my first crush, but it was not on a boy. It was on a teacher, Helen Scott. She was gray-haired, with a distinctive purse to her lips, a determined set to her jaw, and a voice that boomed through the hallways: "Miss So-and-so, stand up straight, button those lips, pipe down!" Mrs. Scott was a whirlwind of feeling and moral inspiration. Her whole heart and soul went into her teaching. She could be fiery and wild; on any given day she might terrorize us with discipline, laugh, cry, coddle us, mother us, or sing to us. She loved and got angry with equal intensity. She had a passion for music and poetry. One day she read to us from Francis Thompson's "The Hound of Heaven": "I fled Him down the nights and down the days, I fled him down the arches of the years. . . ." Her voice was strained with tears, and, not knowing what could be making her so emotional, I felt tears come to my eyes, too. She made us memorize Shakespeare and the Gettysburg Address. She goaded us into debate on moral issues. She demanded, she cajoled, she insisted that we appreciate life and that we learn. I imagined the life she led apart from us and wanted to be part of it. She became the center of my emotional world. I would have laid down my life for this woman: my sole desire was to please her, and nothing mattered so much as being near her.

I began to harbor a daydream that my mother would die and my father would marry Mrs. Scott. I wanted Mrs. Scott to be my mother; I craved her caring, intensity, and emotional presence. She was a model for me. Not only did I want what she could give, but she was the woman I wanted to become.

So I slid into adolescence wondering about love, trying to discern its texture and nuance, thinking of it as a central truth that might elude or catch one by surprise. I knew that I loved, and I knew that I felt the absence of love.

I was twelve when Therese was born. My mother finally gave up her dream of having a male child. My father settled for having three daughters. Things in the family got more and more tense, and we all seemed more distant. I became the family scholar who reminded my father of all his inadequacies. There was never enough money. My father fought with my mother and battled with me over everything, sometimes cruelly trying to control my every thought and feeling. He never did what he said he would do, and I learned that when I needed anything, I had to play a kind of game in which I acted like I didn't need it in order to get it.

And he beat the dog—the dog he had brought home, the dog he had wanted, the dog he wanted desperately to control.

2.

Girl in Blue

"You are young ladies," Sister Mary Claire said, her chestnut eyes full of stern indignation, "and ladies do not wear their skirts rolled up."

Standing at the front of the classroom in the last minutes of our homeroom period, she was referring to our habit of rolling and belting the skirts of our uniforms after school so that they fell above the knee, the current fashion, rather than below it, as school rules required.

"They do not wear excessive makeup. They do not give the impression that they are morally loose. They do not sit on boys' laps. They control their impulses. It is up to you to maintain purity in relationships with boys. You can do it, and they can't. Of equal importance is what you allow to be in your mind. We do not read certain books that would be suggestive and arouse impure thoughts. We carefully screen the books on your reading lists. If you come across a passage that causes you difficulty, skip it and go on."

Sister looked at us with great severity and maintained a lengthy silence for effect. Her face was crushed into a frown, her thick, dark eyebrows furrowed. She was the overseer of freshman homeroom and taught English and Latin to the whole school. She was young—and she seemed hardly out of high school herself. The room was deathly silent. We all stared straight ahead, afraid to look at each other.

"It is easy to tell the girls who are impure," she said ominously.

My insides began to quiver with anxiety. I wondered if I had given myself away somehow.

Sister made a dramatic exit from the room, and we jumped to our feet, the customary ritual of respect when a nun entered or left the class. I turned to my friend Hannah, and we smiled, our eyebrows raised. I knew this little speech would provide the text for tonight's hours-long phone conversation.

"Ye god," Hannah said. "What next?"

"What next is that your mother is going to throw away more of your books because they might be occasions of sin," I said in a stage whisper. Hannah read Nietzsche, Freud, and the *Communist Manifesto*. Her mother had found these books and thrown them in the garbage. Hannah leaned back now, like a cat in a stretch, her hands supporting her back. She sighed, and we picked up our books and trudged to the next class.

When Sister Mary Claire wasn't pontificating on the sins of the flesh, or drilling us on Latin verbs, she was an inspiring teacher. She was at her best teaching literature. I was part of a small group in the class whom she had dubbed the "philosophy club." We were a group of brainy, intellectually precocious social misfits. We always sat together in a row near the windows, as if we needed access to air and light to nourish our hunger for ideas. Mary Claire would beam at us when we commented deftly on the ironies of a passage in Joseph Conrad or challenged the philosophical implications of a poet's work.

The high school building of this exclusive Catholic girls' school was small and intimate. It was connected to the convent by a small chapel that one entered through French doors just off the library. Students could use the chapel, but the convent was off-limits. These women who taught us were mysterious figures, a constant source of speculation and rowdy gossip among us. To me their mystery was compelling. I had vivid flights of fancy about their lives in the private enclosure of the convent.

At this point in my life I was devoutly religious. I found

comfort—identity, even—in the aesthetics of the church and in the refinements of this upper-class school that my parents could not really afford. The small chapel had white pews with dark oak moldings polished to a high gloss. Thick wine-red carpeting muffled all sound and made you feel as if you were walking on tufted lawn. On the altar, a small brass tabernacle housed gold chalices, and during Communion services sudden refractions of light exploded off them like the beacons of privilege they were.

I went to the library often, because I was restless and because I loved books. I went to the chapel because I was lonely. My sense of a relationship with god was almost a mystical one. Prayer was a major emotional outlet. If the love within my family was sparse, I believed that I was loved by god, and so I spent a good deal of time in the chapel keeping him company. I stared at the altar, trying to understand the mysterious process by which one related to someone who was not there.

Maybe it was the presence of Sister Mary Claire, who often sat in the library right outside the chapel door, or maybe it was just my growing confusion about my sexuality, but it was in the convent chapel that I had my first religious crisis about sex, even before I knew much about love. It was a crisis because sex and Catholicism have never made a congenial mix, and I was highly concerned about sex.

Somewhere I had read that women have hymens and that they are broken—ripped to shreds—the first time one has sex. By now I had struggled with masturbating for some time, and my spiritual conflict had reached heroic proportions. I willed myself to stop but couldn't. I tried to give it up for Lent but failed. I would let myself touch just so much, then force myself to stop short of orgasm. If I stopped at a touch it could be considered a venial sin, but if I "went all the way," I knew I had sinned mortally. I thought that having an orgasm had the same effect on a woman's body as intercourse, and so I was convinced that I had broken my own hymen, and that when I went to the doctor he would discover this and tell my mother. In the days following the reading and misunderstanding of whatever book it was, I spent hours after school in the chapel praying to the Blessed Virgin that my mother wouldn't find out. I cried and was dizzy with anxiety. Sister Mary Claire's rousing talk on impurity only frightened me more. I didn't know quite how she could tell, but I knew I was doomed. I fled to confession and vowed never to touch myself again if only god would somehow magically restore my broken hymen to wholeness. I needed a miracle. I said my five Our Fathers and five Hail Marys conscientiously, wondering why the punishment wasn't heavier. I prayed to be relieved of temptation.

From the Church I learned that the body is a rowdy, uncontrolled occasion of sin, and its containment the measure of my value as a woman. Witness the nuns who walked around in starched white boxes, with headpieces that came to a lofty point over their heads. For the rest of us, school rules required that we measure our steps and dress only in the refined and ladylike shades of the blue school uniform. We were to wear white gloves and heels anywhere within a one-mile radius of the school. We were supposed to be models of femininity in the community—in this town where most people worked in mills and factories and didn't even own white gloves.

I was always loath to leave school; I would have lived there had they let me. At home I faced my now almost irrationally hostile father and an ever more distant mother, chronic tension and fighting. So I stayed at school until five or six every day, and when I wasn't at glee club or basketball practice or Sodality, or working on the yearbook, the school paper, or some other project, when I wasn't in the chapel praying over my impure actions, I loitered, hoping to have the chance to talk to Sister K.

K was a tall, lanky woman with bony, angular features. She sprinted down the hallways, her skirts flying, her peaked habit towering like a lightning rod over everything around her. She taught science and was suitably otherworldly. She was awkward about all the practical details of life—a true absentminded professor.

I'd sit in the darkening classroom, idling, occasionally trying to work out a math problem, waiting. Sooner or later I would hear the swish of K's skirts, her galloping walk, the clicking of her beads. She would glide into the classroom, her veil flying, go to her desk, and look at me, smiling.

"Well, fancy meeting you here," she would say ironically, as if this were something new.

"How are you today?" I asked.

"Oh, fair to middlin'. How about you?"

I'd talk about school things, the progress of the yearbook, the latest issue of the school paper.

Eventually K would walk over to my desk, or we would end up standing against the radiator and staring out the window into the courtyard of the convent, standing very close to each other, our arms draped over the top of the window that swung inward at an angle into the room.

Late one damp, gray afternoon, a few weeks before graduation, we stood together, quiet, staring out at the convent courtyard. We had spent many afternoons talking recently. Our conversations had grown more personal, we had become closer even as we realized that soon we'd have to be apart. K finally broke the silence.

"You're pensive today. What's in that mind of yours?" She was smiling.

"I was thinking about you, thinking about our conversation the other day, about your questioning your faith, your talk with Father, wondering what will happen. How will you resolve all this?"

K stared out the window, pensive herself now, a troubled, weighted look on her face.

"Maybe I say too much to you. You shouldn't worry about this."

"What should I worry about, then?"

"I was thinking about what you were telling me about your mother, about your disappointment with her, about wishing she'd show up for some of the extracurricular events here. I was thinking that maybe she fears being out by herself in social situations. She seemed so tense the one time I met her. You need to be less hard on her. We all have our handicaps, our limitations, you know."

She gave a quiet, ironic little laugh. "That's certainly something I know a lot about."

K's voice became softer and lower, almost a whisper. These were the times with her I loved. Warmth started to spread through my body. When her voice dropped like this, I knew she was about to share something very intimate. She stared out the window, her body tense, and I knew she felt pain about something.

"It's very hard at times living so closely with other people. You want things from them that you can't have. There are irritations, needs, longings . . ."

Her voice trailed off. She turned to me and smiled.

"I can't believe how openly I talk to you. It must be something about you—you're very special in that way. Won't it be interesting to see how your life turns out."

"Sometimes my life seems so painful. Do *you* have any idea why? You're older and wiser. Maybe you know something I don't." There was a slight tremble in my voice. I was not used to letting anyone know what I really felt.

"They say we all have our crosses to bear. You're more sensitive than most. I think that someday you may write a book, think of it all as material for a novel. Sartre and Camus say we make our experience what it is, that there is no intrinsic meaning."

"But you read all those books that talk about there being no meaning," I said. "What do you call them—those nihilists."

She gave a little laugh. "Well," she said, "I guess I'd better get over to afternoon prayer."

"I guess I'd better make the five o'clock bus," I said.

She gathered up her books and papers, then looked at me and said softly, "Good night now. I always enjoy talking to you."

"Me too," I said.

She backed away, a shy smile on her face, turned, and was gone. The classroom was dark now. And I went home to another evening of my father yelling and my mother cleaning the stove.

One day I found on my desk a note in K's minute handwriting. It was a quote that had struck her, from a book she had been reading called *Life Against Death*, by Norman O. Brown. "What the great world needs, of course, is a little more Eros and less strife; but the intellectual world needs it just as much. A little more Eros would make conscious the unconscious harmony between dialectical dreamers of all kinds—psychoanalysts, political idealists, mystics, poets, philosophers. . . ."

I didn't know how to interpret this. Part of me thought—wanted to think—that it was a comment on our relationship, a statement that our contact meant something to her, that it freed her, if only briefly, from the bounded intellectual world of teaching and the convent and invited her to feel. We were both dreamers, each in our own way. Now, looking back, I realize it was a warning that she couldn't give me directly.

At the time, I was convinced that it was my vocation to become a nun. I wanted to enter the order of my teachers, strange habits and all. I'm not sure whether my devotion was more to god or to K, whom I assumed I could stay close to if we were both in the same order. K never discouraged me—not directly, anyway. The order required that potential entrants have a year of college. I planned to have my year in college and then enter the novitiate.

Meanwhile, graduation approached. K was going to the West Coast for a while; I was going off on a budget trip to Europe just after graduation with an older male cousin—a gift from my grandmother. K and I talked about how we would keep in touch.

On the last day of school, I found on my desk a copy of a story with a note in it. The main character, Esme, was a troubled woman who was lonely and frightened and facing a crisis in her life. K had signed the note, "From California to Paris, with   , ESME," the space blank where "love" should have been.

At the class party at the convent beach house a few days later, I learned that K was gone. She was leaving the order. She hadn't told me because she didn't want to influence my decision.

I felt stunned. Another nun, her friend, walked the beach with me, trying to console me. My grief was mixed with fear for K's well-being, now that I knew that everything I had sensed about her pain and conflict was true. I also knew that her vulnerability would make this transition back to the world a costly one in terms of her emotions and her soul.

I went off to Europe with my cousin Don, a teacher. He finally asked me whom I kept writing to and what was keeping me so preoccupied. I told him about K and even let him read a letter I wrote to her. He sighed and shook his head. "Such a a lot of wasted energy," he said.

In Europe, I could no longer avoid the compulsory view of myself as a heterosexual woman. In Rome, at the Fountain of Trevi, I wandered by myself around the square. Two slightly older men walked over to me and asked if I wanted to have coffee with them. They kept pointing to the cafe nearby, speaking a combination of Italian and broken English. I kept speaking French, having been forced by the nuns to study four years of it. I finally said, "No, but thanks anyway." I thought of myself as unattractive and it never occurred to me that I would be pursued by strange men.

When I told Don he was amused. "Why didn't you go?" he asked.

"What would those guys want with me?" I retorted. "We don't even speak the same language. Did you ever try to carry on a conversation with an Italian in French?"

"Don't take it too personally, Claud. European men have this idea that all American women are available, that they come here to have sexual adventures."

"Oh, thanks for the education."

"You're not so unattractive, you know. You need to stop wearing those weird dresses, get yourself fixed up a little. Stop reading all the time."

I was accosted by men a couple more times in Rome, and on the train to Florence I didn't know whether to be angry or flattered when I was firmly pinched on the rear. People had warned me about Italian men, but I never thought it would happen to me.

Don apparently believed that as an American male, he should have some European sexual adventures. He was an attractive young Italian himself (despite the receding hairline that ran in the family), a self-made athlete and scholar, Jesuit-educated—a no-nonsense, outspoken person who made up his mind early on to grasp life and make happen what he wanted for himself. He kept running into women who would end up joining us for dinner, and he would laboriously explain that he and I were just cousins and he was escorting me through Europe. There were raised eyebrows—nobody quite believed him. But one night after dinner in Florence, he escorted me back to our fleabag of a *pensione* and then left, saying he was going out to meet the woman with whom we had had dinner.

I took the opportunity to rinse out clothes in the sink and to take a sponge bath, there being no bathtub or shower, but only a filthy "water closet" down the hall that made me wish I had paid attention to my mother's compulsivity in this area and brought along a can of Lysol. Every hour the bells in the Duomo would chime, but I felt too unsettled to think it romantic. Midnight passed and I was still awake. The mattress felt like it was stuffed with straw and the bed sagged in the middle, so that I felt like half of me was lying in a pit. I tossed and turned until three; I was becoming frantic. I tried to think what I would do, an unsophisticated novice traveler, if Don didn't come back. I felt homesick and was close to tears.

At five-thirty, I finally heard a key in the door and Don walked in. He grinned. "Hi, Claud," he said. "What are you doing up?"

"I'm packing. We have a train to catch, and I was trying to figure out how I was going to get there by myself," I said angrily, though since he was back, I was actually more relieved than angry. "Did you have a good time? I thought maybe you were just going to desert me."

"How could you think I wouldn't come back? Cool it, okay?"

"Where did you go?" I demanded.

"Oh, we went to some bars, then spent some time on the grass in the park." He grinned. "You have to live, Claud, have a little fun."

"Oh," I said. I thought, I'm too frightened to live.

We spent the rest of the day sleeping on the train to wherever it was we were going and then toured churches, both of us exhausted from our sleepless night.

In the three weeks of our trip, my cousin had resolutely tried to challenge my pious, constricted views of the world. And to his credit, Don did get me to eat *escargots,* get slightly drunk on the wine we had with our daily lunch of bread and cheese, and learn to laugh at myself.

What this meant was that when I came back from Europe, everything had changed. The loss of K was still like a gaping wound in my life, but being exposed to the world beyond the aluminum cross at Holy Land and my convent school had left me feeling like an anachronism. I didn't dress right, I didn't look right, I didn't think right, and most of all I didn't pay enough attention to the opposite sex. In four years of high school, I had been out on one date. I faced the change from an all-female school of two hundred to a coed state university of ten thousand philosophically—after all, it was only for a year and then I could go off and become a nun.

3.
Labor Pains

It was one of those heart-stirring fall evenings. I could make out the vibrant colors of the trees even in the dark, and the air was ripe with the musky sweetness of earth cooling off. I walked across the campus watching the lights of nearby dorms and passing cars dance on the calm surface of the lake. I was headed to church, to a newly formed theology seminar.

I found a small group of people already huddled in a lounge in the church basement. Father Mike Carey, the head of the Catholic student ministry on campus, was talking with some students. He was smiling broadly and saying things like "That's marvelous, that's wonderful," in his loud but refined voice. I noticed that he focused intently on the people he talked with, was dramatically present, and was very attractive in black.

When the seminar began he introduced himself, asked each of us to say a few words about ourselves, and then launched into his talk for the evening, on Christian ethics. We were quickly riveted by his words. He told the story of a woman whose mother was dying and who had come to him for counsel. She felt she ought to drop everything to care for her mother but didn't want to, and she felt terrible guilt about her selfishness.

"There are two people to be considered here," he said. "This woman sits with me and is in tears because the conflict of this situation is tearing her apart. Clearly she loves her mother, but she also feels she has already sacrificed so much of her life to her mother's needs. She's involved in a new relationship; she has a good job. She doesn't want to go care for her mother. What is ethical, Christian, loving in this situation? Are these woman's needs for a life and a loving relationship as important as her mother's wish that it be her daughter who cares for her?"

It was 1967, the Church was changing, and he posed this question as a challenge to us. He spoke eloquently, and I sensed in him great compassion for the woman's conflict. He was not one of those priests who just told people—particularly women—that they must sacrifice themselves. He talked about the intricacies of theological debate and suggested that morality and love are dependent on context, and that sometimes there are no easy answers.

"There are picture people and drama people," he said. "Picture people look for easy, preordained answers with frames around them. Drama people see life as the emergent, unfolding event that it is. Theology is nothing more than decision-making. Man lives on the basis of probability—nothing is certain. Decision making involves risk. It is inherent in our humanness that we should be capable of making mistakes and that we are fallible."

He looked around to see what we thought of this. I was not thinking; I was watching him. He seemed concerned, intent on shepherding us through this dilemma he had posed. He was at once boyish and masterful, as well as acutely intelligent.

That night, he and I left the church together. He was wearing a black overcoat and his hands were in his pockets. He turned to me.

"So, tell me a little about yourself. You're new on campus?"

"Yes," I said, "just arrived here. I live in the freshman dorm over by the lake."

"Well, that's just next door to where I'm headed. Why don't I give you a ride?"

"Okay, I'd like that," I said, a little nervous.

We walked to his car, a nondescript blue Chevy. It had a huge dent on the back fender.

He looked chagrined. "A little run-in I had coming back from out of town the other day. Haven't had time to have it taken care of." He smiled. "Life is just full of these bits of clutter that distract us from what's important."

"Yes, I know," I said, and I hoped that I conveyed my implicit understanding of what had to be the heavy import beneath these words. I was suddenly feeling an agitation that unnerved me.

"Father, do you do counseling with students? I need to talk some things over, and I wonder if that would be possible."

"Yes, of course, I'd be delighted," he said.

The campus of the university was vast. It was dotted with a combination of ivy-covered turn-of-the-century buildings and modern institutional-looking ones that seemed to be competing for a prize in architectural nondescriptness. The setting was rural; the school had begun as a state agricultural training college. There were rolling fields, sprawling lawns, and two small lakes in the midst of dormitories and classroom buildings. My dorm looked out over one of the lakes, and from my window I faced west into the setting sun. I spent a good deal of time staring out that window, wondering how I had come to be in this alien world.

The loneliness I felt in those first few months overwhelmed me. It seemed to me that everyone else had come here with some notion of how to be a part of college life, but that I was psychologically still curled in the womb of my protected convent school. By now K had made her transition from the convent to the world outside. For a while I survived on her occasional letters. She was my only connection to my past sense of myself.

I wandered the campus enjoying the September mellowness, the richness of the landscape. I sat for hours by the lake. But I was alone. I watched as every other person in view managed to attach himself or herself to someone of the opposite sex. I could sense the aura of sexual misadventure in the air—the constant conversations in the dorm, the displays of couples rolling on the lawns or passionately embracing behind a tree. I fell back on my first line of defense and went to church. And I did what seemed reasonable and safe at the time: I fell in love with Father Carey.

He was midsized, somewhat lanky and gaunt. He had the most

extraordinary blue eyes and graying brown hair that fell rakishly over his forehead. Watching him sweep that lock of errant hair back from his face could trigger a romantic swoon in me. I was destined to be infatuated with him because he talked almost exclusively about love. He read poetry and philosophy from the pulpit. He reminded me of Thomas Merton or one of the Christian mystics. I watched him those first times from the front pews of the church and felt a fascination, a desire to know him that both frightened and captivated me. I had never been drawn to a man before. My interest in the theology seminar came to have much more to do with my curiosity about Father Carey than it did with the intricacies of moral debate.

When I wasn't at church, I was challenged to survive with my peers. I was almost nineteen, virginal, and shy. My roommate found me strange. What seemed most disturbing to her was that I read constantly and that I didn't have a boyfriend.

I felt as lost academically as I did personally. During orientation I went to my adviser and told him I wanted to major in English literature. He glanced at my course selections and shook his head.

"You really want to study English?" he said. "From the looks of this, it seems all you're really interested in doing is reading. You could stay home and do that."

I was not used to this kind of treatment. I felt like crying, but instead I said, "So what courses does an English major take?"

Accordingly, the first class of my college career was in seventeenth-century English literature, a subject I had never had the vaguest interest in. It was taught by David Bowles, an obviously new member of the faculty who may have been even more disoriented than we were. He always dressed in a tweed suit, vest, and neatly pinned tie. He stood stiffly behind a lecturn and read in a husky voice from notes carefully penned and underlined on index cards. His face was overtaken by his horn-rimmed glasses. He was the first person I had met on that campus who seemed more tense than I. He tried to vary the pitch of his voice at times to convey his passion for his work, but it came across somehow as shouting.

When we studied Marvell, I discovered that I had been totally unaware of the apparently pointed references to sexual seduction in "To His Coy Mistress," so I was surprised to hear Bowles lecture for the entire class on Marvell's sexual frustration and on the artful references to lovemaking in the poem. I left the humanities building after class wondering why I hadn't gotten these sexual allusions.

Mr. Bowles came walking up behind me on his way back to his office. Nervous, I commented on the morning's lecture. "The discussion of Marvell was interesting, but I felt pretty silly that it never occurred to me that the poem was about sex."

He looked at me oddly. "Well, now that you're aware of this, it will deepen your understanding of the subject."

It wasn't clear to me whether he meant the subject of Marvell or the subject of sex. We chatted uneasily about the weather, and I made it a point to take a different route back to the dorm from then on.

On weekends I forced myself to show up at the dances held in the men's dorms. They were called mixers. You walked into a room that reeked of beer, and sometimes marijuana, and were greeted by whistles and leers. You stood around trying somehow to look appealing, or even just acceptable, and hoped for a male to come by and ask you to dance so that you could think of yourself as desirable to the opposite sex. You danced and drank and then had to strategize to keep yourself from being asked up to someone's room for what you were sure would be an anonymous and degrading sexual encounter.

One Saturday night a man/boy I had dated briefly finally did convince me to come up to his room. We sat talking and sipping on beer in plastic cups.

Suddenly he put his cup down and turned to face me. "You know, you dress really well," he said.

"I don't think I wear anything very different from anyone else," I responded.

"I mean you're always neat and presentable, attractive, you wear nice colors—that kind of thing, you know? I like to be seen with a girl who dresses well."

He tried to kiss me. I pushed him away.

"Maybe you and I could go to church together," he said.

"Really," I said, pretending to be impressed. "Why would you want to go to church with me?"

"Well, you know, I want you to know I'm a nice guy. I'm ready to do some serious, mature things here."

He tried to kiss me again and I felt his hand slide inside my blouse.

I pushed him away one more time. "I think you're handing me quite a line."

"Oh, c'mon, why so serious? What can I do? Tell me what you want—anything."

"I want to go back to my dorm."

After another half hour or so of this struggle, the bell rang for curfew. I was horrified when he unzipped his pants and ran outside into the hall, pretending to be tucking in his shirt and zipping himself up so that his friends would be impressed. I walked out into the hall to their shrieks and laughter and to a profound sense of humiliation that I took to be simply a part of being a woman.

I couldn't understand why this dating scene was so difficult for me, why it felt so awkward, like an exercise I submitted to with no real interest or motivation. Finally, I decided to schedule the appointment with Father Carey.

That first time we met in the rectory living room.

"I'm here because . . . because I left high school with the intention to enter the convent. I have to have a year of college first. I'm having a very hard time being here. I'm very lonely. I'm very unsure of what I'm doing. I think I should be dating more, but I don't really feel drawn to anyone. It's not that I'm afraid of sex or anything; it's just never happened. I don't know whether I should be exploring that part of my life or not during this year. I really don't know what's right."

There was much more on my mind. I wondered if I should confess my autoerotic activities, if this could somehow be a hindrance to a vocation. But I found that I couldn't. I was too concerned that he should think well of me.

He looked at me with a certain surprise, hesitated, then said, "It sounds like a painful time for you. I understand your loneliness. I'm fairly new here myself, and it can be hard to feel a part of things." He lit his pipe and chewed on it meditatively. "Tell me a little more. What makes you think you have a vocation?"

Wearing his Shetland sweater over his clerical collar, he

seemed every bit the country gentleman. I half expected to see a golden retriever asleep on the hearth. He had an air of studied relaxation, yet he was as intense and eloquent as ever. Of my confusion he said, "The thing is to just keep walking. And in order to do that, you have to stand first on one foot and then on the other. Otherwise, you don't go anywhere."

He had a strange habit of sitting slightly slumped in his chair, his legs outstretched, his hands inside his pants with his thumbs hooked over his belt. This seemed a strangely intimate way to sit, I thought. From then on our meetings usually took place in the afternoons, in the fading light. As the room became dim, I could feel his eyes on me and I looked away. The silences grew uncomfortably intense for me. I felt as if he were studying me, unsure about how to proceed or what to say.

In the times between mass, the theology seminar, and our weekly counseling sessions, I was haunted by a sense of his presence right next door. Proximity makes fantasy all the more acute. At night I imagined him lying lonely in his bed, and I felt guilty about my longings. In our meetings we talked of my confusion about my vocation and my fears about meeting men—my innocence and lack of experience. On Sundays he appeared on the altar in his white and red vestments and would glide gracefully around the sanctuary, his cassock flowing after him. His absorption, his sense of the power of the consecration of the host, was palpable; his sense of compassion and commiseration with suffering was obvious. On some Sundays he looked exhausted and drawn, and he seemed to be suffering himself. On these days his sermons were even more emotional than usual, as if he were reaching out to all of us for some solace from his own pain.

As we got to know each other, I came to assume that many of his words were spoken for me. If I had talked with him about loneliness, somehow loneliness became the theme of his sermon. He would look at me from the lectern, our eyes would meet, and I would know with a terror and a wave of passion all at once that I was in love with this man and that he had somehow read the secrets of my soul. Before long I began to have a hard time making sense of the fact that I had committed myself to becoming a nun and here I was desperately, passionately in love.

One Saturday evening late in the fall, at a loss for anything else to do, I walked with a couple of other girls from the dorm across the campus to a dance. This was not a typical mixer but a major event with a live band held in a large auditorium that was usually used for physical education classes. I walked into the cavernous hall feeling intimidated. The band was loud, and my ears rang with every amplified beat of the drums. People were gyrating around the dance floor. Some were standing around holding paper cups filled with beer. Some were making out in the shadows in the corners of the room. The three of us from my dorm stood in a cluster watching, unable to talk because the music was so loud. I absently watched a woman dancing and thought how fluidly she moved.

At a break in the music, one of my dormmates—barely an acquaintance, surely not a friend—looked at me and said, "Can I ask you a question?"

"Sure," I responded, grateful for the attention.

"Are you odd?"

Was she asking me this because I'd been watching a woman dance? Her words exploded in my ears, and I fell into some empty space inside myself where all the noise and raucous action of the dance receded into a tunnel. "Not that I know of. Why do you ask?"

She smiled insidiously. "I just wondered if you like women instead of men. You don't date much. I just wondered, that's all."

I left the dance and walked back to the dorm by myself. The question stayed with me as a haunting doubt that I first entertained and then dismissed as ridiculous. After all, wasn't I in love with a priest?

I thought back to my years in high school, to K, to my attachments to friends and teachers. I remembered one friend, a doctor's daughter, a beautiful and intelligent member of the "philosophy club" who at one point had commented to me on the intensity of our relationship with each other and questioned whether I thought there was anything odd about us.

"What do you mean, odd?" I had asked.

She turned red, obviously uncomfortable. "Well, you know,

like, I hate to use the word, but . . . queer?" She laughed shakily. "You know, like they say women in prison sometimes turn queer because it's all they can do."

I told her I thought she was being ridiculous. "There is nothing abnormal about caring for one another," I said. It horrified me to think that these feelings and attachments and relationships that I so cherished, and that were so central to my life, could be thought of as odd.

When I talked about this with Father Carey, he acted uncomfortable and dismissed my doubts somewhat cavalierly as something everybody went through at some time in their life. In the haze of my infatuation for him, I dropped the issue entirely, but I always had the sense that people were regarding me as something other than what I thought I was, which was a heterosexual woman who wanted to be a nun.

My infatuation with Father Carey grew. I went to every meeting, every lecture, every mass where I thought he might be. My feelings might not have been so intense had I not gotten the distinct sense that his feelings for me were similar. I told myself that it was presumptuous, but I felt that something was going on between us. Eventually, I couldn't contain these feelings any longer, and I knew I had to say something to him. I felt compelled to let him know. I hoped my talking about it would help it go away. In retrospect, I wonder how innocent I really was, or if I wasn't being brilliantly seductive in my sweet naiveté.

I prepared my confession for days. I wanted to say simply, "Father Mike, I love you." But it had to be more artful, more carefully thought out than this; I couldn't just blurt it out.

Every time I thought about talking with him, a bolt of fear, anxiety, and excitement shot through my body. When the day arrived, I went to see him feeling burdened and somehow ashamed. I said something like "I'm very troubled by my feelings for you. Our talks together mean a great deal to me. I can't seem to get you out of my mind. I'm confused. I don't know what these feelings mean. All I know is that they cause me a lot of pain."

He was quiet as he sat there with his thumbs draped over his belt as usual. When he finally spoke, it was with an air of knowing that this had been coming. "Do these feelings lead to fantasizing? Are they just emotional, or are they sexual as well?" he asked.

"All of the above," I said, trying to be light and charming but feeling shy and exposed.

"Oh," he said, and nodded calmly.

I don't clearly remember the rest of the conversation. I know he was not patronizing, that he was warm and accepting, and that I ended up feeling even closer to him. But the talking didn't help the feelings go away. I left there happy that he now knew how I felt. My passion seemed eternal; I believed it would never not be. I wanted to be with him, to care for him, to talk with him long into the night. And I was no less frustrated.

One afternoon at the end of our counseling session he said, "I have something I need to have taken over to church before the meeting next week. Why don't you come by here Thursday afternoon and pick it up?"

"Yes, okay," I stuttered.

Now, it may have been my imagination, given my lack of experience in such matters, but I felt instinctively that I was being invited to a seduction. I waited for Thursday to arrive in a state of internal agitation. That afternoon, I dressed carefully, put on my raincoat, and made the trek through the back parking lot of the dorm to the front door of the rectory.

I rang several times and nothing happened. I began to think that maybe I'd made all of this up. Finally I heard footsteps. The door opened. Mike Carey stood there and acted surprised to see me.

"Hi," I said. "How was your golf game?" I knew he played golf on Thursday mornings.

"Oh, fine," he said, in his refined, deeply sonorous voice. Now he seemed agitated. There was silence.

"Wasn't there something you wanted me to pick up to take over to church?" I asked. I wondered why I hadn't been asked in. But in an instant, I knew. Footsteps echoed from the hall beyond the door and then Father Leroy appeared.

Mike Carey turned red and said, "Oh, yes, well, I haven't gotten it ready yet. I'll take it over myself. Thanks for coming by."

So much for my seduction fantasy. I didn't know whether to feel disappointment or shame. But in the weeks that followed, my longing for Mike Carey began to eclipse every other feeling: the loneliness, the confusion, the disorientation of being alone surrounded by ten thousand students, the struggles over French class and educational psychology lectures that I hated because they were about rats instead of people. I went to church devotedly, to confession when I knew he was in the box, to his lectures, his workshops. I watched him on the altar—the gracefulness of his walk, the drama of his movements as he said a mass, prayed over the Communion cup, blessed us with deep compassion in his voice. I stared into those intense blue eyes, and I thought I might fall into his soul.

Before long, my frustrated longing turned to anger. He never mentioned the aborted meeting at the rectory, but after that day he kept his distance. As April gave way to May, he seemed distracted and often less available. He alluded to trips to a nearby city and his work with a psychiatrist there. I wondered what was wrong. And I wondered why this man who could talk so eloquently about love and the love of god would confine himself to a life without deeper human contact. How does one speak of love yet remain celibate and out of reach? I began to have my first crisis of faith. What was this love that the Church preached, and what did it have to do with the needs of people like me who were lonely and so needed to be touched and held and cared for, not from a mystical distance but right here on earth and in the flesh?

After the last meeting of the theology seminar, we all went to a local bar for beer and pizza, and Mike Carey joined us. I watched as one of the other women, a wispy senior with long blond hair, flirted with him, leaning across the table and smiling, trying to talk to him over the din. I hated her. The waitress came with the first round of drinks and Carey pulled out some money. But she virtually leapt from her seat, saying, "Oh, no, Father, let us get it."

By now I was angry that he was being so distant with me, paying attention to this other woman and ignoring the men in the group completely. She was talking to him about money.

"But how do you live, what do you live on?" she asked. Before he could answer, I blurted out, the sarcasm rolling from my lips, "Just air. He's very spiritual, and he lives on air."

He glared at me across the table. "Pretty expensive air," he shot back. He was angry. Had he heard my thinly veiled complaint that he was distant and remote, that all he could do was talk about love but not show up for it?

But the anger turned out to be short-lived. On what I didn't know was to be the final time we would see each other, Carey did something that was, at that time, still out of the ordinary in a Catholic church. He had asked all of us in his seminar to meet at the church, and in a small room off the basement we gathered for an impromptu Communion service. We sat around tables that had been set up in the shape of a cross, he at the head, I facing him at the other end. We were all sad, knowing that this was probably the last time we would all meet. Carey was clearly feeling emotional, and his movements were measured and graceful and solemn. He made the sign of the cross and began to pray.

"Father, we're grateful for all that we've shared together this year, for our growth together through one another and through you. We have come to know the depth and beauty of life and of one another, and through this we know more of your presence, more of the sacredness of our lives together. May we continue to be graced by your presence and to touch others with the beauty of our hearts and our actions." He looked directly at me as he said these things; I did not look away.

The atmosphere in the room was charged. We sat transfixed, hypnotized by the ritual and by him. Slowly he poured the wine and consecrated the host. He drank from the chalice, wiped its rim with the ceremonial cloth, then passed it to the student sitting next to him, indicating that it should be given to each of us in turn. This was a bold departure: in a Catholic mass only the priest was to drink the blood of Christ. Carey was looking passionate and intense.

I lifted the chalice and held it up to drink. I remember to this day the cold, stinging sensation that I felt on my lips, as if there were some electricity running through the wine, as if I had been kissed. It was as if his energy burned in waves around that chalice and that, finally, we had touched. The sensation was stunning; it lasted for minutes and was so palpable that it frightened me. At that moment this prayerful last mass seemed, for me, to be a way of making love, a way of sharing a passion as intimate as sex.

The next day, I went to look for him at the church and instead found Father Leroy, who told me Carey had left and would not be coming back.

In those last days of the semester, I spent a lot of time staring out the dorm windows at the rectory next door, wondering about Carey. I wrote a letter to him and asked Father Leroy, who by now clearly understood that I was desperately infatuated, to give it to him. I went home for the summer and wrote long, suffering poetry and letters and journal passages which my mother read and accepted with something close to understanding and sympathy. It didn't help that I had discovered Goethe and read *The Sufferings of Young Werther* to soothe my own tortures. I was obsessed, came down with a case of mono, and spent my summer weak in bed with my mother ministering to me as I waited for word of Mike Carey. My sister Ann and her friends listened to my story with curiosity and waited with me every day for the mail to see if my letter would be answered. My family's attention to my lovesickness surprised me. It was as if these emotional attractions of mine were dramas that took them out of the ordinary dreariness of their days. I was tolerated with a kind of bemused detachment and sometimes actual empathy.

That summer, finally, there were two letters from Carey.

They were beautifully written, in the same graceful, flowing prose, the same refined cadence of his speech. I could almost hear his voice as I read them.

In the first, he empathized with my pain. He called it "labor pain," and spoke of the difficulties of giving birth to oneself. He talked about the ambiguity of personal relationships, he talked of his own fears. And to my great relief, so that I need not spend the rest of my life wondering if I had made it all up, he acknowledged that he had perhaps been misleading in his relationship with me, and that for that, he was sorry.

I wrote back thanking him for this letter, assuring him that I would be all right, that I understood better now what had been.

His first letter had been an apology. The second was a benediction.

He wished me well, and he wished me love.

Some months later I learned that he had left the priesthood and married. A "wonderful gal" was the way he described his wife in his final letter to me. So I had inadvertently picked up on what seemed to be his own conflict, had almost gotten swept into it; wish, still, that I had. Wish that we had made love in a bed instead of in a ritual. Wish that he and I had met at a time when our ages and emotional transitions were not so out of sync. Wish that I knew where he is now. Wish for the intensity again of that first love for a man which was so deeply rooted in my sense of what we shared of the spiritual.

I wrote him, later, that life had become all practicality and responsibility and I wondered what happened to intensity and passion. This letter he didn't answer.

A year or two later I was driving with my husband-to-be and I saw Mike Carey in another car. He saw me, too, and swerved briefly as if to turn around and come after us, but we drove on. And life went on. And whether the kind of love I felt for him, whether the experience we shared, is ageless or has meaning, I still don't know, but I think there is beauty in the question.

4.
Molly

It was the fall of my sophomore year, and though I lived in a new room on a new floor with a new roommate, I still wore a path from the same dorm to the same lake where I went after class to sit on the grass. I felt as imprisoned in my lethargic body as I was in my routine. I had barely recovered from my summer illness, and I was not at all recovered from my bout of unrequited love. I wasn't sure I'd stay the year.

It was a warm Tuesday afternoon, one of those humid Indian summer days, and lying in the cool grass was refreshing. Out of the corner of my eye I noticed a woman from my dorm lounging under an evergreen tree reading. She saw me glance at her and walked over to join me in the grass. She dropped her book down beside her—it was a blue-and-yellow-covered paperback edition of Thomas Mann's *Death in Venice*.

"Hi," she said. "Isn't it beautiful out? Do you remember me from last year? I'm Molly."

"Of course, yes, I remember you. You're living right across the hall from me now, aren't you? How are you doing? I seem to remember that you weren't very happy with school. I'm surprised to see you back."

Molly had lived in the dorm the year before. I'd thought of her as quite standoffish and unfriendly. She had a certain aura of the dramatic about her: her comings and goings seemed secretive and almost furtive. She had a husky, seductive voice and smoked cigarettes in a mannered way that invited a light from any man who happened to be in the vicinity. When one did, she would grasp his hand with her own to steady it, guide it gently, invitingly, while she looked deep into his eyes as if she had known him forever, even if they'd just met.

Toward the end of freshman year she had ended up in my room several times and we'd talked. Molly had been clear that she wanted to get married and have several children. She thought of love as an individual affair: you gave oneself completely to one man and to your children. At that point I still thought I might want to be a nun. I thought of love as a more cosmic affair: you gave love to many, you served others, and you were fulfilled through that giving. We came from totally different worlds. I was Catholic, she was Jewish; I was a virgin, she wasn't. We became acquainted, and when I left for the summer, I never gave her another thought.

Then I had found her somewhat hard looking and too made-up, but today she seemed attractive to me. She was wearing a dark blue shirtwaist dress, and her hair was cut short. Her hair was remarkable—thick, straight, glowing; a rich, deep brown that matched her eyes. She was short and slender and seemed impish to me, almost cute.

"Well," she said, "I guess I didn't know what else to do, so I thought I'd come back and give it another try. And what about you? I thought you were leaving for the convent."

"Well, I guess I changed my mind."

"Ah. What happened?"

"It's a long story. Unrequited love. I decided I'd never be able to keep a vow of chastity. Now I don't know what else to do, either."

She smiled.

"Well, sounds interesting. Unrequited love—that's just what I'm reading about. Have you read Mann?"

"Only *The Magic Mountain*. I loved it. I read it during the summer while I was sick. I felt just like all those people in the sanatorium. I could identify. What have you got there?"

"Death in Venice," she said. "It's about a homosexual relationship. An older man has this passion for a younger one. The older man is dying and believes this passion is a kind of consecration—he is powerless over it and knows it to be all that gives his life meaning. It's beautiful—a really fascinating story."

"Sounds like something I'd enjoy."

"Well, I'll let you borrow it. Now that you're not going to be a nun, we'll have to think up some good things for you to do. C'mon," she said suddenly, "let's play." We decided we'd buy a ball at the local drugstore and play catch by the lake. She grabbed me by the hand and dragged me up the street.

We were walking around the store and couldn't find the toy section. I went up to the man behind the counter and asked politely, "Do you have any balls?"

Molly walked away from me, mortified, and I didn't even realize what I had said until she patiently explained it to me on our way back to the lake.

Molly believed in playing, in loving life, in doing things deliberately and passionately. She believed in living in the moment. She was not so graceful, but she loved to run. She dropped the ball more than she caught it, but she loved to play ball. For the first time since I'd been on this campus I was enjoying myself with someone—I was having fun. I was intrigued that Molly and I shared a fascination for literature and poetry, that there was this sudden comfort and closeness after our distance of last year.

Having finally located a ball, we threw it back and forth for a while and then sat talking in the afternoon light with the trees whispering around us and the westward-moving sun pouring itself into the lake. I felt myself becoming entranced by Molly—by her sense of the dramatic, her playfulness, her seductiveness, her deep-brown eyes, her warmth and aliveness. From this point on we would be lost in an ongoing conversation about love and life. I began to emerge from the depression of unrequited love. I had the sense as I walked through the campus that things were literally brighter, that I saw more acutely than I did before. Slowly, Molly seemed to fill all the empty spaces in my being. Without my even being aware of it, I had fallen in love for the first time with a real person—someone who could be touched and held. It never occurred to me to be concerned about the fact that the person I was in love with was a woman.

That fall, the first signs of student unrest were in the air. The campus was alive with antiwar sentiment and protest. The year began with rallies on the green in front of the student union. I walked to classes watching people carrying placards and listening to distant loudspeakers blaring out over the lawns the jarring, sometimes screechy staccato of that day's speech or demonstration.

As a freshman I had gone to Students for a Democratic Society meetings. It was rumored that anyone who showed up at a rally or an SDS meeting would become known to the FBI. We would go on to our adult, postcollege lives, and somewhere in the crypts of some federal office building there would be a file on us. We all thought it was very risky and very exciting.

Now the rhetoric of free love and antiwar sentiment was being shouted from the wide portico of the student union building. People openly smoked pot. We held sit-ins in various college buildings and demonstrated in front of the president's house. I had hardly emerged from my nunlike sensibilities, and here I was faced with the invitation to sex, drugs, rock and roll, and civil disobedience. In every dorm room on campus, including my own, Beatles music blasted like an emblem of a new civility. The strains of "Yellow Submarine" became a constant background noise in my consciousness. People talked of Timothy Leary and their LSD trips. Everybody had his own druggy point of reference for the popular song "White Rabbit," which played constantly on the radio. My roommate was a Moody Blues devotee, and each evening at dusk we listened to "Nights in White Satin" before heading to the cafeteria for dinner.

Maybe we were all in trance. Maybe love was in the air. But this was the year I liberated myself from the Catholic Church and my virginity. It was my own form of protest. Now I wanted to break through the fear and constriction that had so dominated my life. I wanted to take risks and turn my life into a drama instead of a static picture. My relationship with Molly set all of this in motion. I was ripe for change, and the social unrest swirling around me was the perfect backdrop for my restlessness.

Just off campus was the Campus Restaurant, a stage set where the dramas of our college lives unfolded. It was in a basement, like a Paris jazz *cave,* and was full of smoke. There were white porcelain coffee cups, yellow-vinyl-padded booths with the stuffing falling out, stained gray-brown Formica tables, and greasy cheeseburgers served on flat toasted buns. All of us self-proclaimed bohemian, nontraditional types on campus hung out here, inhaling a lot of first- and secondhand smoke while we listened to the jukebox. You could get a cup of coffee here for 25 cents; one cup could last you three hours, and no one would ask you to leave.

Molly and I spent a lot of time at the "Campus." When she wanted me to know something that would sound too pedestrian if told directly, she played a song on the jukebox. Molly had various signature songs, depending on her mood, on what she needed to say. There was "Scotch and Soda," and Nina Simone singing "My Baby Just Cares for Me," those first few bars set at the tempo of a heartbeat, that sweet jazz, echoing through the greasy spoon, letting me know that Molly was feeling amorous, or just alive and wanting to pull me into her orbit. Molly sat and wrote poetry, or struggled with her physics, or felt intensely about something, and tears would come to her eyes. She would look up at me questioningly, vulnerably, as if she knew I knew. I did know, because I was entranced. Whatever was in her heart I knew, because I willed myself to know. I could feel her pains and her pleasures as if they were my own. I mostly always knew the message in her songs. I knew her sadness and grief at her father's death when she was a young child, the terrible self-destructiveness and confusion she lived with now.

At midnight Molly and I would sit on the hallway floor outside our rooms and convene over cups of tea that we heated in a portable electric kettle. We would whisper because we didn't want to wake our roommates. This had become almost a nightly habit. We would sit in our jeans and T-shirts, or sometimes in our flannel nightgowns, and discuss the problems of the world. We'd had some complaints from other women on the floor who had gotten up to stumble to the bathroom and found it very strange that we stayed up until all hours of the night sitting in the hallway. We giggled and we were very serious. Sometimes we just sat together and studied.

Molly called me Claud, and in her sweet, seductive way she began to try to mentor me, to teach me about sex. In these midnight conversations I heard the very intimate details of Molly's encounters with men: stories about the man who dated her purely for the pleasure of going down on her, which he might do for an entire evening, leaving her on her return to the dorm in some kind of altered state where she was unreachable and preoccupied; stories about the various sizes of penises; stories about the ways in which she had been touched and how she had reacted; stories about her sexual difficulties, and the fact that she had never once had an orgasm.

For some reason Molly needed to tell me all this, and I was her willing audience. I grew to love her more with each conversation, unaware that I was being drawn into an erotic bond with her that would catch me up in its wild, relentless, and unpredictable course through our young and unformed lives. Unaware that she would set me on a path that would define the rest of my life.

Molly had endless curiosity about Catholicism and about my former wish to be a nun. I had endless curiosity about Judaism. She thought of me as the more spiritual. We both believed in the existence of the spiritual, in the primacy of love as a spiritual principle, but by now I knew I could not believe in any religious doctrine that would sentence a person like Molly to eternal damnation because of her sexuality. I felt god must be at least as loving as I was, and I was beginning to love Molly more than anything else in my life.

One afternoon that September, I ran into her as she was leaving the dorm. She seemed agitated.

"Hi. Where are you going?" I asked.

"I'm going to the lake to meditate on my sins."

"Why are you going to do that?"

"Because it's Yom Kippur," she said, "a day of atonement when you think about all the bad things you've done the past year. I was going to do some writing. And I'm glad I ran into you, because I wanted to ask if I could borrow god."

There was an urgency to this, as if she felt she needed forgiveness, was troubled by the thought of her own behavior.

"Yes, he's yours, I lend him to you," I said, smiling. And I sensed that it was my god she wanted, the god of the New Testament, the one who would love her in spite of her desperate confusion and in spite of her desperate search for that love in the minutiae of sexuality.

In the face of my growing and nameless passion for Molly, I decided I must have sex with a man. I had been seeing someone who was actually a friend of Molly's. David and I had met briefly the year before and had had a few desultory dates during which he had made it known that he would like things to get more intimate between us and I had resolutely kept him at bay. When he brought me back to the dorm at night, I literally danced away from him into the elevator without giving him so much as a goodnight hug. I watched him stand there looking forlorn as the door of the elevator closed and wondered why I was being so withholding. Partly I had trouble understanding what David saw in me: I didn't trust his liking me, saw it as some potential flaw in him. Some other part of me thought I was being a good Christian girl and protecting my virtue, even as I had begun to renounce my Catholicism. What didn't occur to me was that I was frightened, totally new to this game of dating and navigating the shoals of sexuality, and I hardly knew what to do.

David and I sat out by the lake one afternoon and I knew with some predatory instinct that I must lose my virginity. We had endlessly discussed the fact that I wanted to be "just friends." David kept on dating me anyway and seemed shocked this afternoon when I suddenly turned to him and asked coyly, "Could I interest you in kissing me?" He put down his book, looked at me fiercely, moved me gently onto my back in the grass, and kissed me—softly at first, then more intently as I responded, until finally his tongue was in my mouth. I vaguely liked this, I decided.

"What's going on?" he questioned.

"Well, I think it's time I stopped talking to everybody about sex and learned something about it firsthand."

He laughed. "I'm only too happy to oblige. How much do you want to know?"

"How much can you teach me?"

"Well, I guess you'll have to wait and find out."

He pulled me back toward him and we kissed longer and more intently.

By the time we were able to be together in a bed, the loss of my virginity was almost anticlimactic. I had had no fear, since I had read enough and talked enough with Molly to know exactly what was happening. From my own erotic explorations, I was used to the responses of my body, yet the experience of touching and being touched by someone else told me something different that was exhilarating and more full. It was a surprise.

I quickly found myself pursuing sex with David with great enthusiasm. It was good sex: it was full, often exciting, and fun. What it never was was passionate, but I didn't know the difference until I made love to a woman.

Slowly I noticed some change in Molly. She seemed more distant, less available. Often when I saw her coming from her room she looked as if she'd been crying. Suddenly she was keeping very erratic hours; there were days when she didn't get to class and didn't show up for meals. I felt hurt and didn't understand why we suddenly weren't as close. I decided that this was yet some new aspect of Molly's life that I would learn about in time, so I waited and watched.

Finally, one night before dinner, we sat in her room with the lights out and the music off. There was a new story. Molly talked about a woman she had become involved with, a senior who lived on one of the upper floors of the dorm. The relationship was troubling to her and to me as well. The woman was a shadowy figure who seemed somehow sinister.

"When we're close it's very exciting to me," Molly said, "but I don't know if I can make a commitment to this."

It was a few moments before I realized what she meant. She and this woman had become lovers.

I felt a mixture of shock, intense curiosity, fear for Molly, and compassion for her pain and conflict. The moment had the quality of a crisis to it. A sense of moral danger took over; my Catholic conscience wondered if even my god could condone this. I needed to save Molly from this terrible situation. What I was unconscious of was my jealousy and my hurt that someone else had what I wanted. "Molly," I said, "this is destructive for you, and I can't stand by and watch it happen. I care too much about you. Give it up, or I can't be your friend." And I meant it. I thought I was being a true friend, willing to sacrifice my own interests for the sake of her well-being.

I left the room and wandered for hours through the dorm, trying to understand my own agitation, pain, and confusion. I had no sense of what might happen, and I was prepared to lose her, though she had become the central part of my life.

Hours later, Molly slid a note under my door. "I'll tell her we have to stop. This will be hard. Can you help me?"

Our intimacy deepened. We spent hours together in the Campus Restaurant. Sometimes she wrote me poems. Molly began telling me that she loved me. She hugged me and sat next to me with her head leaning into my shoulder. Unused to such open displays of affection, I laughed and awkwardly told her I loved her, too. I did, in fact; my heart sang at these times, but it was hard for me to know what all of this feeling meant, and I kept careful control of myself.

Fall began to give way to the chill of the New England winter. I watched Molly make her way around the campus, a standout in the dark raccoon fur coat she had bought at a garage sale, engaging anyone she could with her curiosity and charm. She and I and David now spent a lot of time together; in fact, the bond I had with David had much to do with the fact that he was as entranced by Molly as I. We volunteered together at a nearby training school for the developmentally disabled. We were caught up in examining life together, discussing the horrors we saw in the back wards of the training school, wondering if the life of a person so deformed and disabled had meaning. We worried together about David being drafted. We talked, laughed, and cried together.

Most evenings, Molly went off on a date and I spent time with David. While I fully accepted that this was the way the social contract worked, I knew very well that what I longed for was to be with Molly, and that I wanted only to get to the end of the evening so that we could be together again and talk it all over—so that I could feel reassured that I was still important in Molly's life.

When it came time for Christmas break, I invited Molly to stay with me and my family for one night before she headed home. At dinner my parents were ungracious and cold, as if they sensed there was something different about the two of us. Then it was time to go to bed, and the only place for us to sleep was together on the pull-out couch in the family room, since my grandmother, who had lived with us since my grandfather's death, now used my old room.

We climbed into bed and talked. We were tense. We'd never had this much physical intimacy; the specter of Molly's relationship with the other woman was there between us. I was about to turn over to go to sleep, but I noticed Molly was lying there wide awake, her eyes deep with some feeling I could not place. After a long silence, she inched closer to me in the bed, moved her body against mine, and said, "Claud, I want to kiss you." A shock of longing went through my body along with a shock of fear. The warmth of her was so intoxicating that I couldn't turn away. We kissed and I felt the same burning sensation that I had felt sipping from the chalice the night of the mass with Mike Carey. But the sensation of this kiss was softness, sensual, like melting into down, like falling into water, like leaving my self and losing myself and finding myself in Molly.

Then, I stopped it. "We can't do this," I said.

"I know," she whispered. She turned away, and I lay awake the rest of the night. The next day we tried to talk, but mostly we avoided talking, and the long separation of the vacation gave us time to pretend that nothing had happened. Except that when I thought about her, my body quivered and my mind raced. I was terrified and exhilarated at the same time. I knew that whatever was happening to me, moral or immoral, good or bad, I would give way.

One Saturday morning, my roommate and I were lounging in our beds drinking tea, eating oranges, and talking. There was a knock at the door; it was Molly. She came in and joined us, sitting on my bed. When my roommate left to meet her boyfriend, Molly hugged me. Before long she was stretched out next to me, caressing me and looking into my eyes with that sweet, seductive smile on her lips; fleetingly, her hand grazed my breast. At my sharp intake of breath, she looked at me and said, "But isn't this what you want?"

"Yes . . . no . . . I don't know—we have to stop." I reminded myself that I had threatened to give up my friendship with her to save her from the destructiveness of a lesbian relationship. I saw the folly of my self-righteousness, my moral indignation, my bogus protectiveness of my friend and wondered at my hypocrisy, because I was falling now, out of control, my body and my heart pierced with longing.

One night a few days later, I went to Molly's room. She was alone. I sat next to her on the bed, terrified. "What do you want, Claud?" she asked.

And then our clothes were off, and for the first time I was touching her breasts, being touched, kissing her, no reserve now, and I knew something different from what I had ever known making love with David. All of me was there, present, tender, sensual, impassioned, and I felt held by Molly's heat, caught by the lightness of her touch, I felt her love for me, her sensuality, and in me there was nothing held back. After that first time we cried—with simple relief and with complex feelings of wonder and fear at having finally met here after the months of tension and longing.

We tried, but we couldn't keep from being with each other. Our lovemaking became more intense, more intimate; what had seemed unimaginable to me in terms of the mechanics of making love to a woman now became easy because of the passion I felt, the desire to give everything I could, to be for Molly what no one had been before. For the first time Molly was orgasmic, and I knew it to be a statement of the truth of our caring for each other, the profound connection we felt.

We moved in together. We made love almost nightly. People in the dorm became suspicious about what was going on. We tried to pretend that nothing unusual was happening. Molly still dated men, and I still saw David. I told him about it. David was curious about our lovemaking. "What *do* two women do in bed together?" he asked. "Are there Coke bottles?"

I was enraged. It was a rage that would grow in me as I realized over time how little anyone else could understand—that what I felt with Molly had no parallel anywhere in my experience. How it was all about sex and not about sex at all. How it was about fullness and wholeness and being right with myself. How it was about wanting to take all that I felt for her—the desire, the delight, the deep places in me where I met her pain—and make it real, make it come alive, have a conversation without words that would take us somewhere unimaginable, different every time. How the conversations built, how I understood her and knew her better with each touch, how I let her know me, every hidden and tender place in me, how the knowledge became so deep that my knowing her became part of me and I carried it around with me now, caring for her at the same time I was caring for myself. So that every time I entered her, every time I buried my tongue in her, every time our nipples touched, I knew her life more completely, her secrets became the most true and real bridge between us and my own secrets were opened to her with joy and without reserve. There could be no thought of reserve, because I wanted to give over, give her everything.

Sometimes as I came I saw lights and colors, sometimes I thought I saw god, sometimes I looked out at trees and the whole universe seemed to be alive in me, all the cells dancing. The morning light shuddered in my heart and somewhere deep in my uterus and between my legs, and she was there, holding me, holding all of this feeling. With one touch she could make me come alive, so that we both realized that ecstasy is a part of life, that souls can touch and bodies can meet. And I was not alone anymore.

It could begin with her eyes that looked at me questioningly, smiling, inviting, and then the slightest brush of her lips on mine, the sharp catch of breath as we touched, her moving against me so that I could feel her breasts and her warmth and her life stir, quicken, lean into me as I leaned back. It felt soft as nothing had ever felt soft before. Something moved in me, shifted, gave over as the kisses deepened and my mind left. I became pure feeling and arousal and words began to form in my mind—oh no, what's happening, how can this be happening that I am losing ground here, losing myself in her, that we are floating away together, oh no, oh yes. She whispered that she loved me and I knew it to be true, saw it in her eyes, in the deep tenderness and concentration in her face as she looked at me, seeking me out, wanting to know, to give me to myself as she began to move down my body or I began to move down her body because she knows, I have said that I adore her, that I cherish her, that she is precious to me, that she is what makes my life make sense. And when I said this I was thinking about the way she talks, the way she cries, the way she touches other people, the way she throws her clothes on the floor, the books she loves to read, the poetry she writes, the music we listen to together, the walks outdoors, the muted winter landscape, all of it, all of her. I feel like I'm rocking in a boat while the sun glistens on the surface of the water. Then she moves down my body with her hands and with her tongue with all of her moving tenderly, slowly, till I want to scream to her, please, she touches me and I flood. Then maybe her tongue is on me, her head between my legs, and I look down and watch and stroke her hair moving with her mouth, trying to match her, meet her, and this seems unimaginable, that this can be, every time, but it is true. And I feel her fingers inside of me, exploring and moving, and I feel her excitement, her love for me, she is saying it so clearly, I am embraced by it, and I call out her name because I need to say it, because it is all about her, who she is, the fullness of her being, that I love her so much, that I can be here so out of control and unafraid and open and this may go on for minutes or for hours. We will keep moving together and crying for some relief but wanting it to go on forever. She will cry out and we will grab and hold on to each other and not know whether what is happening is real, whether to let it be just about our bodies or to stay in this state where it keeps being about our souls touching. I move to suck her breasts, or I lie over her grazing her with my own. I can't find enough ways to touch, to carry on this conversation; I can't find enough ways to say it, I love you, every breath, every cell, there is nothing excluded. And she may call out, cry out for me to touch her in a certain way, harder, faster, slower. I move inside of her and try to get the rhythm right, and she cries with pleasure and with the ecstatic pain of being known at her core and embraced. And finally I come or she does, and if she does it feels like I did, it's all the same now. We lie together quietly stroking each other, gently, tenderly, and what has been is ineffable and true. We lie and look into each other's eyes for a long time trying to fathom this, maybe until the sun comes up and the birds start to rouse the world from slumber. Maybe we sleep finally and then get up and drink tea together and pretend that it's just another day. Except that we know that something holy has happened, something ageless and pure, and that no matter what happens, this connection, this knowing between us, can never be taken away. We feel burned through and purified.

And no, David, there is not a Coke bottle in sight.

And then one night, I suppose because it was so intense, because Molly was so frightened, she called me and said she was somewhere off campus with the other woman and would I let her in because she'd be back after the dorm was locked. I was supposed to accept that we were not committed to each other, that we were not exclusive, that she must be free to explore other relationships. I locked Molly out that night. I quickly petitioned the housemother for a new roommate. She was only too happy to oblige. We discovered later that during the semester break, the resident adviser on our floor had gone through our room searching for evidence that we were lovers. They failed to find anything, but the housemother must have taken my defection as a sign that at least one of us had come to our senses. Unknowingly, I had saved us from further investigation and potential dismissal from school.

The system was riddled with hypocrisy. We all broke the university's rules. Men came to our rooms, we went to theirs, we had sex—everybody expected it, and nobody ransacked people's rooms for evidence of illicit heterosexual behavior. When I walked through the dorm with David, I was viewed as a normal, healthy woman on her way to becoming a part of the American dream.

Outside the dorm, as we demonstrated for peace and love, as

the sexual revolution intensified, we protested for the right to love freely. But it was Molly whom I loved and with whom I felt real and connected and alive. Molly was the person I shared the most with, the person who had the most meaning for me, the person who most stirred my heart. But this love was viewed as a grave breach of moral conduct—sick, perverted, dangerous. When we protested for free love, we didn't mean *this* free.

I was forced to question my own values. Was this immoral or wasn't it? I had been taught that love was the central truth of Christianity, the basis of all moral reasoning. I knew I loved Molly. The truth of this for me was unquestionable, immediate; it stood without analysis or reasoning. After all those years of reading about love, I had finally come to understand its meaning. I cherished her; I would do anything for her well-being. She was the only other person in my world who felt as important to me as myself. This love felt completely pure. So I couldn't believe there was anything immoral in what I did, couldn't believe there was something immoral about who I was. If the Catholic Church denounced this, then I could not be Catholic; if the world denounced this, then that was their problem.

Within days, my anger spent by my hasty and dramatic leaving, I began to sneak each night to Molly's single room, hoping I would not be seen. Molly and I struggled to come to terms with what we meant to one another. In all of this it never occurred to me to think of myself as a lesbian. I believed only that I loved Molly.

By April, because she couldn't come to terms with our relationship or with herself, Molly called her mother to come and get her, and she left school. In those last days before she left, I was numb with grief. Molly was sick; I cared for her as she vomited over the side of the bed. I wondered how I would go on without her, wondered how we would stay in touch, if I would ever see her again. She didn't know, just couldn't say. On the day of her departure, I went out to the lake and stared up at the window of the room I knew would be empty when I returned and wondered how one small person could have to endure so much pain. David became my only comfort.

Within a year, Molly was married. I stayed on at the

university and earned a graduate degree. There was never another woman. David and I broke up and, halfheartedly, I dated other men. David and I reunited. What I knew of love I now associated with Molly, and with loss. David was there, and he was steady. I decided to settle for a calmer, less painful path.

5.
David

David and I were married on a cloudy afternoon in December, one week before Christmas. We held the service in a small Lutheran chapel set in the woods just off campus. Neither of us was Catholic any longer, and the Lutheran chapel was starkly beautiful, a small, contemporary wood structure with vaulted ceilings, exposed beams, and high, airy windows. The priest who had come to campus to replace Mike Carey married us in an ecumenical service. Hannah, my old high school friend, was my maid of honor; she and the other bridesmaids and my mother and grandmother wore red velvet. The men were dressed in black tuxedos. The ceremony was a strange mixture of the traditional and the new. I had both my parents walk me to the altar. The organist played traditional wedding music, but David's best man sang a folk song and played the guitar. For the traditional biblical readings we substituted passages from Kahlil Gibran and a Sufi prayer, "Look to this day, it is the day of days," for the Sufis, it seemed, had a great mystical consciousness about love.

David waited for me at the altar with a mixture of pride and devotion on his face. We had written the vows and designed the ceremony ourselves. Up until now I had been caught up with the aesthetics of the wedding, as if I were producing a major theatrical event. Now I faced him squarely, and it must have been that unconsciously I knew that I did not mean what I said.

"David," I started, "I vow to love and honor you, to respect your needs and commit myself unselfishly to your well-being in sickness and in health."

And here I stopped, my voice trembling, thinking I had finished. David looked at me. I waited for him to begin. He was hesitating, and I wasn't sure why. Finally, he recited the identical words addressed to me, except that he finished with what I had forgotten—"for all the days of our lives." I had left off the promise of permanence. I realized this as we walked back down the aisle to the smiles and waves of friends and family. I fleetingly wondered why I forgot my lines. Then I thought about the fact that almost everyone important in my life was here except Molly, the person I cared for most deeply.

From the chapel we drove to an inn closer to my parents' home for an elegant cocktail hour and dinner. It was romantic and aesthetically lovely that a light snow began to fall as the wedding party assembled for photos, but we couldn't ignore the hazards it created for everyone who drove. This contrast of beauty with hazard seemed to me a metaphor for my marriage: everything looked good on the surface, but underneath there was a deep and dangerous fracture in the bond that David and I had vowed to keep. The fracture was my dishonesty with myself, my belief that I was doing the right thing by ignoring my feelings and getting on with the work of being an adult woman. My marriage was only a detour from my true path, and some part of me knew it; but I did it anyway.

I had said to David when he had proposed, "You know it wouldn't be honest for me to say that you're the love of my life. I don't know if I'll ever feel again what I felt for Molly. I don't know if these longings for women will ever entirely leave me. But I care for you, and I think we do well together. If you want me under those circumstances, then, yes, I'll marry you."

"I think you'll come to love me more," he had said. "Love is something that grows. It's not always about passion and intensity."

David and I spent our wedding night in the honeymoon suite of a seedy place called the Red Bull Inn, the best lodging our small town had to offer. Too exhausted to make love that night, we waited until morning. At nine we were interrupted by the housekeeper, who thought we'd left and simply walked in unannounced. It was an intrusion and embarrassing, but we were only doing what was expected for a couple on their honeymoon, so I laughed about it. David yelled as he heard the door opening, and I dove under the covers.

For a time, it felt good to be called "Mrs." It seemed a rite of passage, as if I now had status in a world where I had always felt like an alien presence. The "Mrs." told people who I was, that a man cared for me, that I was acceptable, a conformist, a "good" woman. I checked "Mrs." on my job applications and my credit applications and believed that people looked on me with a new respect. I told myself I was happy to have this conflict over love out of the way and could now get on with my work. Except that what we got on with was David's work. We went where he needed to go, and my own work was put on hold.

Right after Christmas, we moved to the Midwest, where David was pursuing a graduate degree. We lived in a furnished apartment that David had rented for himself a few months earlier. All the carpeting was green and all the furniture dark brown, nondescript, and institutional. As we lay in bed with boxes of my things scattered around the room and David's meager store of personal possessions neatly arranged on the desk and in the bureau, it felt grim to me. But David was elated.

"It's so good that you're finally here. What a relief that I won't have to do my own laundry now and that I'll have you to clean the apartment." He turned his head and I could see a sly grin on his face.

"I'm going to hang a very big sign over the bed," I told him. "It will say, 'I was not put on this earth to be a slave to a man.' In case you didn't know it, I expect you to do fully half the work around here."

"Oh god, okay, I'm sorry." David grabbed his head and feigned distress. "I know you're the original feminist; you invented the term. I'm just kidding. How do you think I survived before you, dear? I'm a very competent housekeeper." He jabbed me in the ribs.

"Sure, that's why we came back here to a month's worth of mold in the refrigerator. Some reception you planned for me."

I was half teasing, but there was anger in my voice, and it wasn't fair to David. He tried to jostle me out of my lonely, dark mood. In fact, he had cleaned the entire colony of mold out of the refrigerator and had been more upset than I when we found it.

David took up his graduate program again, and I stocked shelves in a department store, because, my graduate degree notwithstanding, I was unable to find work in my field. He structured his time at school so that he was free to be with me in the evenings. He made me feel secure and protected. He was physically big and cuddly, like a teddy bear. It was just that most evenings, he sat and stared for hours at the television. He didn't generate much that was new or active in our life. I was lonely. In this foreign place I was adrift without familiar anchors. There were no more classes, no more seminars, no more books that I was required to read. There was no family and there were no friends. I hated working in the department store. I began to invent reasons to be angry with him, and he was always patient with me and never got mad.

After a year, because I was so miserable, David decided we would move back east. He enrolled in another graduate program and we both got jobs and lived in the city in a studio apartment. Still I was discontented. Nothing satisfied me—not taking classes, not my new editorial job, not the exhilaration of the cultural life of the city.

David now called me, affectionately, "bug," short for "you bug me." This was his only concession to anger with me. He bore my discontent with typical patience and good-natured joking. He tried to be supportive, but he was never sure what precisely to support.

On Friday nights it became our habit to eat an inexpensive dinner out and wander through town listening to the music that drifted from the jazz clubs. We'd end up in a coffeehouse and sit playing chess or watching people come and go until we were tired enough to go home. Over coffee one Friday night, David looked at me across the chessboard and said, "There's something I want to tell you. I've talked to Molly."

"What do you mean, you've talked to Molly? When did you talk to her? And why?" I had not been in contact with Molly in over four years.

David started to play absently with chess pieces. He moved his queen around in small circles on the board. "Well, before we moved back, when I was out here interviewing for the job, I called her and asked her to meet me for a cup of coffee at the airport. I missed her and wanted to know how she was. She asked about you. When I told her we were moving back here, she said, 'Well, maybe we can all get together sometime.'

"So, last week I called her again. She and Phil would like to get together. I said I'd check with you and call her back, but I suggested they come in and have dinner with us next week. What do you think?"

"I think I wish you'd told me earlier."

"I didn't know how you'd feel about it."

"I'm not sure I do know. She said she didn't want to have any contact with me anymore. Why has she changed her mind?"

"Well," David said, "she was surprised to find out we were married. I think she feels that the past is the past and that now we could all be friends."

"Is that how you feel?" I asked, somewhat incredulous.

"Sure, why not. I thought it would make you happy to see her again. I know that you two were good friends. Maybe you need a friend in your life."

I remembered the letter Molly had sent me some time after her last visit to me at school, just before her marriage. I had saved it carefully in a box with letters from K and Mike Carey and Helen Scott and other people I'd been close to. I thought of this as a box of love letters that I would pore over when I was old and was trying to figure out all that had happened in my life.

"I can't continue to be in touch with you," she had written. "I think we kind of soaked everything we could of each other." She had sent me a wedding picture. The last line of the letter said, "I was talking about you to some friends at work today, and I began to cry. I'm not even going to try to figure out why."

Molly and I hugged. "Hi, Claud," she said, with an air of "let's acknowledge but forget everything that's been in our past." And then she introduced Phil, whom neither David nor I had met. He was an attractive, tall, lean, dark man. He was overeffusive, I thought, clearly nervous. We quickly set about serving drinks. I noticed Molly wanted scotch on the rocks, not a sedate glass of wine.

She had changed. She was tense and overly formal, and she avoided looking directly at me. Her intensity was gone. She talked about houses and budgets and recipes. She rambled on at great length about her recipe for beef bourguignon. Every once in a while the old spark of her was there, and I remembered what I had felt. We carefully kept our distance. We were married ladies now, not the same people who had been passionately involved. We had chosen a different path.

The four of us developed a kind of social friendship. We'd visit their apartment and their cabin upstate. But when David and I made a decision to move from the city to the suburbs, Molly and I went back to being two women friends and our foursome dissolved. David and Phil had little in common. Molly and I would meet for lunch in the city. Sometimes she would take a train to our apartment. We wrote letters. We were friends, and I accepted that this was all we were.

Except for one fleeting night when she stayed over because David was out of town. I had vaguely conscious hopes for this visit. Some part of me knew that I could easily be unfaithful to David. I saw the fear of this possibility in Molly's eyes. For a moment we looked at each other, we held each other, then she quickly pulled away.

But for the first time we talked about the past, about what we had been to each other.

"I miss making love to a woman, Molly. Things have never been the same for me since you. I walk around feeling like there's this hole in me, and I wonder if only a woman can fill it. Maybe what I need is a child. But some days I find myself wondering if I am to go through my whole life never being with a woman again. The thought of that makes me very sad. I wish I could get over wanting it."

"I would be very jealous if you were with another woman," she said. "I need you, Claud, I want you in my life, but not as a lover. And I don't think you're gay. I think you take David too much for granted. He needs to be more demanding with you, not so accepting of everything you do. If he were firmer with you, you would respect him more."

I found this ironic, that she didn't want me herself but in some way thought of us as exclusively tied, that it would disturb her if there were to be another woman in my life. And while she talked endlessly about Phil, it seemed to me that it was our emotional connection that she wanted. I was the one who was privy to the landscape of her emotional life, and she to mine. It seemed we simply had sex with these men we had married. When I let myself, I could acknowledge that I was deeply envious of Phil and that I still wanted Molly.

Since we lived in the suburbs and had only one car, David took the train every day to his job in the city and I picked him up at the station. He always made the 5:28, always jumped into the car and kissed me, and always asked, "How was your day, bug?"

I was always depressed. Sometimes I wouldn't answer.

"Oh, another one of those days, huh? Is there anything I can do?"

Usually at these times I'd tell him I needed a change and suggest we get fast food for dinner. The routines of our life felt deadening to me. We'd eat in stony silence, and when we got home he would retreat to the TV.

A few times, he tried to talk about what it felt like for him.

"You know, sometimes it really bothers me that I never know how you're going to be. Either you're mad or you're depressed or something has gone wrong at work. You don't seem to care much about what's going on with me. It's not too pleasant to have to wonder every day what I'm going to have to face when I get in the car."

I would struggle not to cry, feeling completely misunderstood. "I'm bored, I hate my job, we have no money. I have a graduate degree and I can't get a decent job. You go off to work every day and are with people you like. You do interesting things and you're working toward a degree. I'm stuck in a goddamned office where they ring a bell to tell you it's okay to go to the bathroom, and I sit writing blurbs for library books over and over for eight hours a day. I'm sorry I'm not happier, I'm sorry. I'm just miserable, and I don't know what to do."

David became more and more frustrated with my unhappiness. Nothing he tried seemed to help. What he didn't know was that I spent much of my time when he wasn't home lying on top of our bed crying. I kept thinking, knowing, that I had to leave him, but I wasn't able to imagine how I could. He was good to me; it was I who created the problems, I who still loved Molly and who spent my days at work fantasizing about some woman who might take her place, trying to fill up the hours till it was time to go home. Finally, I decided to see a therapist.

In therapy, I tried to learn how to be married and be happy. What used to be spiritual and moral questions for me about the meaning of love now became psychological ones. Though my therapist was a feminist and going through her own divorce, therapy began to make me think I was sick. I learned that I expected too much from marriage, that my depression was really suppressed anger at David, that I needed to build a life separate from him. I learned that I had trouble with intimacy, that my lesbian longings could be tamed by a concerted effort at fostering my own emotional development, and that I simply had to grow up.

I convinced myself that I must go back to being the good wife. Once again, I tried to settle for the trappings of a domestic life. I looked for activities to keep myself occupied. I joined an evening volleyball group. I invited friends out for lunch. I found a church group for us to join. I began to feel mature and responsible and mentally healthy again, though not significantly less depressed.

David and I felt that a crisis had passed, except now our marriage was about separateness—his life, my life. We seemed to spend more time apart than together.

Then, in that bleak suburban community we lived in that sprawled for miles without definition, that seemed like a cultural wasteland where only car dealerships and fast-food restaurants could thrive, I located a consciousness-raising group. It met in a large, rundown house on the main street of town—one of those prewar Victorians with three floors that seem to go on forever.

The group was made up of women, many of whom, like me, had not confined their sexual experimenting to men. Some were on their second or third marriages. We were all struggling to know how to "do" a relationship and having very little success at being happy. Some were flirting with drug addiction—their own or their partner's. We worked our way through the standard set of consciousness-raising questions, pored over our pasts, and explored the ways we'd been hurt by the sexist biases of society. We followed the format carefully, talking in turn, listening to one another's stories, not interrupting, not giving advice. We cried and got angry for one another. And after the formal part of the group was done, we had coffee and soda and sometimes wine or beer or a joint, and we carried on about the trials of our current lives and the way love just never seemed to go right.

One of the married women in the group felt drawn to another woman, but the attraction wasn't mutual. Each week I waited to see how she handled wanting a woman she couldn't have. She always seemed depressed, too. Some weeks she cried, and the other women in the group who knew her better held her and rocked her until her sobbing stopped.

Now I had a political perspective to counter my newfound therapeutic one. I saw that the others didn't seem to struggle like me to be psychologically correct. When I got home I described to David what was happening in the group and told him that it made me reconsider all my questions about wanting a woman. Hearing that the group rekindled my preoccupation with women made him very uneasy.

"Well, what do you want from me?" he asked. "What does this mean for us?"

"It means that I need a woman in my life I can be close to. I don't know what it means beyond that. Sometimes I think I want to have a female lover. I can't seem to get past this."

I felt that I must be honest with David, that it was only fair to let him know the truth. It created more and more distance between us. Whenever I got close to a woman, he knew that more energy went into my longing than into our marriage. He listened endlessly to my conflicts, my doubts, my obsessions. Finally he said, "Maybe if this is what you need you have to act on it. Then you'll know."

"And what about you?" I asked.

"I think I could handle it. If it makes you happy, it could actually help our relationship."

"So you think we could be married and I could have a relationship with a woman 'on the side'?"

"I want you to be happy."

I found David's offer perplexing because I couldn't imagine how this could work for him. In reality I knew that should a woman come into my life, all my energies would be devoted to her. I could not envision living a split existence.

Each week I faithfully went to therapy sessions. We never dealt directly with the possibility that I needed to make a choice, that maybe I simply had an emotional preference for women. We kept trying to understand what was wrong with me. I kept trying to talk about what made me so angry with David. My therapist suggested that maybe a couples' group would help.

Two therapists ran the group. After a few initial sessions, they asked each of the women to act out a scene from our childhoods that reflected our feelings about our relationship with our father.

When it was my turn, I picked one of the men in the group to be the stand-in for my father and had him sit quietly and told him to look judgmental and harsh. I left the room, and as I opened the door and walked back in, I could feel the same fear and constriction I used to feel around my father. I crouched and began to make my way around the outskirts of the room, like an animal, stealthy, trying to keep from attracting notice, watching, trying to keep myself safe. At some point I stood with my back to the wall and crept, my back arched, as people do in movie scenes when they are terrified, and avoided my father's gaze, trying only to get away from him. I could feel the rigidity of my body, my fear, and at the same time my wanting just to get away, to be free of his control.

The group sat quietly, stunned by this vivid performance of my fear. I knew what I would hear from the therapists before they could say it.

"But David's not your father."

Indeed he was not my father; he was everything my father was not. But I didn't love him. All the therapy and marriage counseling our community mental-health center had to offer couldn't change that. We had a workable, friendly, and civilized relationship, if not an emotionally gratifying one. I couldn't understand why I could desire David sexually, be driven by lust, by enjoyment of his body and my own, yet be totally absorbed by and obsessed with whatever woman happened to be in my heart. For a while I thought the problem was that I needed a different man. But no other man attracted me. It was only women who fascinated.

When I was in high school I overheard my mother having a conversation one night with my father about a student in the senior class. She made an offhand sarcastic comment, in the way my mother would: "Oh, her. I hear she's one of *those.*" Somehow I knew instinctively that she meant this girl was a lesbian. I could hear my mother reporting bitterly to some faceless someone one day about me, "Oh, she's one of those." *Or saying nothing, denying my existence.*

I didn't want to be "one of those." My journal, full of my obsessive longings for various women and my conflict about not loving David, began to reflect my increasing awareness that I had to give some language, a name, to what I was feeling.

> *I think that I must say, I am gay. I think. There would be a tremendously freeing power to that declaration. A direction, an identity—allowing myself to need women in the way I need them. Giving up the struggle to be a man's woman. Would I make it in a gay world? Can I make it as I am now? Isn't the basic issue one of coming out to people in general, being who I am, even beyond defining a sexual preference?*
>
> *I wish there were some easy way or someone to help. I wish I could take David and find for him what he needs and what could make him happy so that I would lessen the pain of causing him pain. I wish I could lessen the pain of having to give up what he is to me. Is there some way to deal with all this? Right now I don't see it, but I know it is time, sooner or later—there is a frightening inevitability.*

David began to travel more on business. I began to allow the word "gay" to enter my consciousness, but somehow I couldn't bring myself to think "lesbian." With David out of town, I read *The Well of Loneliness* and whatever other few books I could find. The psychology texts were all clear that lesbians were pathological and immature. In a book called *On Women* by the psychoanalyst

Clara Thompson I read: "Adult love seems to be a rare experience in our culture anyway and would doubtless be even more rare among homosexuals because a person with the necessary degree of maturity would probably prefer a heterosexual relation."

I felt shame. I felt relegated to the emotional status of a child.

I searched the libraries and the pages of alternative newspapers for references to gay events and gay activities. But this was the seventies; there was still little language, few words, almost no events. In one paper I found a listing for a meeting of the Daughters of Bilitis, an organization, it said, of women who loved women. The name put me off. What did my feelings, which were pure and intense and tender, have to do with a word like "Bilitis," or with a word like "lesbian," which seemed somehow medieval and stirred in me images of perversion, women in black leather with whips, women who rode motorcycles and pretended to be men. These were not words that conjured images that spoke to what I felt.

It went back and forth like this. For a time I was mature, married, and committed; then I slipped back into questioning, knowing that I couldn't be happy and married to a man.

The sense of inevitability I had written about in my journal was like a weight that I could not jettison. But for me there is always a vast gulf of time between inevitability and action. I took another detour. I decided to go back to graduate school to get training in a profession in which I could make a living. I decided to become a therapist myself.

Graduate school was not the rural idyll of my college life. The campus, set in the middle of a city, was cluttered and obstructed with traffic, and there was never anywhere to park. This was no ivory tower for the study of literary criticism or philosophy; this was a working degree I was studying for. When I wasn't in class I was interning at clinics. Ironically, I found myself training in a clinic with alcoholics and drug addicts.

Feminist consciousness was completely lacking in the school curriculum. We were still taught a medically driven, pathology-based model of treatment that almost completely avoided looking at larger social issues that oppressed our women clients. Some of the other women students and I decided to form a consciousness-raising group at school. But what started out as an effort to look at women's issues became a support group. We began to meet over dinner at one another's homes. We talked about our husbands, our problems with marriage, how there was never enough time to do anything, how Professor So-and-so was incredibly sexist. One night I said to these women, one of whom in particular had become a good friend, "Well, what about being gay?" It was the first time this subject has been broached.

"What about it?" Ellen wanted to know.

"Have any of you ever thought you might want to be with a woman?"

"Sure," one of the other women said. "I tried it once. I just like sex with men too much."

"Well, do you think it's immature and pathological, like all the books say?"

"Who cares? If it's who you are, it's who you are. I don't think gay people are sick and pathological. It's a social prejudice, just like racism and sexism."

I was quiet as I listened to them, and finally Ellen turned to me and asked gently, "Is there something else that's troubling you?"

I poured out my story about Molly, about David, about my still-unresolved conflicts. Now they listened to me seriously.

"Sometimes I think I want to be with a woman. But it's a frightening thought. What about a family? What about having someone you can depend on to be there in the way you depend on a spouse?"

"Ha!" one woman said. "From what I can see, marriages aren't exactly dependable these days."

Ellen looked at me as if she didn't understand. "But wouldn't you have this if you met the right woman?"

"I don't know," I said. "I just don't know."

I had never told David about my pilgrimage to the woman in the chemistry lab. When the women in my group heard what she had said—that I might not be strong enough to be gay—they told me that was ridiculous and they were sorry I had listened to her. But they could offer no help for me other than encouragement that it was okay, that I was okay. They didn't know anything about how gay people "came out." In the whole of the graduate school curriculum, there was not one course that dealt with homosexuality except to make vague references to its deviance. The old despair, the chronic depression and questioning of myself, set in again.

"Bug, you need to come home. I just got a call from your mother. Your father's in the hospital, in intensive care. It's something about his liver. He's very jaundiced, and they don't know if he's going to make it. I'd walk down and meet you, but I'm going to start packing the car."

It was the end of the day and I was down the street having coffee with Diane, my redheaded, funny, down-to-earth best friend. We had been close since the end of my relationship with Molly in college. We had spent much of the summer after sitting in a rowboat in the middle of a lake leaning over a chessboard we propped between us on a box. I felt I might not have survived the breakup without her. She knew all the ups and downs, all the neurotic and not-so-neurotic conflicts of my life.

She walked me to the door, her hand on my shoulder. "Please call if there's anything I can do," she said. From an alcoholic family herself, she knew what this was like—the sudden crises, the never knowing whether or not things were a matter of life or death. She hugged me and I walked back up the street, banging the ground with a stick in frustration, knowing I didn't want my father to die.

It was a cool night in early October. I sat mutely in the passenger side of the car as we headed up the parkway trying to absorb the reality that my father might die at the same time that I tried to deny it. My mother had said only, "Come now, they're taking him to intensive care." The past weeks had been tentative, with his seeming to be very sick and then seeming not so. We had been back and forth to visit several times. I had waited for and dreaded the phone call: Come, your father is dying. Come, your father is dying because he drinks too much. Come, your father is dying because he is an alcoholic and hides liquor under the seats of the car and can't get home from work because he drives into telephone poles and doesn't want to live because his children have grown up and left home and there is nothing more for him to live for.

My father had been drinking himself to death and I could not understand it, refused to understand it. So I sat and watched the October moon lighten the edges of passing clouds in that otherwise clear night sky.

My sister Ann and her husband arrived at the hospital before we did. My mother and Therese, only thirteen years old, were already there. We found them standing outside a room that was not intensive care but a private isolation unit. We were going to be asked to participate in a charade. We had to put on masks and gowns to go in to see him. They were calling it hepatitis.

We learned later that the doctor had admitted him under a false diagnosis so that our family name would not be tarnished. Three generations of our family had been born in that hospital, had been sick there, had been visitors there, and our faces were too familiar to let anybody know the truth. The truth was that my father had made an attempt to stop drinking and had gone into D.T.'s. The doctor had given him Librium to help him through it, but he had only become sicker. I walked into the room to find my father lying in a white gown under white sheets, his face yellow-green and puffy. I stood at the foot of his bed and he struggled to greet me with the familiar gesture that was half a wave. The intravenous dripped silently into his veins. I said, "Hi, Dad," and I wanted to tell him I loved him but I couldn't. Late into that night there was no change, so we left the hospital and went to my parents' house.

My mother was pretending to be very strong, but my sisters and I knew better. We trailed her home on the interstate. When she walked through the door she headed straight to the liquor cabinet and downed a glass of wine. She didn't even take off her coat. My grandmother was there and we all watched this but didn't comment.

"Maybe I called you to come too soon," she mumbled to us, "but the doctor said it was very bad. Then, after you had both already left, his blood count changed. But that's not why they didn't take him to intensive care. The doctors said it wouldn't do any good. You must be hungry. Get something to eat."

David went to the refrigerator and pulled out leftovers. We all sat around the table. A heavy sense of inevitability came over me again. As I sat there eating a cheese sandwich, I pretended my father was dead. Then I noticed that tears had begun to stream down my mother's face, and I became enraged. This was more of the same inconsistency, the same confusion of love and hate that I had lived with for years.

I slammed the sandwich down onto the plate. "What are you crying about?" I yelled. "For years you've said that you'd like to leave him, that he makes you miserable, that you can't live with him. When he cracked up the car, you were upset about the car, not him. This will be a chance to end it, to start over, and I really don't understand why now you cry. All you've ever been able to do is complain."

My mother sat sideways to the table, her legs crossed, her head bowed and leaning on her left hand. She spoke very softly for once.

"But this is the only life I've ever known. I don't know anything else. My life with your father is the only thing I have."

The hospital did not call that night, and by morning my father was still alive. My sister Ann grimly acknowledged that maybe he would make it, and she hoped so because she didn't know how she would manage without him. Weak and abusive as he had been, he was the emotional center of her life. She felt she was the only one who really understood him.

When we went back to the hospital my mother was there combing his hair. There was now some reddish solution dripping through the IV, which they told us was a kind of vitamin. It seemed to be saving his life. He survived that day and the next. David and I went back home.

At the clinic where I did my fieldwork there was a woman named Alice who was an alcoholism specialist. The day I returned from my father's bedside, I walked into her office, sat down, faced her squarely, and demanded, "Why?"

"Why what?" she said, startled.

"Why, when somebody knows they're dying because of their drinking, do they keep doing it?"

That question marked the beginning of a relationship in which I was to learn the answer to that and many other questions whose answers were deep and complex and inscrutable. Only some were about alcoholism. The others were about love.

6.
Alice

"I'm going away for three weeks," Alice said, "but when I come back, let's have lunch. We can talk about this more."

I sidled out of her office, tentative and shy now in the face of my aggressive entrance. "Yes, I'd like that," I said.

Alice Osborne O'Neill was legendary in the local health community. Wherever I went, people talked about her with awe: she had a reputation for her work, for being bright and powerful, and for being hard at times. She could handle the most difficult cases with warmth and humor. She had forced the center to develop a program for indigent alcoholics. Every week a handful of unkempt, often homeless men arrived at the clinic. She did group work with them, encouraged them to give up booze, and when nothing else worked, she pushed the system to provide services for them. Her work often took her out into the projects, where she confronted drug pushers, prostitutes, and psychotic people living in squalor. There was no client she couldn't engage, and they all came to love her.

Shortly after I arrived as a student at the clinic, a national television station showed up to film a documentary on therapy. Alice was chosen to be the therapist. I watched her work what seemed to me a kind of magic with a mother and her daughter. In minutes she took two people who were tense, frightened, and angry with each other and had them tearful, looking at each other tenderly, clearly caring deeply. Alice walked over to the daughter, put a hand on her shoulder, and said, "I know what you're feeling, I know how painful it is, I know how hard it is to want something from your mother and not know how to get it."

I believed her. The daughter believed her, too. This capacity to make a profound emotional connection, to break right through people's armor and touch their pain, seemed amazing to me. I began to invest Alice with almost mythical healing powers. She could be tender and soft; she had the power to get past a person's reserve and pull him out; she knew what pain meant; and not only did she know about feelings, but she could handle them. Nobody in my life had ever had these powers except possibly Molly. Alice had the emotional intensity I craved. The more I recognized this, the more curious about her I became. It was why I went to her desperate to know what she knew about why people drink.

And there was something else. Rumor had it that she might be gay.

I often worked nights at the clinic. While Alice was gone those three weeks, between interviews I wandered the hallways absently. Always I stopped right outside her office. The door was open. When nobody else was around, I got into the habit of stepping inside and switching on the light. I sat in her chair and stared at the piles of papers on her desk. Then I went around to the other side of the desk and sat facing her chair. I got up and slowly circled the room, studying the photos on her wall. There was a picture of a dog, a little mutt with sandy hair and woeful eyes. There were pictures of surf and ocean, and of a beautiful, mythical-looking place, and of herself there looking out, alone. I fantasized that she was lonely, just like me.

Alice was a small woman. She was attractive in a patrician sort of way, with her short, straight, brown-blond hair and finely edged features. She had compelling blue-green eyes and a smile that lit up her face. When she wore lipstick, her face radiated warmth and color; when she didn't, she could look pale and drawn. She wore knit shirts that were low-cut and subtly drew attention to her breasts and long skirts that made her look taller than she was. She had an infectious laugh and seemed always to be darting places.

I had always fantasized about a woman I would meet on a beach, her outline indistinct, no more than a hypnotic reverie. She was a woman I would be submerged in, much as I could be engulfed by the ocean if I let myself. We would be all softness and pliancy; we could careen around in the churning surf together, loosely, gently, but connected, our eyes meeting in knowledge, in intimacy and love. Something in the photos in Alice's office stirred this fantasy; I recognized a mood, a soulfulness. I created a story in my mind about Alice, and on a subliminal level, as if I could sense this from sitting in her chair and looking at the pictures on her wall, I started to let myself believe that she was gay.

"I'm so glad we could finally get together," Alice said as we rushed across the street to a greasy spoon called Bonnie's, where most of the staff congregated for lunch. I was half rehearsing my conversation with her; I wanted to make a good impression. I tried to think about what I had learned so far about addiction and about being a therapist, because I wondered what else we could talk about.

As we were making our way through the intersection, she said, "I'm sorry we won't have as much time as I would have liked. I have to get back to meet this woman who wants to borrow some money from me. I'm really irritated, but I have to do it. By the way, I'm gay, you know."

"By the way, I'm gay, you know . . ."—so offhand.

"I don't often make a habit of telling people that. I'm actually not sure why I'm telling you."

"Well, no, I didn't know," I said, and a surge of mingled fear and confirmation shot through me.

By now we were inside the restaurant and had taken a table for two in the front near the door. It reminded me of the Campus Restaurant, except that it was small and cluttered and smelled of fried onions. There was no jukebox and no soft jazz playing.

"This woman and I are just at the bitter end of a relationship, and we're in the process of separating," Alice explained.

"That's an issue I struggle with myself," I stuttered.

"What's that?"

"My feelings for women."

"Oh. I'm surprised to hear you say that. I thought you were married."

"I am, but I think I may be gay. I had a lover in college, and I'm pretty much in turmoil about it. What I keep asking myself is, Should I leave my husband?"

There was a long pause in the conversation. Alice looked at me in that penetrating, intent style that she used to get into you. She pushed her plate forward slightly, moved her water glass further to the side, leaned into the table, and said, "Well, how can I help?"

We never did talk about alcoholism or therapy. We talked about my marriage, my conflict, my fear of letting myself get involved with a woman. We talked about there being no easy way into a gay life and a gay community. We talked and talked and at some point we stopped eating without being aware of it, except that when Alice realized it was time to go, half our food was still on our plates but neither of us was hungry. We walked back to the office, awkward with each other. She said we should talk more; I said I'd like that. It seemed to me that there was some heat between us, that something had caught. But then I thought it might be my overactive imagination and my overdue longing for a woman that was making me think that something mutual had happened.

Alice went back to her office to meet her ex-lover, and I walked back to the student office to write case notes. I had trouble concentrating, and after about twenty minutes the phone rang. It was Alice.

"You can either keep being frightened or you can come home with me for dinner," she said.

That night when I went home, David and I had a talk. I wasn't sure what to say to him, but I knew it was inevitable that Alice and I would become involved and I wanted to be honest with him.

"David, today I had lunch with Alice, that woman I've been telling you about on the unit—the one I've been wanting to talk to about my father's drinking."

He nodded. He smoked a pipe now, and he was fiddling with it, casting around in its bowl with something that looked like a nail.

"She told me she's gay and she invited me to have dinner with her and I want to go."

He crossed his legs and put the pipe in his mouth unlit.

"Okay," he said slowly. "Are you attracted to her?"

"Yes, I think I am. But I can't really say. I just want to pursue it, that's all."

"It makes me a little uneasy, but I'm glad it's finally happening. Maybe it will help you get this out of your system."

Slightly over a week later, I followed Alice down the thruway to her house. It was just dusk and raining, teeming. I was in my suburban boat of a station wagon and she was in her small foreign station wagon, and I noticed that she darted when she drove in the same way she did when she walked. I had brought her flowers, chrysanthemums in fall colors. For days I had been in a state of sexual agitation. I called her the day before and she said in a voice full of warmth and invitation, "Gee, I'm glad you called." I thrilled to this, to the sense that she was happy to hear from me. I wouldn't let myself think about it directly, but on some level I assumed this dinner was an invitation to a seduction.

She lived in an old rented bungalow that had been a summer cottage before it was converted. When we walked into the house I was charmed by its quaintness, its cluttered, unfinished quality, its eccentric layout. There was a small foyer dominated by a washer and dryer and piles of coats and shoes and an odd assortment of paper bags. The foyer led to a kitchen that had brown carpeting, old metal cabinets, a counter that slanted, and large windows looking out into the backyard. Alice's refrigerator was an ancient Kelvinator and it was covered with pencil markings, drawings, and phone numbers. She saw me stare at it and she explained that her ex-lover was fond of writing on it because the phone was there. "We fought about it all the time," she said.

The wallpaper in the bathroom was peeling. The floors all sagged and ran at strange angles: the head of the bed was lower than the foot.

A vacuum cleaner sat in the middle of the dining-room floor.

Alice apologized. "Cleaning just isn't that important to me. I hope you don't mind. I had every intention of vacuuming before you came, but then I just got caught up with something else. I don't remember what." She looked at me with a grin, shrugged, and clearly had no doubt that I would accept her haphazard housekeeping.

Her furniture was all mismatched, and much of it quite shabby, the chairs torn and clawed by her cat, Christopher, a mean-looking black-and-white creature who glared at me and then retreated to the top of the refrigerator.

She took the flowers, obviously pleased. "I really thought you'd probably forget about dinner tonight."

"How could you think that? I've been nervous about it all week, looking forward to it."

"Really? Oh, c'mon, why would you be nervous?"

"Well, you're such a legend on the unit, you know. I couldn't quite believe you would ask me to dinner."

"Yeah, I'm notorious, no legend, and I'd like to get to know you better," she said.

She darted around the kitchen to find a vase for the flowers.

The week before when she had asked what kind of food I liked, I had told her anything but fish. She cooked shrimp—shrimp creole, hot and spicy, with rice that clumped together because she cooked it in too small a pot. That very night, I acquired a taste for shrimp, for much that I had never had a taste for. I overlooked all that might have disturbed me in my other life—even the cat litter scattered all over the porch floor. In my life as a wife, I had been known to be quite irritable with David for not being neat, but here, with this woman, her very messiness became a part of her charm.

We sat at dinner in the large, carpeted kitchen that looked out onto a backyard full of flower boxes and the fall remnants of a garden. She looked across the table at me, those blue-green eyes bright in the candlelight, her talk punctuated with laughter and with quick smiles at me. She poured me a glass of wine, but she drank water.

"Not drinking tonight?" I asked.

"The first thing you should know about me is that I don't drink. I've seen too much of the destruction alcohol can cause. I came too close to being destroyed by it myself. I strictly avoid the stuff. Does that surprise you?"

"No, not at all," I said. "I guess it gives me greater respect for you. I wish people in my family had gotten help with their drinking."

"Well, maybe someday your family will get help. Meanwhile, nobody overcomes alcoholism. They stay sober one day at a time. Once an alcoholic, always an alcoholic, that's what they say. I believe that, and I think AA is one of the only real solutions for alcoholism. But let's talk about more interesting things. You look very nice tonight."

I was wearing slacks and a turtleneck sweater and brown wooden beads. My hair was long and pulled back with a leather clip. I had dressed carefully for the occasion. I was trying to look sexy but not obvious. I didn't know what lesbians wore. I made some offhand comment about not having very much money to spend on clothes so that I had to be creative, and Alice laughed.

"I want to know about you," I said. "Have you always lived here? What's your family like?"

"I grew up in the Midwest, outside of St. Louis. My parents are still there, and so is my brother. He's older and married, and politically he positions himself somewhat to the right of Attila the Hun. Needless to say, he is incensed that I am gay, so I don't see much of him. My parents tolerate my gayness uneasily. It's been a long struggle. I am their only daughter, the apple of my father's eye, and my mother believes I am an extension of her. My lesbianism is not what she had in mind for herself—and besides, the neighbors might not approve."

Alice laughed, an ironic, pained chortle.

"I came east to go to school. Afterward I moved here because I craved water. Literally and figuratively, the Midwest was just too dry for me."

Alice kept talking till she was almost breathless. Her speech was rapid-fire, intense, animated. I listened, wide-eyed and impressed, thinking how articulate she was. The candles were burning down. Finally, she jumped from her chair to get herself another glass of water.

Then she changed the topic abruptly. "So tell me about this woman you were involved with in college. What happened?"

"Well, we were very involved, it was very intense, and then she left school. She always questioned whether she was gay, and finally she couldn't take the conflict anymore. She got sick and had her mother come to take her home. And within a year she was married."

"Are you still in touch with her?"

"Yes," I said, "we see each other now and then. She and David were good friends, too."

"Is there anything still between you?"

"No, not really. She wants children and doesn't think that I'm really gay. I guess she doesn't think she is either. She's been a little uncomfortable with me since I've gone back to school. I think she feels it separates us somehow."

"So are you?" she asked.

"Am I what?"

"Gay."

"That's what I'd like to know. I think so. I know I feel a deep need to be with a woman. It's been a problem in my marriage. I have this recurring fantasy . . ."

I told Alice about my dreams of meeting a woman, how it would feel, what it would mean to me. I was a little loosened by the wine and feeling emotional. Perhaps she sensed it; she seemed to soften and smiled at me across the table.

Then she talked about the woman who had just left her, about the pain of the rejection. I told her about David and his TV watching.

"Do you know how you can tell a relationship is going bad?" she said. "I'll tell you. Judy watched the entire Fischer–Spassky chess match on TV and during all those days she never once talked to me—just sullenly stared at the tube and wouldn't even respond if I asked her a question. I nearly went crazy and finally had to leave the house to keep from blowing up."

I nodded with understanding. "That must have been awful."

Alice talked much more—about her friends, about her work, about books and movies. I got a glimpse of her softer, more vulnerable side. I felt warmed and comfortable with her, almost at home.

After dinner, she insisted that we had to see the town. I knew she wasn't sure what else to do. But much of our talking had been about her gardens, her love of the out-of-doors, so it seemed important that I get a sense of this place, even though it was raining and dark outside.

We walked under umbrellas to the end of her street. Less than a quarter mile from her house was an access area to a river. There was a boat ramp and several small sailboats stored for the winter. There was marshland that trailed off into a small backwater stream, an inland finger of the river. Alice told me that the river was one of two that circled the town and that we were only a few miles from the ocean.

In the foggy light of a street lamp I could see cattails and brush just turning brown in the October air. The night was damp and heavy with the smell of salt—ocean air.

We walked back from the river, got into her car, and rode through the town. It was one mile square and quaint, bordered by the river, yacht clubs, and expensive homes. Understated boutiques and interesting shops lined the main street.

"I came here eight years ago from a job in Albany," Alice said. "I taught for a while in the school on the other side of town. I love it here because it's on the water. Wherever you go there's water."

In the half light of street lamps and headlights, I caught a glimpse of Alice's world. It was a combination of pretentious and unpretentious, stylish and quaint. It was a water world defined by river and ocean and the vast array of life that lived in and on and around it. We headed now farther out of town to the ocean. She kept up a running monologue as we drove.

"For a while before I moved here I lived in another part of the county, where there are rolling fields and horse farms. I rented a little house on a farm—I was single at the time—and one night I woke to noises outside my window. I was terrified; I thought somebody was trying to break in. I got up and turned on the floodlight and what do you suppose was standing there trying to poke its head in?"

"I can't imagine," I said.

"A huge old horse." She laughed.

I smiled.

Warming to her subject, she told me about the birds that

congregated by the bridge, about seeing herons near the river, black ducks and flickers by the sailing club. At night sometimes, she said, she could hear an owl hooting in the distance.

Finally we crossed a bridge over the river and headed south to a town on the ocean. We pulled into the public beach area. The rain had stopped, so we got out to walk near the water.

We ambled down the beach and came to a breakwater of rocks piled high. The tide was going out. We were finally forced to stop our relentless motion. We turned to face each other, neither of us knowing what to do next. I looked at her and smiled. She moved toward me almost imperceptibly, and suddenly we were kissing, and in that kiss I was saying, Yes, I see you, I know, I understand what you love here. What she was saying, I don't know. It was a cool kiss—cool with the dampness of the night, cool with the first drops of rain that had just begun to fall. It was a slight kiss—tentative, searching.

The rain fell harder and we raced back to the car. "I don't know what else to show you," she said. "Would you like to go to some gay bars? I'm not sure just what to do now." She was cute and seemed vulnerable, sweet in her discomfort.

Emboldened by the kiss, by the ocean, by the rain, by what I don't know, I said, "I think I have some idea what to do. Let's just go back to your house."

As we pulled into the driveway, she said, "But you're a student."

I smiled. "I'm not your student, and in two months I'll be graduating."

"I'm older than you."

"There are so many things that separate people, let's not let age be one of them." I was holding her as we stood in the driveway in the rain, impressed by my own boldness. "Why don't we go inside?" I suggested.

She was visibly nervous. But I was full of confidence and conviction. I felt that this was, after all, what her invitation had been about. We had talked and toured and gotten to know something about each other. Now I was desperate to be held and touched by a woman—by this woman.

Our first embrace was awkward. We moved slowly to the bed and struggled out of our clothes. I paused at that first sight of her breasts, paused to touch gently, to press against her, to languish in that first knowledge of bodies touching. I felt myself letting go, being as forthright and as fluid as I wished to be, relishing the softness and sensuality of being with a woman again, almost overcome by the pure pleasure of it, feeling that I was home. I kept stroking her hair and her face and looking into her eyes, as if to reassure myself that she was real. As I held her to me, caressing her back, I realized that I was taking another tour, this one not just of her body, but through a chamber of her heart. And through a closed-off chamber of my own, which opened now, leaving me breathless and suddenly weak and vulnerable—and, I think, in love.

This night of lovemaking seemed to go on and on. We laughed, we read poetry to each other, we cried. There was relief, there was excitement, there was tenderness, and there was pain about the unfinished relationships in our past. Sometimes it seemed that both Molly and David accompanied me to bed.

Finally I said, "I think I'd better call David. Would you like me to stay?"

"Yes, please stay, please . . ."

I called our number, ready to tell David that I wouldn't be home. But I didn't have to.

"Why don't you stay the night," he said. "I'm really concerned about you driving in this rain."

Alice and I slept briefly, wrapped around each other in the sloping bed, and by morning my world was changed. I felt washed by a drenching rain and dried, sweet-smelling and fresh in the sun, and I didn't know what to do.

"We need a romantic weekend away," Alice said. "Let's go to the mountains."

We drove on a Friday afternoon in the off-season to an antiquated lake resort high in the mountains upstate. "Look in the bag in the backseat," Alice said, turning to look at me instead of the road. There were chocolate cupcakes and popcorn.

"Ah, trying to seduce me, I see."

She laughed and grabbed my hand.

"No, I just want to give you what you like—as much of it as I can."

We arrived in the last light of the day. We looked out onto the lawn as we sat in the dining room having tea. On the shuffleboard court, the Queen of Hearts was pushing at a puck and the Mad Hatter made crazy gestures beside her. Somebody in the distance was filming. The character who was Alice stood to the side watching. I looked at my Alice, thinking maybe I had become psychotic, but she was staring too, obviously seeing what I saw, and before long she burst into raucous laughter. We raced out to the lawn to watch this odd spectacle. An amateur film company was staging a shoot here, and for the rest of the weekend the characters from *Alice in Wonderland* walked through the grounds treating us to surreal images that completely captured the tone and ambiance of our affair.

In the resort's grand and sweeping sitting room furnished with Victorian antiques I played one of the few pieces I knew on the piano. Alice walked over and whispered to me, "I'm falling in love with your hands. Do you know what lovely fingers you have?" That night we made love with a small fire flickering in the fireplace in our room, a sagging mattress barely supporting us as we moved into and away from each other delicately, intently. Later we popped the popcorn in the fire.

The next morning we walked out to the lake to sit on rocks that stretched like steppingstones away from the shore. Alice was unusually quiet, in a reflective mood. I sensed her distance.

"Claud, I'm scared. It's hard to say this, but, you know, I'm not sure I'm very good at commitment. I walk around thinking to myself, 'I'm in big trouble here.' It's hard for me to believe how I feel about you. It's so soon. I was feeling good, less upset than I expected about the breakup with Judy; my life was going along better than I had thought it would. And then there you were. I just didn't expect this. Maybe I'm not ready for you. What if I'm not good for you?"

"It's fast," I responded, "but I'm not afraid of commitment. I've been waiting a long time for this, and I'm ready. I don't have any doubts about what I feel for you. I'm very loyal, and when I see what I want I go after it and I make it work."

"You know, lesbians are notorious for getting together fast and then breaking up. How do you know you love me?"

"I know." I looked at her. My whole being seemed on familiar ground with her. At that moment I knew that Alice was the woman of the water, that I could sink, could fall into her and that her depths would challenge and feed me. I thought of all that we had in common—our work, our values, our quick minds that seemed so in tune intellectually that we could talk for hours without tiring. I thought of her intensity, her aliveness, the way she seemed to know her way around feelings and around me. I relished the way she was taking me back to my childhood love of the out-of-doors, leading me like a small child through woods and ponds and oceans and lakes, teaching me all that she knew of the natural world. There was a certain moment during our love-making when I felt, yes, this is real, I am loved. I broke into tears as a surge of gratefulness and relief overcame me, because it was so unlikely for me to feel cared for. I knew there was something special about us, that something about our love for each other could overflow and reach out to embrace and encompass many other people. I felt that we had common energy. This, it seemed to me, would be the love that I had searched for—the love that was intensely personal and erotic yet would open me to service in the world as well. I had a vision of what we might become, and even though I didn't know how it would evolve, I knew that it would.

In those early weeks this certainty of mine rarely wavered. Alice wavered, but whenever I felt frightened, I simply told myself that fear was something I needed to overcome.

"Don't you think you need some time to be alone, on your own?" Alice challenged. "This is how it will happen. We'll be together for a couple of years, and then you'll decide you don't know who you are, that you need to explore other relationships with women—or with men. I'm older. You'll get tired of me. This isn't like marriage, you know. Gay relationships last, on average, three years. We'll just be one more statistic."

"This is different," I protested, horrified at her thinking that our relationship could be anything but permanent. "I want to build a life with you. I'm willing to do what I have to do to make it work. We don't have to be like all the other lesbians. Do you think of me as so immature?"

Alice sighed. "Maybe it's myself I don't trust."

For weeks we dated and we went to work together and we

made love. In spite of Alice's fears, we found that we couldn't be apart. Some nights, driving down the parkway from work or from a date or from a particularly stirring show in the city, we couldn't wait to get to the house and we'd pull over to make love on the side of the road, aware every minute of the danger of being seen. We walked to the river and to the ocean beaches in the daylight now. Life with Alice was constant motion and newness, filled with people, activity, and stimulation, and I grasped at it, took it all in like a person starved for life.

"David, I can't do this anymore. I can't live this split life. I want to be with Alice. We have to divorce."

He looked at me with panic, the color draining from his face. "But why?" he demanded. "You can be with her. Why do you need to leave me? I don't understand. I thought this was what you wanted. How can you be sure about this?"

"I want to live with her. I want to build a life with her. We can't stay married; it just won't work anymore."

"Oh, great," he said, angry now. "For years I've put up with this from you, turned myself inside out to support you, and this is what you do, just walk away."

"I'm sorry, but I've always been honest with you about what I've been feeling. I've struggled, too, to try to make it work."

"Oh, just because you've been honest, that makes it okay, right?"

I had known from the first night with Alice that it was over for David and me. He was patient with my seeing her. We still made love. He thought of this as the arrangement he had said he was willing to accept. But now I knew there was no avoiding this anger, this pain. I felt loathsome—so much so that part of me just shut down and I watched all this as if it were happening to someone else.

David kept asking, "Why? Why do you have to leave?"

I didn't want to have to tell him what was true: that I loved Alice and didn't love him.

In January, I gathered my few belongings and half of our wedding gifts, packed them in the station wagon, and left to live with Alice. Overcome as I was by my excitement about being in love, I had thought very little of the consequences for the rest of my life. At some point I called my mother to let her know what was happening. "I'm leaving David, Mother, I'm just not happy."

She was angry. "Since when do you leave somebody just because you're unhappy?"

The biggest shock, though, was David. His anger finally came to the surface, and we got into endless disputes over who would take what debts from the marriage, arguing over the ownership of each long-distance call on the phone bill.

Diane wanted to be supportive. She walked into the apartment one day as I was packing. She hadn't known Alice would be there and was faced with meeting her for the first time. She took one look at the two of us, burst into tears, and left the house. Within a few months, she was totally gone from my life, as if I could no longer have both a female lover and a best friend.

Molly left my life because I cut her out of it. Alice felt threatened by her. Seeing me involved with another woman, Molly had stepped up her contact, clearly jealous and upset. She questioned my decision. Finally I asked her not to call. I responded to her letters with a biting rejection. "Do us both a favor and drop this," I wrote, totally unaware, in my protectiveness of my life with Alice, of the pain I was causing her.

I graduated with my social work degree and quickly found a job a few miles away from Alice's house, the house we would share. We stored my boxes in a corner of the small study and made some room for my clothes in the cluttered closet.

In spite of the losses, I felt that my life had finally righted itself. The depression was gone. The emptiness was gone. I had been let out of prison. Almost for the first time, I knew what it felt like to be happy. I watched Alice putter around the kitchen dressed in her weekend garb, flannel shirt and jeans, thick wool socks and Clark's shoes, and I felt delight, I felt home. I knew what it meant to be truly myself and to have somewhere to put my passion. My questions about my sexuality were over.

But there was no wedding, no file to keep details organized; our families wouldn't even know for some time. There would be no elegant evening affair, no bridesmaids in red velvet, and no honeymoon in Vermont. There would be no outward celebration of this coming together.

That first night, we sat in the kitchen talking. Suddenly Alice got up, peeled herself an orange, walked into the living room, and turned off the light behind her, leaving me sitting in the dark. "Hey," I yelled, "I'm here, remember?"

"Oh god, I'm sorry." She raced into the kitchen and turned the light back on. "This doesn't mean anything, really."

I knew very well it did mean something. I sensed tension and distance in her. But I put it out of my mind, and that night we held each other tenderly and tentatively in the sloping bed.

7.
The House with the White Picket Fence

For various weeks of each year, Alice had rented a cottage on a bay in Maine. It was her soul's home because of its sweeping, rock-clad beauty. The photos covering her office wall that had intrigued me in the early days of our courtship had been taken there.

One weekend in early spring, after we'd lived together for four months, Alice insisted that we visit this place. I understood that this was a test, as great in significance as being brought home to meet the family. It was a test of our spiritual compatibility, because, although she hadn't said it, I knew Alice feared she could not be with a person who didn't love Maine.

Crossing the bridge from New Hampshire into Kittery that day, we met with clouds and fog and a slight drizzle that followed us all the way up the coast. The approach to the "camp," as it was called, was a long dirt fire road that wound downward through a thick forest of spruce and hemlock, pine and birch.

We drove down this right-of-way through the trees. Alice opened the car windows. The dank, musky fragrance of the woods, the scent of evergreens in the rain, was intoxicating.

Beyond the stands of trees there was an opening. The breathtaking surprise was to suddenly have a commanding view of water, of the gently landscaped lawn of the camp, of the spruce forest on the opposite shore, and of a stand of brightly colored lupine at the edge of the lawn. It was low tide, and I could see rock outcroppings covered with birds, gulls and cormorants, an osprey flying overhead.

Alice stopped the car in the gravel drive and leapt out like a child too excited to sit still any longer. "C'mon!" she yelled. She showed me all the spots where flowers would bloom in another few weeks, stands of wild rugosa roses, impatiens, window boxes that would be full of geraniums and blue lobelia. She pointed out sheltered spots to the east side of the cottage where one could bask in warm sun out of the wind on more blustery days. For the heat of the summer there was a large, expansive deck to lie on and a broad lawn to the west where one could take in the full openness of the bay. The cottage itself was right at the water. At high tide and full-moon tide, Alice said, two of the steps leading from the beach to the deck would be fully submerged. "Wait," she said. "In the front bedroom, you're going to feel like you're on a boat at sea."

That day the gray of the water merged with the gray of the sky, and I knew only because Alice told me that the mountains of Mount Desert were in the distance. In the house we lit a fire in the fireplace. And for a day or two we didn't leave, because the rain never stopped. I stared out the window at the cormorants and other birds that made their way back and forth along the shore. I watched the water roll in and out, the pools that took shape onshore at low tide. The place was magical. My identification with it was immediate and intense.

I wrote in my journal about the overwhelming beauty there, the deep solitude and silence. It was painful, this beauty. It touched that meditative part of me that yearned to simply become a part of the landscape around me.

In the evening we lay on a blanket by the fire. Slowly, we made love. I took a pine branch that had come in with the firewood, its needles still wet from the rain, and caressed her body with it gently, tenderly.

"I love it here, Alice. It makes me feel so close to you. It is incredibly beautiful. I can't believe I've lived all these years without knowing this was here."

Her eyes shone in the light of the fire. She stared back at me, not needing to say anything. It was a kind of consecration, an acknowledgment. In this lovemaking, we seemed to touch more deeply than before. I know she felt this too, and then we slept.

In all five days that trip, we never saw the sun. Alice woke up on the third day and said, "This is it. We're getting out of here today. We'll go into town and buy rain gear and we'll hike in the rain."

My pace had slowed. Alice was frantic now to be outdoors, and her energy was jarring. But within the hour she had packed tuna sandwiches and poured hot tomato soup into a thermos. We stowed everything we'd need in a day pack. In town we bought boots and rain ponchos to cover our heavy sweaters and jeans.

We headed to Mount Desert, where we picked a trail that skirted the shore and hiked in the rain, all the time drinking in the fog and the damp and the smell of the sea. The bell buoys sounded in the distance, foghorns rang out; occasionally we could hear the motors of lobster boats that we couldn't see through the fog as fishermen plied their weary, unromantic trade.

Rain and all, I still thought it was beautiful. Alice was chattering. "This is bunchberry, this is black spruce, and do you know what these are called, Claud?"

"No," I said, "but I know you can tell me." I smiled. They were tiny, bright red dots shooting up out of a clump of moss.

"British soldiers," she said proudly. "Aren't they cute?" Alice instructed as we walked. We'd bend over to look at some minute piece of plant life, and the rain would come pouring off our ponchos and drench us. But on we hiked.

It was teeming; we were cold and hungry. Finally I said, "Let's get in a tree and have lunch."

"How can we do that?" Alice wanted to know.

"Just like this." The evergreens were gigantic and had wide, spreading branches. I found one that I could crawl into and pulled Alice in with me. We sat near the trunk dodging needles, sheltered from the downpour.

Nestled in the tree, we laughed and kissed through drops of

rain, drinking the moisture off each other's lips. We ate our tuna sandwiches and drank the tomato soup.

"I could live here," I said, sighing. Rain and all, I felt deeply peaceful. "Why shouldn't one be surrounded by this beauty every day?"

"Maybe someday we will live here," Alice said. "I've come here every summer since I was fifteen, and I've always felt someday I would move here. Could you handle having vacations here for now? There's so much more to show you."

"Yes, I could handle that. I feel like I want to explore every inch of it, like I want to inhale it. I've never felt this way about a place before."

"Somehow I knew you would love it here, Claud."

"I guess that means we can stay together, right?"

"I guess it does."

In late summer we went back to Maine, as we would each summer after. We explored coves and lakes; we learned the contours of the national park better than the rangers who worked in it. We found special spots farther up the coast that we journeyed to on days when our moods called for different vistas, different sets of rocks, more solitude. We took our books, our paints, our journals, and our tuna sandwiches and sat for hours on rocks by the sea, sometimes inland, sometimes needing the open and dramatic crashing of the surf. We read, meditated, and just stared off into space together. We explored, coming to know the land as if it were a common lover, slowly, with curiosity, taking our time, never wanting to let our eyes rest, sensing its different rhythms, wanting with a passion to merge with it, become a part of it.

In this place and in our way of being together there, I reclaimed some sense of the spiritual in my life. What came to replace the lost god of my youth was the very live presence in me of love for a woman and passion for a place that moved me. The world became sacred to me again. Life itself, all the ineffable beauty seen and unseen, was sacred. I felt alive. I felt like singing, like dancing in the sun. This place bound us to each other. Our souls had found a home together.

Shortly after the late-summer trip to Maine, Alice called me unexpectedly one day at work.

"Can you leave a little early today to meet me in town? We're going to buy a house."

"What?"

"We're going to go house hunting. I've decided it's time."

"Today?"

"Yes, honey, today."

"Did we talk about this?"

"Well, I've kind of mentioned it. I've got enough money saved for a down payment, and I just think it's time for me to stop being a renter. Today's the day."

"But, Alice, we've only been together eight months, and I don't have any money. There are my school loans, and I barely have enough money to pay my bills."

"Don't worry about it," she told me, laughing that infectious laugh of hers. "I'll get the mortgage. It won't cost you any more than it would for your share of the rent."

At four o'clock that afternoon we walked into one of the realty offices in town. A friend of Alice's had sent us. He told us that Jan was the best realtor in the area. She was a gracious older woman who acted as if she couldn't be happier that we had called. Alice told her what we could afford. "I want to stay here in town," she said.

"Well, I think that's a wonderful choice. I live here myself, and I just love it. Now let's see what we can find for you." Jan pulled out her listing book. She and Alice chatted amiably about the town.

"Where do you live, Jan?" Alice asked.

Soon Alice had Jan talking about her house by the river, her family, her husband, and her reasons for being in real estate. By the time we got into her car to see some of the listings she'd pulled from her book, we were like old friends, a congenial little group out to find a good buy in housing.

Since I was new here and didn't have any money to contribute, I didn't feel I had much of a say in the house decision. Staying in town seemed fine to me. It was a beautiful area, but it was also a very Republican, conservative, family-oriented town. There were no other gay people around except the men who ran the flower shop. It was a community of stockbrokers and bankers, refugees from the world of high finance who commuted daily on the uncomfortable, late, and crowded trains to avoid living in the city. It was suburbia, and I wondered how this very Waspy heterosexual woman really felt about us, if she knew we were lesbians. I wondered if anybody would sell two lesbians a house.

But Jan was utterly charming and genuinely helpful. She was patient with Alice's anxiety. She seemed to like us. This was my first experience with being visibly a couple in the community. It was reassuring. I thought to myself, driving around in Jan's luxury car, maybe we can make our way in the world and be lesbians. At least this one person doesn't seem to mind.

Alice required a fireplace, a good-sized yard, and, if possible, a basement. We saw two or three houses in our price range: a small bungalow, well renovated, but, we decided, too small; an older Victorian nearer the river that needed too much work; and then, in an older development of very middle-class homes, a small cape with something very charming about it. The listing said it had a fireplace and there was a large picture window, a screened-in porch off the back, and a huge maple tree in the front yard. It was surrounded by a white picket fence and had a rose trellis that arched over the gate leading to a large backyard.

"Well, this looks interesting," Jan said as we pulled up.

"Actually, I've always admired this house," I said.

"Let's take a look." Jan pulled out her lock-box key and we walked in.

The house had a good feel to it. Sun poured in through the plant-filled picture window, and there was a lovely fireplace with a handmade mantel that Jan said would stay with the house. There were hardwood floors.

The owners had tried to be creative with some of the older features of the house. The old metal kitchen cabinets were painted a bright orange, while the wallpaper was a black-and-white check. The doors in the hallway leading to the bedroom and den were painted orange on top and yellow on bottom. The living room was covered with a vivid wallpaper that looked like a Native American print, full of zigzags in browns and blacks. The kitchen was old and small, and there was no dining room. But there was a fireplace, a yard, a garage, and a porch, and the price was right. There was enough space for each of us to have a study and still have a small den.

No one was home, and we wandered around for quite a while checking the furnace and the plumbing and the roof.

"What do you think, Claud?" Alice finally asked.

"Well, I think with a little work it could be great."

"Do you love it, though?"

"I love it."

Alice turned to Jan. "We want it. Do you think we can get it?"

Just like that. Three houses and we'd made up our minds.

We drove by the house two or three times every night while we waited to know if our offer would be accepted. We had fantasies and dreams about what it would be like to live there. The owners were musicians who were leaving because one of them had been accepted to a prestigious music academy. They cried when Jan told them she had a buyer; they loved the house and didn't really want to give it up. But they accepted our offer.

Alice and I talked about this house becoming the reference point for our lives together. I was happy to think that its rooms had been filled with music. We would fill it with people. Alice would plant flowers in the yard. We would make love in front of the fireplace with the lights out and soft music on the stereo. We would love each other here. It would be our sanctuary, our home.

Now Alice faced the task of getting a mortgage. Did they lend money to lesbians? I wondered. And yet the more basic question was, Do they lend money to single women? It was 1976—not the year of the woman.

But Alice had friends who had connections. The day of her meeting with the bank president, she dressed in her most feminine, classic Wasp outfit and headed to town. She was her most charming, engaging self. She told the man flirtatiously as she shook his hand, "I've never met a bank president before." She mentioned her two degrees and her new job as an administrator in a health center. She got the mortgage. She was a lesbian who knew how to play the game. Or was she a lesbian who didn't think much about the fact that she was one? In either case, I was filled with admiration at her skill in navigating the world. Here we were, two women in love, and in this most heterosexual, patriarchal of communities, we—or she—owned a house. I thought of this not as a right but as a lucky break. See, it's not so hard being gay after all.

We moved in fits and starts with all the help we could muster from friends. We lay in bed our first night there, exhausted from carting boxes and dragging the few pieces of heavy furniture we owned. We held each other and felt a mixture of excitement and fear. Could we afford this, would the furnace blow up, were there secrets about this house that the inspection didn't turn up, were we really grown-up enough to do this? How would we live comfortably with our neighbors on either side a mere ten or twenty feet away? How could we be two women living in the middle of straight suburbia and make it? This time I did the reassuring.

"I love you, Alice, we love each other. Whatever happens, we'll handle it together. We'll learn what we need to know. Trust me, I'm pretty good with house things. And nobody's going to burn crosses on our lawn because we're gay. We have our first house; it's ours. That is really amazing."

I loved this woman, and we were going to make it all work. My sense of commitment and dedication to our life together was fierce. As frightened as I was, my idealism was stronger. Love would conquer all. We could be models—gay people who lived happily and comfortably in an alien world. We would teach people that we were just like everyone else, that what defined us was our love for each other, that there was nothing about us to be feared. Something about moving into this house meant to me that we were stable and married and that all those statistics that said gay relationships can't last were just plain wrong. I felt this; I believed it.

In the course of our pre-closing trips to measure and inspect, we'd already met most of our neighbors, who had showed up, curious about us, to introduce themselves. Across the street were a New York TV producer and his wife. Our other close neighbors were an oceanographer, an airline pilot, a widow, and a strange couple who at Halloween dressed in black hooded gowns as witches and warlocks and frightened the neighborhood children with pranks and incantations that seemed entirely too sinister to be only about fun. Down the street was the family whose children would care for our dog and shovel our walk in the winter. And farther down the street were the people who sold drugs and who invited frequent visits from the town police. In time we were entirely accepted in this neighborhood. We bought Girl Scout cookies and supported the local school athletic events. We gave out bags and bags of candy at Halloween. We stood in the middle of the street and talked to our neighbors. They become friends. We had them in for coffee; we talked about their troubles; we commiserated about the problems in the town government, about the declining services and the higher taxes. We raced outside to check with each other when the lights went out and after fierce storms. We exchanged little gifts at Christmas. We shouted to each other as we mowed our lawns and raked our leaves. We were lesbians and it didn't matter: we were part of this neighborhood; we lived in this town and felt safe and embraced.

We never had separate bedrooms to deceive our families or company into thinking that we were really just roommates. Every time Alice's mother visited, she walked through the house on inspection and her first question was "Where does Claudia sleep?" Alice would deflect the ominous insinuation with humor. Her mother knew perfectly well where I slept. It never occurred to us that we should try to pretend that we were not what we were—a lesbian couple in love.

"Is there dinner tonight?" Alice yelled as she walked in the door. She made her way into the kitchen and saw I was cleaning the floor.

"Oh my god, not again. How many times are you going to do this? Why can't you just get it that it's not going to turn white?"

"I'm sorry. It bothers me."

"Everything in this house bothers you."

"Well, it's got to bother somebody. You certainly don't care what it looks like. Why don't you try hanging up your jacket instead of throwing it on a chair?"

"I'll hang it up when I'm ready to. Why does everything have to be on your timetable?"

"Because with you, eternity is the only measure of time."

"You know what, you're a real nag. Is there ever going to be any dinner, or are you just going to scrub the floor all night?"

"Fix it yourself," I shouted, and left the kitchen in a huff, leaving my mop and pail behind.

I was obsessed with the kitchen floor. We had no money to replace it, so I tried to clean it. It was white and full of what I thought was dirt. It made me uncomfortable to look at it. I bought various cleaners and reconditioners, and by the time we had been in the house a few weeks, I had tried no fewer than twenty times to clean this floor with little success. I was forced to accept its dingy, gray, mottled look.

In this new house, our life settled into a predictable domestic routine, but our differences began to chafe. By now I was working as a social worker in a school system. Each day at mid-afternoon I came home from work and succumbed to what would become my lifelong preoccupation with home improvement. I began to have my first experience of acute attacks of householditis—that is, an irritating preoccupation with having to make my environment visually and aesthetically appealing, neat and clean and comfortable. It extended to the outside as well. In fall I raked leaves endlessly; in spring I pruned and reseeded the lawn and cleared away weeds. Some of my happiest times involved cleaning the garage.

The orange cabinets begin to haunt me, and so did the yellow-and-orange doors. My house obsession started to haunt Alice. On weekends, when she wanted to be outdoors, I wanted to be home working on the house. Of course, I believed that my preference for neatness was superior to her preference for activity. "There is no dust in heaven," I would say with an air of moral superiority. It was an old Shaker maxim that I had learned in our travels. I delighted in repeating it to her.

I painted and puttered and planned renovations and redecorations, and in my frustration with what I couldn't do I would fantasize endlessly about the house on the ocean that I would someday design to my—or our—exact specifications. It would be the perfect environment, my ideal space, and it would contain all that we loved. It would have windows that brought the outdoors in; it would have natural woods; it would have open spaces and bookshelves and the warmth of woodstoves and fireplaces. It was so real to me, I could feel it, and I kept trying to achieve the effect without having the real thing.

Alice tried to make concessions to my house obsession, but she did not see dirt or clutter. She was as undomesticated as any human being could be. She was totally a person of the outdoors, and the inside of a house was alien to her. When she walked into a room, clothes, books, papers flew in all directions, and unless someone else created order, there was steady chaos. With some alarm I started to realize that on the night of our first seduction, I should have paid more attention to the clothes heaped on her closet floor. I should have been more conscious of the vacuum in the middle of the dining room, of the cat litter strewn everywhere on the porch. I should have realized that someone would have to pick all this up and that it was not likely to be her. The more she demonstrated her messiness, the more obsessed with order I became. Domesticity was the first battleground of our otherwise loving relationship. It was to be a long, hard, never-resolved battle. The fights that erupted because of it pushed me to suggest we see a therapist.

A few sessions into the therapy, I finally bared my soul to Alvin, our psychiatrist, a compassionate, jocular gay man.

"I feel like the nagging wife, Alvin. She walks in the door and just drops her jacket and leaves it there, and when I ask her if she's going to pick it up, she ignores me or she gets mad and tells me to stop nagging her, and we end up fighting about this stupid jacket. I'm beginning to feel worse than a wife, like the maid. I always used to tell my ex-husband that I was not put on this earth to be a slave to him, and now I'm becoming a domestic servant to a woman."

Alvin nodded with understanding. He let both of us go on venting, but then the time was up. I was unsure of what he could or would say to help, but I sensed that he was on my side. Perhaps, I hoped to myself, he believed that jackets belong in closets too.

We got up to leave, and Alice headed for the ladies' room. Alvin took this opportunity to walk to the coat rack in his waiting room, where Alice's red jacket was hanging at a precarious pitch.

I watched as he picked up the jacket and dropped it ceremoniously in the middle of his waiting-room floor. He retreated to a corner and stood there with his arms crossed, waiting.

Alice came out of the bathroom and was startled to see her red jacket clumped up in the middle of the floor. She looked at me. I was trying not to laugh. Then she looked at Alvin.

With raised eyebrows, a grin forming at the edge of his lips, he said to her, challenging, "Does this jacket belong to you? I wonder who's going to pick it up. I'm not."

We all laughed. From then on Alice put away her red jacket, but little else.

My complaints to Alvin weren't limited to red jackets. More and more I found myself seeing him alone. I was riddled with a vague uneasiness. I felt like my own life was lost to me.

"I feel like if Alice says jump, I ask, 'How high?' " I said to him. "When I was married I refused to be controlled by David in any way. Now I wonder if I'm doing just the opposite with Alice."

"How does this happen?" he asked. "What kinds of situations come up that make you feel this way?"

"Well, if I want to do something by myself, often it's a struggle. The other night I was going to go out to a lecture at the college. Alice got mad because she was working and wouldn't be able to go. She was convinced I had some ulterior motive for wanting to go. She accused me of never wanting to do things when she's available. By the time she was done, I felt so guilty about wanting to go without her that I just stayed home. Alice objects to a lot that I want to do, or she comes up with reasons why I shouldn't want to do it. I give in because it's easier than fighting about it. So more and more I feel like I revolve in her orbit. We do what she wants, we go where she wants. And if I don't have any clear sense of what I want myself, I just go along."

"Hmm," Alvin said, nodding. "How would it be if you did these things anyway?"

"Oh," I said after a long few minutes staring out his window. "I suppose I'm scared of how it would be. Maybe she wouldn't want me anymore. I have a hard time dealing with her anger. Sometimes I think that maybe if I didn't do so much of the work, give in to so much, maybe there'd be no real reason for her to want me."

"Now that's something for you to look at," Alvin said.

But my fears were always neutralized by the very distractions that caused them. Alice was a whirlwind of ideas and activity. How could I object to evenings at the theater, tramping through the woods bird-watching, summer weekends at the small house at the shore—boating, swimming, visiting friends, traveling to wonderful places I had never been to before, the idylls of our visits to Maine? This seemed like a charmed life to me. The fear that I was lost to myself would go underground, drowned out by the activities of the day, by the focus on the house, the garage that needed cleaning, my work. I stole rare moments for myself to read or to bicycle through town, and most of the time I managed to avoid my uneasiness about the degree of my focus on Alice.

The year we moved into the house, we went our separate ways for Christmas. We were not very far along in the process of defining ourselves as a couple to our families. It was still a tense, difficult issue for us both.

I called home to try to work out a plan that would give me both time with my family and time with Alice.

"Mom," I said, "this year what I'd like to do is come home Christmas day rather than Christmas eve. I wondered if we could have dinner early in the day rather than later so I could be back here by evening for a party we've been invited to."

There was icy silence on the other end.

"Will that be okay? Will Ann and Therese mind?"

"Do what you want, Claudia. You know how hurt your father will be not to have you here Christmas eve."

"Mother, I know this will be a change for all of us. I want to be there, but I also want to spend some of the holiday with Alice and with friends. So I'm asking if we could change things around a little."

"Do what you want," she said, and hung up.

Early Christmas morning, I drove the three hours to my parents' home. They had moved to a large condo in the woods. Finally my grandmother had a room that was hers, but the condos were so far out of town that she couldn't get out much and was depressed at her isolation. Therese was in high school now and had a boyfriend who spent most of his free time there with her. I couldn't understand why my parents left the home I had grown up in. The condo seemed poorly constructed; it was riddled with problems. My mother had decorated the kitchen with a garish orange-flowered wallpaper that I could barely look at. Both my parents were actively drinking now, and I couldn't help thinking that the move had been an attempt at a geographical cure.

I arrived to a grim, less-than-warm reception.

"Hello, Claudia," my mother said in her coldest, most sarcastic tones. My father gave me a perfunctory kiss on the cheek. It was tense and furtive and felt like a small attack.

"How was your drive? Was the car okay?" he said, and then he walked away.

My mother, who had always looked much younger than her age, was for some reason now wearing a blond wig. Her face was puffy and she had gained weight, which on her slim frame made her look slightly misshapen. My father's face was a pasty yellow-white. His dark black hair was just beginning to gray. He had lost weight and looked frail and unhealthy.

My grandmother didn't come down from her room for a long while. I knew that she wasn't angry with me but that she was upset and had probably been fighting with my mother.

Ann's husband, Bob, was the most cordial. He and Ann had been there since late the night before, after his own family's Christmas eve. He and Therese's boyfriend helped carry packages in from my car. It was late morning. The dining-room table wasn't set. The tension in the air mounted as I realized that dinner was not going to be early this year.

Talk was strained. No one asked about Alice. Finally, about midafternoon, we opened packages. I sat there the whole time feeling like I wanted to cry, wondering what I should say, if I should tell anyone how hurt I was.

After the last gift had been opened, I said, "Well, I'm afraid it's time for me to go."

"You're going to leave?" Ann said. "You haven't had dinner."

"I know. But I asked if we could eat earlier in the day. There's a party I want to get back for; it's Christmas, I want to be with Alice. I'm sorry, but I really have to go."

I got my things together and left.

Alice's family had not been any easier. She spent two hours with them at the motel where they stayed because they refused to come to our house. For the rest of the day she was alone.

That night, after Alice and I were back from the open house at her friend's, the phone rang. It was Ann.

"I called to make sure you got there all right." She was cold, angry sounding. "I also wanted to thank you for ruining everybody's Christmas."

"I don't know what you mean," I said, defensive. "I was the one who had to leave without dinner."

"Well, nobody enjoyed it very much with you walking out. You know how important Christmas is to Mother and Father. How could you just go? Why couldn't you have come last night? Is this what we can expect from now on?"

"Ann, I tried to work this out with Mother weeks ago. I asked to have dinner early. I explained that I wanted to spend some time with Alice. Is that so hard to understand? Would you want to have to spend Christmas with your family and leave your husband home?"

"Well, I hardly think it's the same."

"Why isn't it the same? You all are going to have to accept that we're together. This is the last time I'll do this. Next year either Alice will have to be included or I won't come home at all."

I was trying very hard to keep myself from simply hanging up. Then I heard a shift in Ann's voice. She wavered, softened a bit.

"Well, I don't know if they're going to be able to accept that. I can, but . . ."

I could hear Ann crying on the other end of the line, which was completely out of the ordinary for her. She was rarely emotional.

"Ann, what's happening?" I said, moved by her tears. "What is so hard for you about this? I still love you all. I'm not rejecting you; you're rejecting me."

"I don't want to lose you. I thought you would be a part of my life." She was sobbing.

I realized Ann thought that my choice to be with Alice meant I would leave my family, and her, behind. And I couldn't understand that she, and they, didn't know how much I needed and wanted to be included.

"Ann, Ann . . . I want you in my life too, I always have. But it can't be at the expense of my relationship with Alice. She's too important to me."

"Okay," she said, calmer now. "I know we'll have to work this out. Please just promise you'll always be here for Christmas."

"I always will, always."

Alice was angry with my family, and I was angry with hers.

"We're going to have to start early to deal with things for next year, you know," I said to her. "This can't go on this way."

"With my mother, it can," she said. "I've been struggling with this with her for years."

"Well, now we have our own home. I'd like to be in it for Christmas. Let's have your family here Christmas eve and Christmas morning, and then we can drive to mine for the rest of the day."

"You don't know what you're asking," Alice said.

"I'm asking to be treated like every other couple in the world. I won't spend Christmas without you again."

We got into our nightgowns and lay on the floor in front of our Christmas tree, looking up into the lights. The cats came and purred, nuzzling our heads, and the dog lay at our side.

"I love you, Alice. I love you . . . well . . . desperately," I told her shyly.

"I think you're the best thing that ever happened to me," she said. "With you I can do anything. We'll work this out, won't we Claud?"

"Yes," I said. "Yes."

8.
The Love of Work and the Work of Love

I walked in the door of the suite of offices we shared on the main street of town, cup of coffee in hand, and heard Alice's voice in a low monotone drifting like fog out from under her office door. At home, on the kitchen table, I had found a note: "Claud, pleeeease bring coffee. Your sweetheart, Alice."

I knocked gently on her door; I heard her and her client laughing. She opened the door a crack, pushed her hand through, and smiled. "Thanks, Claud."

I had the office at the front of the building. I loved it because for most of the day it was full of light. From my chair I could look out over the carefully landscaped parking lot. It was rimmed with lampposts that looked like Victorian gaslights. Beyond it, I could see up the road into the bustle of our small town. It was spring. I watched the linden trees come into bloom, the azalea bushes flair, and the daffodils come up. I opened my window and I could almost smell the damp, sweetish brine of the river half a block away.

Our offices were adjoining. This morning I was distracted by Alice. Her voice was loud and insistent, and her laughter kept intruding. I loved her laugh; sometimes it was the most endearing thing about her. But today I just couldn't understand what could be so funny, and it irritated me.

It was gloriously sunny and bright out as I settled down into my oversized stuffed desk chair to wait for my first client. She came in a few minutes late as always, but today I decided not to comment. She was looking tense, and I knew something was wrong. People always come to therapy because something is wrong, but on certain days the crisis or the pain is more acute. The strain shows; the emotions aren't contained.

By lunchtime I had seen three different people. There was this first woman in crisis. There was a woman going through a divorce who talked about her hatred for her husband and the bitter warfare between their two lawyers. My third client of the morning was a woman who felt too economically dependent on her husband to leave him. She had affairs that she kept a secret from him. I struggled with my own attitudes about this decision of hers, because I believed that the secret was keeping her stuck and was unfair to him.

By evening I would have done six hours more of therapy, some with couples, some with families, all equally difficult and demanding. I would confront the pain of people struggling with addiction, children acting out, women who felt oppressed by their marriages but didn't have the resources to leave or the belief in their own right to demand equality. Some were very wealthy; some were very poor; all were very confused. And I needed to help them to see alternatives, to help generate hope that there were solutions to their problems. Most days my optimism and sense of purpose got me through. On other days, secretly, I looked to my clients to distract me from my own troubles.

But it was noon now, and I headed out for lunch. I picked up sandwiches at the nearby deli. Alice met me at the river in her car. We walked to a bench facing the water. We didn't do this every day; it was a ritual reserved for times when we both needed to get away from the pressure or when the weather was especially beautiful. I always looked forward to these lunch meetings. I looked forward to being with her in the midst of these draining workdays.

"So, what were you laughing about in there all morning?" I asked her.

"My client was telling me stories about her family. Claud, you would not believe it. This woman has such a sense of humor, and she talked about this straitlaced family confronted with the antics of a completely rebellious, wild son. It was so hilarious, I couldn't help but laugh. I thought, Gee, I should have tried that with my mother . . . Are you going to eat your pickle?"

"No, Alice, you know I never eat them."

"So, anyway, we got the copy of the new lease. The rent is going up again; it's almost more than the mortgage. . . ."

Alice talked on without taking a breath. Finally, I interrupted.

"Al, could we talk a minute about a case of mine?"

"Let me finish about the rent."

I grimaced and looked put out.

"Okay, so what do you want to talk about?"

"I need to run something past you about a client who's being abused."

"She needs to call the police."

"I know. Could you wait and hear what I'm asking?"

"Okay, okay, go ahead."

Alice looked irritated now, impatient.

"Never mind, just forget it." I decided to be sullen and distant.

"No, I'm sorry, go on. I've been thinking about the way I've just left you to your own devices since we've been working together, I know we should talk more about cases. I want to give you support, go ahead."

I was not quite sure whether to hang on to my irritation with Alice or to go on talking, because I was always confronted with both these dynamics in our conversations: the abrupt interruptions and cutoffs, and then the supportive encouragement to go on. This was too much to sort out over lunch.

"I just wanted your ideas about where to go with this. She won't call the police. She won't even call me."

But by now it was time to get back to the office.

"Look, we'll talk about this more over dinner, okay?"

"Okay, I'll see you later. What time are you done?"

From the beginning, I had viewed our relationship as an offering from the gods. I simply had the sense that love overflowed, moved one outward from oneself. I wanted us to be generative, I wanted to feel that we could do good for the world. I wanted it known that two dykes could be as selfless and as valuable contributors to society as the heterosexuals who scorned us.

In the early days what I admired most in Alice was her generosity. She was always giving, always responsive. Her energy was infectious and impressive; she gave without guile. It seemed to cost her so little. I loved her for this; I gave vicariously through her. I kept thinking how remarkable she was, how lucky I was to be with her.

Gradually, we had built a private counseling practice together, first Alice, then me joining her. She was the general contractor, the energy behind the plan. I followed when my level of experience and training caught up. It was meaningful to me that we worked together. This was one more link we had to each other: we were partners in work as well as in love.

The work that I really wanted to do was write. Or, rather, I obsessed about writing, dreamed of writing, lived in continual turmoil and pain about not writing, and drove all my friends and Alice in particular nearly mad because all I did was talk about writing but never did it.

Alice's friend June finally got impatient with listening to me lament about it—it had gone on for years.

"When the hell are you going to stop talking about this and get it that you have to sit down and do it—that you have to make a commitment? All you do is sit and moan about why you can't do it and why you'll never be good enough and how you have to make a living and all that shit. This is all I've ever heard you say you wanted to do, so what are you going to do about it?"

"But I don't know what to write about," I whined. "I need ideas. I need time. All I do is see clients."

By now June was at the edge of exasperation, but she was being patient with me.

"Okay. What do you want, Claudia?"

"I want to write books."

"Why do you want this?"

"I've always wanted it. I started out wanting it. Books were my first passion."

"What's stopping you from doing it now?"

"My crazy, neurotic self. I know I won't be good enough . . ." I secretly wished June would tell me I'd be wonderful, but she didn't. "And . . . ideas, I need ideas."

"So write about your work, write about what you're doing now with clients, for Christ's sake. Get on with it, do it! You've got to start somewhere. Now tell me what steps you're going to take. What's step one?"

This made sense to me. This grilling June put me through felt like the process I had put myself through when I came out. There was the continual talking, the obsessing, the forcing myself to verbalize, to say, "I want this, this is who I am," and then the words finally leading to action and commitment, to naming myself as a lesbian. I began to envision myself actually sitting down and putting pen to paper in some strucutured, directed way. From this point on, I reminded myself of June's words every day—*You've got to make a commitment.* I set a schedule. I wrote an outline and then a proposal. Before long, I got a contract. I was elated.

Alice and I set to work. This would be a joint project based on our work together. For seven years we had run groups, mostly of women, each of whom had been either the daughter, wife, or mother of an addicted person, or a recovering drinker herself. Thanks to Alice's foresight and to her aggressive pursuit of the information she knew would be useful, we had audiotaped every single session of every group. She had videotaped many of her couple and individual sessions as well. Now we set about putting into words what we had learned. It became the focus of our life together, this ongoing conversation about our work.

The book really began to take shape that summer in Maine. We walked the rocky beach, sat on the deck of the house, and talked as the gulls swirled over our heads and the water flowed over and receded from the sand.

"I think we want to make this a book that bridges two worlds. There is no coherent theory about how addiction affects families."

"Yes," I said, "and it has to be intellectually rigorous and very substantive theoretically; otherwise, nobody will pay any attention to it. We have to give people a reason to get beyond their prejudices about addiction being just like any other symptom in a system."

"The most important piece, Claud, is the gender issue. No one has made those connections. The fact that women have been told they're enabling when they do what they've been trained to do, which is caretake everyone . . ."

". . . and the fact that when men drink it's considered manly, but when women drink, they're pathologized for being out of control. We'll begin to describe a typology of interaction based on the Bateson stuff, and then we can talk about the ways that addiction takes those behaviors to an extreme."

"Isn't this exciting, Claud?" Alice looked at me with an intense, pleased stare.

"Yes, it is." I smiled back and looked out over the water, thinking that I had never been happier.

Being in this place of exquisite beauty engaged with ideas, creating something new together, something that was larger than us and an expression of us at the same time, was exhilarating. In sync intellectually, we could complete each other's sentences. Alice had flights of ideas and I embellished and articulated them, took them further until we could both say, "Yes, that's it!" It felt intimate, this work—a meeting of minds that enriched the contact of our bodies and hearts.

At the cottage I set up a workspace in the small bunkhouse that sat next to the cottage, and Alice worked on the deck. We yelled ideas back and forth. We spent our vacations writing. Sometimes we fought. The book took shape, and our work with clients was energized, took on a new importance and meaning. I needed this work with ideas, with my own mind, and I needed to write, to articulate it all, to say it. I felt centered and alive, and so did Alice. We quipped with each other. "Well, other people have babies; we have books."

The book was born after a year's hard labor. The publication brought with it invitations to speak. We now found ourselves adding travel and speaking to an already packed schedule. The experience was, as always, mixed. We had wonderful trips together and met wonderful new people. But our lives began to blur into a series of hotel rooms and meetings. Back home, we had to hire a cleaning person who came two times a week—once to clean and once to buy groceries and run all the other errands we now couldn't get to.

At the height of the book's success, and her own, Alice was invited to speak at a national conference to an audience of three or four thousand people. She woke up the morning of the speech with raging anxiety. She had been up most of the night and was irritable and frantic.

"God, my stomach hurts. How can I work with my stomach so upset?" She flung clothes all over the room looking for her slip. "Where the hell are my earrings?"

I was trying to finish my breakfast. She turned and glared at me. "Could you help? Would you mind finding something for me?"

"Okay, okay, I'm going to help you. Stop yelling."

I raced around trying to find what was lost and dug out Pepto-Bismol for her stomach. I felt caught between my natural inclination to try to reassure her and my irritation with this chronic state of tension that had crept into our lives. Before I knew how it happened, we were fighting, attacking each other, and I was distraught and distant. And within an hour, she needed to make this presentation.

Somehow we calmed ourselves down.

"Good luck, Al. I know you'll be great."

I straightened the collar on her blouse. I smoothed the lapels of her jacket. But she didn't soften. She was guarded, defensive, looking at me with a kind of hardness that often crept into her face when she was certain that I couldn't possibly wish her well, that I couldn't possibly care for her.

We went downstairs to the grand ballroom. The room was filling up. It was a massive space. The din and roar of people filing in was muffled by the thick hotel carpeting. Rows of chairs stretched endlessly across the vast cavern of the room. Huge crystal chandeliers hung over our heads. This is big, I thought to myself. This is a big deal. How did our life get here so suddenly?

Alice went backstage to consult with the video person. On the stage there were mammoth screens. Alice's face would be projected on them out into the vast corners of this ballroom. I found friends and we sat together, all of us probably more nervous than Alice was at this moment.

Finally, the proceedings began. Alice was on the stage looking calm and wonderful. She began her talk and within seconds she had the audience laughing with her. Her stage presence was remarkable, her voice strong and compelling, her intelligence and wit and power immediately apparent. Our friends and I began to relax and I felt that old feeling of awe at Alice surge over me, that rush of pleasure at her charm and charisma and the sheer acuteness of her mind. I heard her outline so clearly, so concretely all the ideas we had worked on for so long. She showed videotapes of her work. And what she did best was to infuse her talk with the deep conviction and sense of passion that we had felt in our work together. I was in awe at the way she could do this, at her power.

She finished, and then most of the audience was on its feet. I was not the only one moved. The talk was a wild success. People rushed up to the stage to talk with her, to offer their congratulations. From a distance I could see the flash of her smile. I could almost hear her laugh as she greeted people.

She was a public persona now, and for the rest of the conference she was pursued by people. I began to have the strange sense that she was not mine anymore, that something had come between us. It frightened me. Gradually, imperceptibly, I began to pull away from Alice because I was terrified that I was losing her.

"Maybe you don't need me," I whined. "I get feeling inadequate. You have so much presence, so much more visibility. And it feels unfair that my contribution to our work goes so unnoticed. Somebody came up to me after the talk and said, 'Where can I get a copy of Alice's book?' That hurt."

"Well, I get resentful that I have to take care of your feelings all the time, that if I get some attention I have to worry how it's going to make you feel."

The invitations to teach or speak often came to Alice. She was senior, more visible in the field, a more experienced speaker. But I was the primary author of the book. Neither of us knew how to handle the resentments we experienced. I felt like a background person; she felt guilty that she was in the limelight when I was a full partner in the work. We tried various ways to think about and handle the inequity. Eventually we accepted only invitations that included the two of us. But this didn't really address the underlying feelings of competition and envy that each of us struggled with.

Our dependency on each other as collaborators in our career life began to chafe. We were, in fact, a great team; we each contributed skills to our work. But we weren't mature enough to feel good about it. We lived with chronic anxiety and fear, as if the other were an enemy who somehow limited our individual power.

Added to the practical and emotional stress we faced, there was the new experience of being thrown together in public arenas, where our coupleness was always visible, if not overtly defined. We had published an earlier paper on work with lesbian couples. A professional colleague and friend called one day and asked us to speak at a conference as part of a panel on women's psychology.

"Of course, you'll come out," she said. "I think it's important for you to be models that it's positive not to remain silent. It's important to what we're trying to accomplish on this panel."

Elinor was a well-known feminist writer. In the past she had taken us to task for not consistently coming out when we spoke. Alice finally couldn't hold back her irritation any longer.

"Elinor," Alice said, "of course we'll come out, because it's right and we believe we make a contribution by doing it. But it bothers me that you're so cavalier about pushing it. You're straight and you're married. You can be supportive of our lifestyle, but it doesn't cost you anything. You have no appreciation of the potential losses for us, of the discomfort of having to put your life out there on display because you happen to be part of an oppressed group. There are consequences sometimes, you know. Not everyone is as accepting as you. Anybody who has your liberal turn of mind, liberal politics, can talk easily about being accepting of homosexual lifestyles, but you'll never know what it's like to live it from the inside. The world we walk through is a different place. The way we are, who we are, is completely normal and routine inside the confines of our house and in the open spaces of our souls. But when we walk out the door, we become something else, and we're always vulnerable to the public scrutiny of those who hate us."

"Well," Elinor responded, "you're right that I'll never know what you experience, because it's not what I live, and that I don't have to live with the consequences, as you do. But I think there are consequences, too, for being silent—not just for you but for other lesbians, for all women. I'm sorry if I've been insensitive to you, but I still want you to do it, honey."

"Aggh!" Alice yelled. "It's a good thing I love you."

That panel was a training ground, because the question about whether or not to come out would be ongoing. Some time later, we were invited to teach a continuing-education course on gay and lesbian life at a prestigious New England graduate school. It was the very first time this course had been taught at this school, which was, ironically, known as a hotbed of radical lifestyles. We didn't immediately come out.

By the second class, there was obvious tension in the room. Students sat silent and were not particularly responsive to any issue we raised for discussion. Finally I said, "Does anyone want to speak to the silence in here this morning? I'd like to invite you to let us know if there's some problem that's getting in the way of our talking more freely today."

After a long pause, one of the women in the back of the room spoke up.

"Well," she said, "I'm feeling kind of ripped off and very disempowered. When we went around the room introducing ourselves, I made it a point to come out as a lesbian. I don't feel any support for that. The atmosphere in here doesn't feel safe to me."

Alice jumped in now. I could tell she was getting mad.

"Say more. What makes it feel unsafe?"

The woman who had spoken wasn't about to say more. Another woman jumped in.

"Well, this is a course on gay and lesbian lifestyles. You two are very well known writers, most of us probably make the assumption that you're a couple, yet you didn't come out, and that feels like a pretty negative message about your willingness to practice what you preach."

"Okay," I said, trying to prevent a defensive response from Alice. "Does anybody else want to comment?"

Another woman chimed in. "Yes. I think it would be completely innappropriate for you to come out. I don't think it's relevant. Nobody makes an announcement that they're heterosexual before teaching a class. It's a private issue, and I'm angry that we're taking class time on it."

We would be caught in this bind for the rest of our professional career. If we came out directly, immediately, we were accused of being too radical, of "flaunting it." If we were circumspect and more discreet, never failing to talk about the "we-ness" of our lives together but not saying, "By the way, we're lesbians," we were told that we were cowards and politically incorrect. No one seemed to think that coming out should be something we controlled, that its timing and form should respond to our own intuitive sense of safety and appropriateness, to the context and purpose of the disclosure. So we walked some irregular line between feeling radical and politically incorrect.

One day I left the room in the middle of our class to find a bathroom. I startled someone standing behind our open classroom door, apparently eavesdropping on our teaching. She was crouched in the corner, somewhat hidden by the door, with her ear to the opening near the doorjamb. It was one of the old, conservative faculty members, a bastion of psychoanalytic thought who had written on the pathology of homosexuality. She must have been listening for heresy—or maybe she was curious, or envious, I don't know. She scuttled away while I floated past on my way to the ladies' room, pretending not to have seen her.

While much of our work had nothing directly to do with our lesbianism or the fact that we were a couple, we always were conscious of the realities that marked us as different. We worked as family and marital therapists in a community of largely straight, conservative people. Occasionally someone would come in and ask, "Are you married?" Alice was fond of saying, "No, I live in sin." I usually told them, "No, I'm divorced." Asked if I had a family, I would say, "No, but I grew up in one." And if a client came in and started talking about how much he or she hated queers, I wouldn't really know what to do. About myself. With them I could explore what they meant by that and what the prejudices were. But I never knew what to do with my own pain. With the dishonesty of not telling them they were talking to one. I didn't have courage in those days, and I also didn't have the support of a community of gay therapists.

With all the other pressures that working with the emotional lives of people entailed, this was one that nagged at us constantly—what would they think if they knew? It was a measure of our own homophobia, our own fear. We worried about lawsuits. What would happen if we worked with an adolescent to come out or a young adult to make a lesbian relationship a reality and irate parents found out we were gay and sued us?

We struggled with ways to address political realities, oppression, homophobia, the literature that pathologized us, that pathologized women. We lived in a cauldron of pressures bubbling, reducing us. What nourished us was the effort to add some new response, some new consciousness, some new piece of work that shed light on the clinical realities of our days. We wanted to throw a new idea into the pot and stir, and the more we could teach and write, the more meaningful our work felt.

But what nourished also divided us. Our personal selves became more and more separated from our professional selves. Distance crept insidiously into our relationsip. One night I put an album on the stereo, and I made Alice sit and listen to a song that captured for me something of what I felt was happening to us. It was a James Taylor song and in it a lyric about loss, about good times slipping away, kept repeating itself, insinuating itself into my mind as it played over and over, wringing my heart. I played the song and cried and pleaded with her to understand what I was saying, because slowly I was beginning to feel that I was losing her. She listened, but she didn't respond. I wasn't sure whether she didn't understand or whether she just needed to avoid what I was saying.

A few weeks later we were in a plane on our way to a vacation in Bermuda. We had been fighting and we were furious and distant. We wanted to be mad at each other, but we wanted to have a good time, too. There was a desperateness to get back in touch.

Alice turned from her resolute staring out the plane window and said, "Look, couldn't we just pretend that we're somebody else? We could have alter egos and we'll pretend we're them. That way we don't have to be mad, we can go back to it when we get home. C'mon. Who do you want to be?"

I looked at her with my face twisted into disapproval, one of those "you've got to be kidding" expressions that she hated. But some part of me liked the idea. I'd have loved not to be myself. I decided I wanted drama—to be somebody with flair. I wanted to escape the professional and personal roles that were making me feel as if I had lost myself.

"Camille," I said. "I am Camille. And I have a rose in my teeth. And I sing. And I wear frilly, lacy skirts that swirl when I walk. And I'm passionate and sometimes you like me."

"Okay, that's good," she said, relieved that I was willing to go along with this gambit. "Who should I be?"

"Not only do I have to carry your bags, I have to pick your alter ego for you, too?"

"Yeah. Do you think it would kill you?" Anger flared briefly again on Alice's face. I realized I couldn't push this too far.

"Okay. Elizabeth. You are Elizabeth."

"You always did like that name," she said. "Was there a woman or something?"

"Possibly in a past life," I said.

"Okay, Camille, do you think you could ask the flight attendant for a glass of water for me?"

From then on, Camille and Elizabeth materialized whenever we were unable to make contact with each other and we wanted to. The harder we worked, the more tense we became. We could rarely relax together, and sometimes Camille and Elizabeth had to do it for us.

"Camille, get up. I want to get going." It was 6:00 A.M. on a Saturday morning.

"Oh, Elizabeth, where do you want to go, my dear?"

"I want to go to look at birds. We agreed, Camille."

"But it's so early. Can't I sleep just a little longer? I hate the dark. I hate to get up in the dark. Come back to bed with me, Elizabeth." Camille stretched out her arms and tried to seduce Elizabeth back into the bed. Elizabeth jumped away from her.

Twenty minutes later. "Camille, get up, here's your coffee. Do you know how lucky you are to have a lover who every morning of your life brings you coffee in bed?"

"Yes, Elizabeth, I know I am the luckiest woman in the world, I know it. Do you know how lucky you are to have a woman who keeps your house so clean and your closets straight?"

"What are you mumbling?"

"I keep your closets straight." Camille's head was still in her pillow.

"Yes, we're both lucky, Camille. Now get out of that bed."

Elizabeth threw the covers off Camille, who groaned and dragged herself slowly from the bed.

Later. "Look, Camille, snow geese, thousands of them." Camille and Elizabeth were driving through the wildlife refuge.

"Yes, Elizabeth, I see them. Oh, there they go!" Hundreds of the birds burst into flight. The sky was full of cascading, waving lines of white.

"Look, over there—bufflehead and red merganser!" Elizabeth pointed to the tidal marsh and scanned the water with her binoculars.

"Elizabeth, give me the binoculars. Ah yes, I see."

Later, lying on the grass in the November sun.

"Claud, I'm glad we came today. I feel better, do you?"

"Yes, Elizabeth—Alice, even if you did drag me out of bed."

I turned and smiled at Alice, grabbed her hand, felt it warm in the heat of the sunlight, felt warmed by this touch. I had the impulse to kiss her, but the timing didn't seem right. "Do you think we should talk about the fight?"

"Yeah, I guess we should."

Each Monday morning we went back to work, and each Monday afternoon we met with the group of women who had been the first subjects of our book. Today there were seven women, some of whom we had known for years now, some of whom we had worked with only recently. Alice and I sat facing them, ready to hear the day's problems. All of these women were struggling—with husbands who drank, with children who weren't thriving, with the insidious self-destructiveness that comes from inside that made it nearly impossible for them to care for themselves.

"Who wants to start today?" I asked after we'd chatted about the details of the day.

Everyone was silent, and when I looked around, I realized that one of the women was in tears, crying softly, her cheeks moist. Everyone was watching her, waiting.

The story she told us was about a sudden, unexpected, and profound loss that had happened just two days earlier.

We were all shocked. The rest of the group leaned toward her in empathy. Alice and I waited, silent, to respect the power of her emotion, to let her feel it.

It was spring and outside the office there was an apple tree in bloom. As my client sobbed, I glanced out the window, and I saw that the wind had carried two apple-blossom petals down between our offices and the building next door. They floated, purely, serenely, past the office window. I could just make out the tinge of pink in them in the afternoon light. The woman sobbed, I watched, and I was struck by this juxtaposition of pain with beauty, the ripping of a soul and the gentleness of a breeze. Somehow these two petals floating gently past the window comforted me, gave me perspective, and I turned back to the group feeling more compassion.

And on the good days, I knew that something had been given, something shared, something of beauty, that we each took part in very small ways in the transformation that is life. Alice and I, in spite of our own struggles, shared this—with our clients, with each other. This was a great gift. And that we lived this experience, I realized, had nothing at all to do with being lesbians. This had to do with being people who knew what it felt like to suffer and to love.

9.

Scenes from a Marriage

Elizabeth and Camille were sitting on a plane whose destination was Los Angeles. Elizabeth was complaining that her hormones were jumping. She couldn't understand why last night she felt so happy and full of energy and today she felt like a slug—"just like a bug crawling up the side of a tomato plant." Camille laughed.

Camille, for her part, had felt like a slug since last night herself. She felt like a slug because of Elizabeth. She and Elizabeth were emotionally estranged—had been for months. Camille couldn't get over her sadness about this. Neither could she bring herself to be more pleasant to Elizabeth. Poor Camille.

The plane was stuffy and uncomfortable. Camille was disgruntled that she was seated only two rows in front of the smoking section. She couldn't quite breathe and decided to exercise in leapfrog fashion on her seat to keep the circulation going in her legs. Elizabeth sat immobile on the vinyl car seat she had brought from home, her neck in a soft collar. She had been injured by their dog, Amelia, who lunged to chase a squirrel when Elizabeth was walking her and nearly pulled her arm out of its socket.

Elizabeth was in perpetual discomfort. Periodically, she asked Camille to massage her back. Reluctantly, Camille obliged.

Camille really did feel sad—a sadness that reached deep into the marrow of her bones and into the inaccessible strands of her veins. Camille wondered what it was that happened to love, or what love was in the first place. Everybody wondered that. But to Camille it felt like sitting alone naked in the desert now under the plane, or like scaling the mountains she saw in the distance. It felt like all the pain that ever was anywhere had by anybody. And Camille couldn't think what to do.

Elizabeth wanted Camille to open her bag of peanuts for her. Reluctantly, Camille did. Then Elizabeth told Camille how bad she felt for eating the peanuts. Elizabeth always felt guilty about things, but never enough not to do them.

The plane was approaching Los Angeles, and the people in the stuffy compartment were getting restless, milling. Camille thought to herself that the pad of paper she was writing on could get burned in a plane crash. Or it could survive a plane crash and somebody would just shove it into the garbage. And it would be kind of the way she felt about her life—like all her feelings were just so many scraps that would get burned up or thrown away. Poor Camille.

Then Camille noticed that she threw her own feelings on a scrap heap. She was having that nagging sense again of being unloved and unimportant. There weren't too many places a person could go with feelings like that. So, she wondered, what kind of a relationship can two alter egos have on a plane speeding toward Los Angeles, a destination on the edge.

Elizabeth was a fiery, eccentric person whose behavior at times verged on lunacy. Her hormones tended to get the better of her. She demanded attention all the time and generally got it. She sang; she had sparks of brilliance; she danced toward and away from people, leaving a lot of emotional dust in her wake. She talked about slugs on tomato plants. She was plain crazy except when she tied herself down with illness or injury. Sometimes she might not want Camille around, but clearly she needed Camille's peaceful, serene countenance, her reasoned, polite manner. The sensitive, considerate saint who would always remember the niceties toward people that Elizabeth forgot. Elizabeth needed someone to pick up after her, tie her down a bit, keep her energy within the bounds of reason. She was outrageous, verbose, loud in her desperation.

Camille was a reserved and shy person. She was staid, poker-faced, tense. She was quiet, given to excessive rumination and quiet despair. Camille didn't think much of herself and really wanted to be Elizabeth. She would slink away, trying her best to be invisible.

Another Day, Not on a Plane

> ***Elizabeth:*** *I love you.*
> ***Camille:*** *I love you more.*
> ***E:*** *No you don't.*
> ***C:*** *Yes I do. It's funny. To have you, I don't have to compete with other people; I have to compete with places and the events of the day. Like places and recreation are your real loves.*
> ***E:*** *But you'll go away one day.*
> ***C:*** *No I won't, but the day will go away.*
> ***E:*** *But the day is who I am.*
> ***C:*** *Then I love you more because the day is not who I am. The day is better because of you.*
> ***E:*** *Then we have the perfect relationship, because each of us feels that we love more than the other, and neither of us has the burden of feeling more loved.*
> ***C:*** *I love you more.*

Elizabeth climbed up from where she had stood wedged on a float beneath the dock. She had been looking for crabs that might be crawling on the bottom there, where it was very shallow. She was poking in the water with a stick. She grabbed Camille's hand to pull herself onto the dock. She wrapped her arm around Camille's waist and they walked arm in arm down the length of the pier and back onto shore.

Later the Afternoon of the Same Day, on the Beach

> *E: Something's happening with you and I don't know what, but I notice it.*

Silence. Camille was watching something, preoccupied.

On the beach a few feet from their blanket there was a woman in a brief green bathing suit. She was preoccupied with adjusting its top to cover her breasts, its bottom to conform to the shape of her upper thighs. When she was not adjusting her bathing suit she was studying herself in her compact mirror, making minor adjustments to her makeup. She alternated between adjusting and lying stomach-to-blanket, staring over the top of her magazine at three men who had deposited themselves on towels some distance up the beach. Furtively she watched them from behind the cover of *Cosmo*, and when they got up to walk down the beach, she got up nonchalantly, adjusted her bathing suit again, and ambled to the water. The three men walked, lazy and just as nonchalant, in the opposite direction, not noticing her. At last glance she was pacing back and forth at the water's edge. The tide was going out and the three men were gone.

> *C: (having observed this mini-drama, which had interested her acutely) No, nothing's happening with me.*
> *E: Do you mind if I go down to the water?*
> *C: (nonchalantly) No, go ahead.*

Elizabeth ambled down to the water. When she was sure Camille was watching, she jumped in and floated around and waved and jumped around some more with a big grin on her face, wanting Camille to admire and delight in her. Camille smiled watching her and thought, I'm sure she couldn't possibly love me more.

Meanwhile, the woman in the green bathing suit had returned to her blanket and *Cosmo*. Camille glanced over at her and somehow felt lucky and smug. And then Camille went down to the water, because she knew Elizabeth wanted her to. She got wet and they jumped around together playing in the water. Elizabeth said she loved to see Camille so relaxed, loved to be in the water with her, it was the only time she saw her smile. And then they went back to their blanket to lie on the warm beach talking and reading, and it felt like a good day.

The Evening of the Same Day, Dinner

I had just put a forkful of food into my mouth, and, as was her habit, Alice said, "That was an awfully big mouthful you took." Alice always watched me eat—and commented disapprovingly. I hated this and tried to ignore it. I said nothing.

> **Alice:** *What are you feeling right now?*
> **Claudia:** *I'm not feeling anything right now.*
> **A:** *You can't be not feeling anything. One is always feeling something. If you were honest, you would just say, "I don't want to tell you what I'm feeling right now."*
> **C:** *I don't want to tell you what I'm feeling right now.*
> **A:** *So you want to be distant?*
> **C:** *I'm not being distant.*
> **A:** *So you're afraid to be close to me. I knew I loved you more.*
> **C:** *(a deep and weary sigh)*

The Night of the Same Day, in Bed

Up in the loft bedroom of the old house. The trees outside the window rustled in the breeze. It was warm. We had only a sheet over us. We were lying there and my sense was that we were going to make love. It would be usual, the usual routine, always here in this house. Finally, I said, "Would you like to make love?" Softly, questioning.

> **A:** *Would you?*
> **C:** *I could.*
> **A:** *Maybe we'll just lie here and see what happens.*

I felt some frustration, as I was sure the mood was right. But I couldn't be direct, because this would create pressure.

> **A:** *I'm afraid.*
> **C:** *What are you afraid of?*

I thought she was saying that she was afraid of making love.

> **A:** *Of death. I fear it every day of my life.*

I thought we were going to make love, and suddenly here we were talking about death.

> **C:** *Well, death is scary, but it's going to happen to all of us. Are you more afraid of me dying or of you dying?*
> A: *It makes me anxious to talk like this.*
> C: *Oh, well . . .*
> A: *Well, do you have any response? Do you think about death?*
> C: *You just said it made you anxious . . .*
> A: *Do you think you could ever tell me how you feel?*

Now I began to feel tense. There was something happening that confused me, but I wasn't sure what it was.

> **C:** *Yes, I fear death, too, but I fear your death more than my own.*
> **A:** *I'm not going to die.*
> **C:** *I'll probably die first—you've got better genes. Or we could plan to die together. Let's die together and then neither of us has to feel alone.*
> **A:** *If I died, you'd probably be with somebody else in a minute.*
> **C:** *No, I don't think so. I can't imagine not being with you.*
> **A:** *Oh, what about all those other girls you've had your eye on? What if somebody tried to seduce you?*
> **C:** *That would never happen.*
> **A:** *(sharply) That's not the right answer, Alice.*

I was getting tense again.

> ***C:*** *I love you, and I only want you. Is that the right answer?*
> ***A:*** *Well, are you going to make love to me or not?*

Taken aback now, my arousal almost gone, I said yes, of course. I reached for Alice, and she sensed the tension and held back and closed her eyes, and it was a while before either of us could get past this wall enough to give in to the moment. And it went like the day, the lovemaking, moments of connection and arousal interrupted by whatever it was between us that got in the way.

But in spite of myself, slowly I let go. I heard myself call out Alice's name, whispering it, "Al, Alice." Alice said "What?" and I had to tell her for the hundredth time, more of the ritual, that I just wanted to say her name. As we touched, I looked out the window and watched the tree against the night sky, felt the summer breeze blow across the bed over my now-hot body. I sank into that feeling of oneness with everything around me and with the whole of the day, the beach, the water, the dinner with Boccherini playing in the background, the talk of death, the irritations, the insinuations. I was ready to be beside myself, and I just wanted Alice to look at me and hold it all with me, go out of control with me, not leave me here alone with this fullness, with this awareness of everything.

But tonight it was too much to ask. Alice was jumpy and uneven, and she was not looking, she was not in touch. Maybe she was thinking about death, or angry with me. I didn't make an issue of it, because I was afraid to.

I thought, Maybe Alice is right. Maybe I have never been honest because if I were, it would hurt her or make her anxious. Or maybe I don't know what's really true sometimes and I can't tell her what she wants to know and there's no leeway for me to be unsure. Maybe I try harder to please her than to be direct myself. Partly out of love and partly out of fear, I felt that there was no room here to just be myself—the consequences would be too awful. Alice wanted me to be something, somebody, I couldn't always be. But I didn't say that. I just kept trying and kept getting mad, or knowing it and keeping it a secret. Of course Alice sensed this and kept trying to get at what I was thinking, even though she didn't really want to know.

An orgasm slipped out of me, and I felt alone with myself. But when Alice asked I said it was fine, and then we went to sleep.

The next morning was a fine summer day and I knew that Alice would want to go to the beach, then to the lake, then take a bicycle ride. Resentment sat in me like day-old bread, because I would have liked a day just to putter, to have no schedule, nothing I had to do, and I couldn't say this because I was afraid, or a wimp—because it was a given that if I had no clear sense of something, then Alice must have her way.

Another Day, Another Year on Maple Avenue

It was a quiet night on Maple Avenue. I was lying with a hot-water bottle pressed to my face; my sinuses hurt. The cat was studying me intently from a perch near my feet. If I moved, the cat would glare at me sternly. It took very little to disturb the cat's peace.

An evening at home, I was thinking—a rarity. Tonight we were like all normal married couples in the world. Alice paid bills, I was ensconced in bed with books and TV. Who would have thought many years ago that two lesbians could find peace and contentment in the middle of suburbia? Who would have thought that Maple Avenue could become home?

I was ruminating. I thought, One could be comfortably sick only at home with a person with whom one was familiar enough to be weak. There were no pretenses any longer between me and Alice. Life was full and meaningful in its ordinariness. We had our little house with its routine weekly clutter, its old and motley furnishings, and the bare spots outside that needed paint. We had one serious and sensitive cat, one mischievous and elusive one, and one dog who was little, loyal, and sweet. We had two cars, a messy garage, and piles of newspapers that needed to be placed at the curb. We worked very hard and struggled to relax. We fought very badly at times and cared for each other very much.

Some nights we would lie in bed together and listen to the rain pouring from the roof down over the gutters filled with leaves and onto the windows near our heads. On these kind of nights I often woke at three in the morning and grabbed Alice and woke her to be with me because I felt lonely and frightened in the dark. Alice was never angry at those times because she knew I needed her. Other, less lucky times Alice might stomp to the couch with her sleeping bag simply because I tossed and turned in the bed. But fundamentally I knew that Alice was a person who would be there for me in the middle of the night. Insofar as we could both evade death and destructiveness. It could be a great relief to give up the pretenses and just be ordinarily vulnerable. Sometimes it could be one of life's simple pleasures to be home sick in the evening with the cat on the bed and your lover nearby, with peace and quiet and fall making their night approach to an ordinary street in the suburbs.

10.
A Family of Friends

Alice was turned facing the backseat of the car, her body poised for conflict. Marsha, the object of her irritation, leaned with her head against the window as if she'd like to leave.

"Marsha," Alice said, "I started this program. I'm not going to just let the agency take it over now that I've gotten it up and running."

"You imply that we can't run it without you. You've trained us, and now you're saying that we're not competent to run it ourselves."

"But why should you?" I could feel Alice turn toward me. I was driving, so I kept my eyes squarely on the road. "What's your feeling about this, Claud?"

"Yeah, Jeffrey," Marsha interrupted, poking him, pleading in the child voice she used when she was trying to engage him, "what's your feeling?"

We were midway down the Delmarva Peninsula heading south to the Outer Banks of North Carolina. We'd left the turnpike and were traveling through a stretch of Delaware that was a line of interminable stoplights, traffic, and fast-food restaurants.

Alice and Marsha were wrangling, as they often did, about

work, about their joint training project, about something Marsha had said that Alice didn't like. This was a familiar scene by now; Jeff and I were used to it. But nevertheless, the tension in the car was becoming uncomfortable. Each of them tried to engage us, the spouses, in the battle, and Jeff and I tried tactfully to stay neutral. We were all therapists, after all, and we knew what not to do, even if we often ignored it.

Marsha had been testy and moody since we set out. Now she started to cry, and I pulled quickly into the nearest fast-food restaurant. We needed a change of pace; we needed food. None of us wanted this vacation to be spoiled. We were on our way to a small island just off Cape Hatteras to visit our two other best friends, Pat and Jane.

Over burgers, Marsha apologized. "You know, I'm realizing that this is the anniversary of my father's death. I guess the old depression just caught me without my being aware of it."

"I was wondering when you were going to remember that," Jeff said gently. The tears now flowed uncontrollably. Marsha's father had died when she was a young girl, and she had never recovered from the loss, followed as it was a short time later by her brother's death from a drug overdose. Alice was now all kindness and compassion, and I was empathizing with Marsha's depression, having felt so much of it myself.

This was how it went among the four of us. Our relationship as couples was charged with a kind of chemistry that none of us understood completely; we just knew that we cared deeply for one another. We were connected in a way that went beyond simple friendship. Alice and Jeff had worked together in a mental health clinic. Marsha and Alice now ran a training program together. The four of us had met for the first time at a Halloween party at Jeff and Marsha's home. Alice and I had dressed as Ichabod Crane and the Headless Horseman. Jeff and Marsha were pirate and gypsy.

Marsha was, in reality, all romanticism and flights of fancy. She hated routine and spent her days in search of variety, always looking forward to the next trip, the next event, to remove her from the dreariness of the daily. She was a dark, Jewish beauty with flashing eyes, a broad-lipped smile, and a flair for stylish dressing. She had a warm, enthusiastic laugh and was often the center of conversation in a group. She was a violinist who had put her music aside for a time to devote her energy to her marriage and her career.

A small, attractive man with a receding hairline, Jeff was equally a romantic. He was a sculptor and an artist in his spare time. He was more introspective than Marsha; intellectual and sensitive; and passionate about her. He dressed with impeccable style in a way that emphasized his masculinity and his aesthetic sensibility at the same time.

From the first it seemed there was a hint of eroticism in our attraction as two couples. I could not say who felt erotic toward whom; it was a charge to our coupleness that was curious to us. We talked about it at one point, and then left it alone. It became one of those mysterious realities of our lives together and of the permeability of the boundaries between straight and gay. For the longest time neither Alice nor I could understand how it was that our closest friends were a heterosexual couple.

We became family to one another. We celebrated Hanukkah with them and they helped us trim our Christmas tree. We had joint Passover and Easter rituals. We spent Thanksgiving together, and they told us shyly at one point that when they had a child, they wanted us to be the godparents. With them we felt our coupleness respected and valued; they understood the depth of our feeling for each other in a way that most others did not. It was entirely natural for Alice and me to show affection for each other when they were around. All the differences seemed blurred and irrelevant. There was unquestioning acceptance.

Pat and Jane, whose home we were heading toward, had been together for over twenty-five years. They were both old friends of Alice's who had discovered each other in a burst of passion. I had become very attached to them. They were older, and we called them our fairy godmothers. They tried to instruct us in the ways of leading a happy lesbian life. Pat and Alice were very close. Pat told Alice at one point, "I wouldn't much want to live in a world that didn't have you in it."

Pat could be crotchety, but she was one of the most intelligent women I'd ever known, and I was a little in awe of her. Now in her sixties, she was very aristocratic, from a Mainline Philadelphia family. Pat grew up tended by nannies and servants. Her mother had died shortly after her birth in a flu epidemic. She was shuffled off to boarding schools, and when she was a teenager on one visit home, Grandfather (as she called him) found her in the library reading *The Well of Loneliness*. He took it from her and later summoned her to his office. His words to her were "I want you to know that people like this do not exist." And he forbade her to read any further.

Pat started to drink. She left school and "chased a woman all over Europe," as she put it. The drinking got worse.

Eventually she was committed to a plush Philadelphia mental hospital, where her family assumed she would remain for life. She was thought to be deranged, and even at the hospital nobody thought to diagnose her alcoholism. Knowing she was perfectly sane but that she would never convince anyone of that by acting that way, she devised a plan. Having been sullen and withdrawn and uncooperative for weeks, she suddenly became the model patient. And then she asked to be brought knitting needles and yarn and evidenced a strong interest in knitting. The staff was very pleased, thinking their treatments were finally beginning to work and that Patricia was indeed improving.

But everything Patricia knitted was in miniature size—mittens, she told them, but mittens that would be too small even for the smallest infant. Intrigued, the staff began to watch her more closely. They followed every click of her needles with growing interest. Finally, one day she requested clothespins and asked to be taken outside to the hospital grounds. With great seriousness and caution because of her delicate mental condition, they asked her what she might need clothespins for.

"Why, to hang the mittens on the trees for the squirrels," she told them, "so that they should be able to survive the winter."

The next person to visit her was the head psychiatrist. They talked, and Patricia was released from the hospital.

From the coffers of her family's vast fortune, Pat was granted a meager independent income. She got sober and settled down to live with a woman who died young of a heart attack.

Then she met Jane. Jane had been married and raised two children when, in middle age, she realized she was a lesbian. Jane went back to school to become a nurse. Pat took care of every single detail of their lives together. She had the linens starched and ironed, kept the apartment in perfect order, sent Jane's uniforms out to be cleaned. They both loved the water, and when Jane retired they moved to their North Carolina island to be near the sea. They lived on high ground in a mobile home that Pat, with her fine sensibility, made livable and comfortable within the constraints of a limited budget. Later, they bought a used boat.

The trailer had a guest room that she named after Alice and me, because we tried to visit often and were best friends. We would sit in the trailer at night talking, Pat perched in her leather recliner, Jane sitting on the couch, her glasses settled low on her nose, usually a cat in her lap. We would listen to classical music or read poetry or listen to Pat hold forth about her latest interest or her latest irritation or tell stories of the island people, whom she had come to love. Being with them like this always made me feel as if I were back in the sheltering protection of a family.

That day, we pulled up to the trailer off the sandy back island road and honked the horn. Pat was waving as she came out onto the small deck that fronted the trailer. "Hiya!" she called out, grinning. She was wearing her typical summer garb—a man's light-blue, short-sleeved sport shirt with the tails hanging out, striped shorts held up with a man's belt, and boat shoes. She was a patrician, heavyset, dykey-looking woman who was most comfortable in these men's clothes that she ordered through the mail from fine shops. In the winter she wore only cashmere sweaters. She put only fine linens on the bed. It took little time to understand that Pat still lived as if she were the privileged child she had been. When she wanted to confuse people about her sexual orientation, she would simply wear lipstick, assuming most people to be so simpleminded that this was enough to help them avoid knowing what they didn't want to know.

"Well, so nice to meet you," Marsha was saying as we unloaded the car. "Though I must say Claudia and Alice have talked so much about you that I feel like we're already old friends."

"Same here," Pat said. "Jane, where the heck are you? Come on out here."

Jeff pulled his camera out of a bag and tried to capture this reunion in photos. He was to spend much of the rest of the weekend taking pictures and sketching scenes from the trailer. His pictures show us all standing on the deck of the trailer, our arms around one another, smiling broadly, looking young and happy.

We hadn't been there very long when Pat piled us all into what she called her beach buggy and drove us to the town landing. She said we had to "blow the city out of us." She had arranged with Gordon, an old island native, to take us out on Pamlico Sound in his fishing boat to watch the sunset. On the boat she had stocked champagne, nonalcoholic drinks, chilled clams on the half-shell, and an array of gourmet cheeses and crackers. We traveled out a few miles and watched dolphins jumping on the horizon as streaks of purple and pink began to paint the sky to the west. We relaxed and talked, joked with Gordon, and came back to a supper of boiled shrimp taken that day from the very waters we had just been sailing in. It was one of Pat's strong beliefs that living well is the best revenge. The other was that any woman could be had.

By day we would hop into the rusted-out beach buggy and ride the sands of the national seashore, all eighteen miles of it, bird-watching, shell collecting, fishing, swimming in warm tidal pools that formed in the wake of rough surf. We watched plovers skittering along the water's edge, and Pat kept yelling, *"Rynchops niger, Rynchops niger!"*—the formal name of the black skimmers that darted across the surface of the water. In the evenings we sat and listened to Pat's endless stories about her life in Europe and the trials of life on an island. She told Marsha and Jeff how she and Jane had come to have the old Franklin stove installed in the trailer living room, how she had had special reinforcements built around the trailer to keep it from blowing away in a hurricane, and she talked of the origins of the few antiques that she still held on to from her family.

Marsha and Jeff were congenial, open, warm. Pat and Jane were funny, obstreperous, gracious. Marsha and Jeff slept on the pull-out couch in the small living room and tolerated our stepping over them in the night or early mornings with good-natured humor. Our stay was short—three nights. On the last evening we talked until eleven or so and then, unwilling to let ourselves feel the separation pangs that would come in the morning, we impulsively decided to go out to the beach in the buggy.

The moon had just turned full and the sky was cloudless. The whole island was washed in an eerie kind of light, as if dawn were not far off. By the trailer, the moonflowers, which bloom white and full each night in the dark, were half shut, confused by the illusory brightness.

We crossed the yard to get into the buggy. Looking back at the trailer, I had a vision that nearly stopped my heart. In the window of the spare room, staring out at me, was the image of my grandmother, her face etched against the window shade. I looked again, then looked away, but the vision stayed. I got in the car with the others, trying to understand what I had seen. With this disturbing image fixed in my mind, I rode with the others to the beach.

There was little wind, and the ocean was gentle and rhythmic. We needed no light to see as we stood at the edge of the water watching the waves roll in and out. We were feeling a kind of sentimental attachment to one another, a connection that was genderless and deep with our shared histories. I don't know who first began to sing—probably Marsha, who seemed always to be bursting into song. But before long we had all begun to sing, and by some unspoken telepathic connection it was understood that we would sing only songs about the moon. We stood there, arms draped around one another, forming a circle and swaying together, even the reserved Pat, singing every moon song anyone of us could remember until we ran out of songs. "Blue Moon," "Moon Over Miami," "By the Light of the Silvery Moon," "Moon River," "Old Devil Moon"—on and on. Like druids or some ancient tribal band, we were immersed in our own full-moon ritual, totally transfixed by that landscape, by the power of the water and of the shadowy light, and by our love for one another.

Then it was over; there were no more songs. Silently we hugged, then very slowly climbed back into the buggy for the drive back to the trailer.

While we sang I prayed my grandmother was all right. Later I learned that that night she had been hospitalized with an unfamiliar, undiagnosable illness that had left her at the edge of death. She recovered, barely.

There are some experiences in life that are mysterious and magical; this was one. That we shared it with these friends at two poles of our experience, straight and gay, male and female, old and young, was typical for Alice and me. We could never form friends solely on the basis of political correctness or the lesbianism we might have in common. We seemed to seek out these deeper, less understandable bonds that operated much as the light of the moon had that night, connecting us in a deep, inscrutable way to some truth as indiscernible at the time as the coming dawn.

For years, Alice had owned a tiny hundred-year-old house in a seaside community about an hour's drive from our home. It had been deeded to her by her family. It was red, run-down, and sat right next door to a Methodist church. We went there most summer weekends to relax. One morning, we were in the upstairs bedroom looking out at the sky from the bed. It was hot and steamy, so we lounged there with all the covers thrown off, lying askew at a strange angle on the bed, completely naked. We heard the clicking of bicycle chains approaching from a distance, and then the moaning of brakes.

"Get up, you hussies!"

It was our friend Frank. In the pandemonium of the dog barking and the cats scattering, we laughed and got up to throw on clothes to make Frank, the old queen, his cup of morning tea.

"Good morning, girls. I'll have my usual cup of tea, if you're awake enough to make it. Hope I didn't interrupt anything. Damon's still home in bed. Ooh, did we have a wonderful time last night!"

"I'm going to make breakfast, Frank. Will you have some?" I asked.

"No, no thank you, I've had my cereal."

"How about some orange juice?"

"Well, maybe just half a glass with water. The doctor says if I'm not careful, my kidney stones will come back."

"So how's it going with Damon?" Alice asked.

"Well, the usual. He lives in one place, I live in another. We fool around, it's great, then he goes home. I don't want to give up my place, and he doesn't want to give up his. So we're in this holding pattern. I guess it will just stay that way for now. That's the problem with being two old queers set in our ways."

Frank owned a little summer house just around the corner. Some weekends we'd see him for tea; others he'd have us over to his house for dinner and a viewing of his latest pornographic video. Frank believed that all gay people were sick, much as we tried to convince him otherwise. Yet he was one of the most caring, loving men in our lives. A public school teacher, he had lived at home caring for both his parents while they died long, agonizing deaths from cancer. He struggled to help Damon with his various family and personal problems, and eventually retired from teaching to become a hospital volunteer who increasingly worked with AIDS patients. He shared my householditis. Together he and I tried to patch up Alice's old house to make it more livable. We pulled out the ivy growing in the makeshift shower and covered the walls with salvage vinyl tile. We redid the old bathroom floor and painted what we could of the sagging, mildewed walls.

The next Sunday, my friend Ellen, one of the members of my old feminist support group from my graduate school days, was visiting with her husband, Jerry. The house at the shore was a gathering place for all of our friends. They came to visit, swim, boat, and crab in the bay. We cooked and ate all the crabs we caught; we barbecued in the backyard; we sat on the wide screened-in porch and watched the comings and goings of the small town. Frank made his usual Sunday-morning call, but this time Damon was with him. We went out to the backyard with our coffee and tea and sat around a small fire in the barbecue pit to chase off the early-morning chill. Frank was listening to the bells of the Methodist church next door chiming. He suddenly shrieked with laughter.

"Good god, what would they do if they realized they had a bunch of queers sitting next door!"

Every Sunday morning we were treated to carillon bells playing selected Christian hymns to the town. It was disconcerting to be upstairs in the bedroom making love when the faithful were piling into the parking lot to attend services. We kept waiting to be struck dead for our immorality. I always thought that we were simply engaged in our own form of worship, the erotic being as valid a way of knowing god as any.

"Now, Frank, we're not all queers," I said. "There are some of the redeemed here among us."

"Yeah," Alice said. "Look at us. It's really amazing when you think about the continuum of sexual experience we've had. I do think we represent all the points along the Kinsey scale from exclusively gay to exclusively straight and all the stops in between."

"That's me," Frank said, "exclusively gay. I have never once had any even fleeting impulse to be with a woman. Damon here, though, tried it for a while, didn't you, dear?"

Damon was shy, less gregarious than Frank. "Yeah," he offered, "but it was never as good as with you, dear," he quipped.

"You better believe it." Frank slapped him on the leg.

"And Ellen," Alice said, "is the perfectly straight female. Have you ever been attracted to a woman, Ellen?"

Ellen was a sensitive, gently feminine woman, bright and articulate. Jerry, her husband, had been exclusively gay until he met her, and then his love for her and the desire to have a family motivated him to ask her to marry him. In contrast with Ellen's softness, his manner seemed very masculine. He and Ellen had the most stable relationship of any of us there.

"Why, no," Ellen responded. "I don't think I ever have. I can't think of a time when that would have been true for me. It's never really entered my mind."

"And then there's us in the middle, Claud," Alice said. "You've been married, and I almost was."

"Yeah, I had a thing for priests, and you for ministers. What is it about spiritual types that is so compelling as a detour from gayness, I wonder?"

"Well, you're either a saint or a sinner, right?" Frank commented. "What could be better when you're trying to fight off lust and queerness than to be attracted to a man of the cloth?"

"I think it's deeper than that," Jerry challenged, jumping into the conversation for the first time. He rarely talked about his conversion, his change of preference. It was simply clear that he loved Ellen deeply. "I think we're all looking for something spiritual, and for a while we seek it outside instead of inside ourselves.

And let's face it, it's not exactly easy to accept that you're gay and still think you're a spiritual person."

"That's for sure," Damon said with a wry glance at Frank.

Back from our weekend retreat, I would seek the community of Connie's Cafe. Most working days I would walk around the corner from the office for lunch at her shop, which was the hub of community life. Everybody in town ended up there at some point during the day, for breakfast or lunch, or sometimes both. Coming here was like coming home to Mom for lunch. When we were upset, temperamental, angry, impatient, Connie was the first to know, whether she wanted to or not. We knew most people in the coffee shop, and most people knew us. We were regulars, and I always felt almost like a regular person here. We loved Connie and she loved us. Nor was it unusual for us to run into our therapy clients or friends, who always greeted us warmly. I thought, Gee, isn't it nice to live in a town where we're so accepted.

Except that one morning I walked into Connie's for breakfast and noticed a group of women whom I knew only vaguely, though I'd seen them there before. I had always had a kind of negative visceral reaction to them, for no reason that I could understand.

That day, in Connie's small shop, I overheard them discussing an article in the morning paper about homosexuality. Then one of them—the one I least liked the looks of, the one who looked hard and too made-up—said in an exaggeratedly loud voice, "Oh, those queers. Isn't it good that AIDS is killing them all?" And they all laughed a bitter, harsh laugh, a laugh of agreement and blunt hatred, for no reason, no reason at all. At that moment I had a horrifying jolt of awareness of the danger, the evil, of these kinds of attitudes. I wondered if those people even knew what it was they were rejecting or why. They didn't know me or Alice or Frank or Jerry. Or Alvin, or any of the people I knew and cared for. So how could they be happy that AIDS was killing us all? How could they hate someone, anyone, they didn't know? How could they wish for our deaths on general principle?

My failure was that I didn't say anything to them, nor did I stop going to Connie's. It was too important a ritual to me. But it was never the same again. I told Connie about it, and she was upset. I was reminded not to think of myself as wholly accepted in this world, not to give in to the illusion that it made no difference that I was a lesbian. Connie's would never be home again, and I remembered that there are no more mothers—not when you're gay. Nobody safe who loves you unconditionally. Because even the most loving are uncomfortable at some unvoiced level with this sexual differentness, with any difference. Even your lover. Even yourself. And, I wondered, why has this fear and hatred been so bred into our cells that we're capable of killing one another off? For no reason. Over breakfast.

As many friends as we had, I felt a pervasive loneliness at times. I felt somehow unacceptable, uncared for, isolated. Was it just the depression that seemed to haunt me chronically, or was it that in my own mind I was never good enough because I was gay? I kept remembering my mother's comment to me some time after I had come out: "You're my daughter, and even if you were a murderer I would still love you."

I took my loneliness and my pains to my therapy with Alvin. Each week I sat in the small outer room of his office suite and studied the art on the walls and the mementos of his many trips.

Alvin was deliberately old-fashioned. On hot days an antiquated black fan with fraying wires twisted solemnly back and forth, blowing a comforting but not cool stream of air into the waiting room. On his desk there was an old black rotary-dial telephone with a curved earpiece. Even in the middle of a session, Alvin answered the phone himself, and when I asked once why he did things this way, he looked pensive and said, "Well, because my analyst did."

Alvin had been with his male lover for over thirty years. He was a stabilizing influence in my relationship with Alice. He was a model for us—a model that gay relationships could work, could be full, wonderful, and lasting. While in many places in our lives, especially in our families, we confronted hatred and suspiciousness, with him we felt validation and caring.

Alvin became my spiritual father, a replacement and substitute for the man who was my biological one. For all the richness of Alvin's own life, I knew he could be plagued by loneliness, too. I felt deeply connected to him, as if we shared some fundamental knowledge about life that few others had.

It was an outing to go to the city to see him—an excuse for Alice and me, when she came, to have a day together. Alvin's office was in the heart of the gay section of town. We'd stop at the gourmet shop and buy delicacies, or we'd walk down the avenue to the French pastry shop that had flown croissants to presidents. We would tramp window shopping around the gay boutiques and have coffee at the Peacock Cafe. We would visit gay bookstores and women's bookstores, and end our day in what was at the time one of the few bars open exclusively to women. We would buy each other presents, each of us always eager to please the other. We would eat in some literary cafe and pretend that we were well-known writers, and we would see theater, as much as possible, because it was Alice's first love and she wanted to be a playwright. We would hear jazz. We would report our plans to Alvin, who sometimes played concierge and offered suggestions for new restaurants or movies or plays we should see. He seemed to delight in our drinking in of the pleasures of the city. Often we would run into him and his lover at a movie, or we would spend half a session talking about a new book or play.

So my loneliness would alternate with feeling richly connected. And though Alvin was our psychiatrist, I thought of him as a crucial part of our lives.

For our tenth anniversary, Alice and I had a party. It was a celebration in lieu of the marriage ceremony we hadn't had. In ten years we'd done a lot of living. We had traveled; we had built a business; we had written a book and book chapters; we had bought and renovated a house; we had made a home. We had acquired many good friends, and tonight we invited all of them. Pat and Jane couldn't make it from North Carolina. But that afternoon a dozen red long-stemmed roses arrived from them. "Darlings," the card read, "we love you dearly and are deeply sorry we can't be there. Here's to the next ten."

Connie catered the affair. It was a rainy Saturday night in November, much like the night of our first date. Connie and her husband, Ted, braved the driving rain to arrive early with stores of hors d'oeuvres and champagne. Jeff and Marsha were there already, helping us set up the house. Jeff paced, nervous because we'd asked him to offer a toast. Marsha helped us primp and approved our choice of dress for the occasion. June arrived with her husband, Ben, who had taught Alice how to fish. And Jerry and Ellen and Frank and Damon were there, along with several of our lesbian couple friends from town and from the city. There were straight couples who were part of Alice's old work network. Some friends were new; some were old. What was amazing was the love and warmth and genuine happiness for us people expressed.

We mingled while the gifts piled up on the living room floor. Finally Jeff tapped a glass with a spoon and we all gathered for the toast.

He was dressed even more smartly than usual, in a fine wool suit and black leather vest.

"Well," he said, "it feels like a real honor to me to be here tonight. I've known Alice and Claudia for many years, I've watched them struggle and grow together, and they are probably two of the most honest, courageous women I know, as well as being two of my closest friends. I hope they know how profoundly I respect them when I say that of all the people in my life, they are the ones I look to most as models for making a relationship work. I'd like to offer a toast to them tonight on this tenth anniversary. May their love continue to grow, and may we all continue to have the good fortune to be a part of their lives."

We raised our glasses. Alice and I kissed. People cried. And then Marsha sang a song—a love song to me written by Alice, part of the score of a musical comedy Alice had been writing for the past few months in her spare time.

And then I read "A Brief History of the First Ten Years," a mildly satirical piece about the two of us I composed for the occasion, in which I told all of the people there how important they were to us and to the survival of our relationship. "Although we've suffered our share of turmoil and trauma with one another, and although we threaten to divorce about every other day, it's been a stable, rich, and rewarding ten years for us," I read. "This party is really a renewal of our commitment to one another. I think of us as blessed, and I hope we'll grow in wisdom and compassion and handle whatever it is life hands us in the next ten years with grace and courage. I hope that we see all of you here again ten years hence."

My own "song" to Alice was borrowed from a poem by Adrienne Rich. As if Rich had shared a similar love, the poem "Paula Becker to Clara Westhoff" captured for me what I so deeply wanted Alice, and the others, to know: that I celebrated her, that I celebrated us, the work we had done together, and the lives and home we had built. That our relationship, the good and the bad of it, was deeply meaningful to me because we had struggled so hard to have it. And that somehow my self both rested and came alive in her because I could, finally, be known.

The next morning, one of our older straight friends called to thank us and to tell us how her husband had reacted to the party. What he said to her was "I never knew that two women could love each other so deeply. Maybe they do love more than a man and a woman can." This was a conservative and prejudiced man. Rigid and unthinking as he often was, he had seen something in our ceremony that night that gave him pause, that moved him. Somehow our differences hadn't mattered. Our love for one another rang true.

Camille would take Elizabeth's hand.

"We're very lucky, Elizabeth."

"Yes we are, Camille. And don't you forget it."

PART TWO

11. Love in a Dying Body

We were in Philadelphia in a run-down inn, the kind of hotel where the windows don't open and the air is bad. We were across from the University of Pennsylvania Hospital, scheduled to see a specialist there the next morning. Alice had developed a rare autoimmune disorder that spread patches of itchy, red pustules across her body whenever she got a cold sore. Her body overreacted to the herpes virus that lived dormant within it. At any time she had an outbreak of cold sores, which she did often, this red and menacing rash started to appear on her body, first in small, slight lesions, and then in larger, angry ones that itched so horribly that she would lie in the bed next to me screaming out, clenching her teeth in an effort not to scratch. I would try to soothe her, to comfort her; we'd put cold compresses and ice and anything we could think of on her that would distract her from the itch. She took cortisone, which made her puffy and bloated; she took a strange medication called Atarax, which made her labile and irritable. But a doctor who consulted with her over the phone, one of the many she would talk to trying to get control of her out-of-control immune system, told her this condition was potentially life-threatening, that the lesions could form in the mouth and block the airways. She must take the medication; she had no choice.

That year the photographs of Alice in our albums showed her looking blimpish and moon-face, almost not recognizable as the person I loved. Her eyes seemed vacant hollows in her puffy face, and there were dark shadows under them.

We drove to Pennsylvania through the late-November fields down to the turnpike, in the evening after we'd already worked a full day with clients. We ate dinner at Mom's Diner and found our lurching way through the city only to end up lost in the Navy Yard. We finally reached the inn well after ten o'clock.

The room was dingy, with spots on the walls, peeling wallpaper, lampshades that twisted at odd angles, and dirty carpeting. By the time we made our way around the worn and dirty spots on the carpet to pour ourselves into the bed that had one thin blanket on it and paper-thin sheets, Alice was feeling very ill. She had one of the first attacks of what we would later learn was asthma. She was feverish and uncomfortable, had difficulty breathing, and was coughing violently, trying to get her breath. She thought it was bronchitis, but she feared it was pneumonia. Maybe it was part of the systemic illness that was running rampant in her system. We were in this godforsaken hotel in this unfamiliar city, and I was lying in the bed with that creepy feeling my skin gets when I'm not sure I'm in a clean bed or breathing clean air. I was terrified that Alice was going to die. I was afraid she might not make it through this night.

I asked, "Should we go to the emergency room?"

"No, I'll be all right. Hold me." Then the plea: "Rub my back." This reassured me. It was part of the routine and must mean we were still both among the living.

I held her through her racking coughing, her back pressed against me. I rubbed her back, trying to keep her from feeling my body tremble. It was not trembling from desire this time; it was trembling from fear and the cold, clammy air of the room. We got as close as we could, as if only this blunt physical connection could save us from anxiety, illness, and the fact that we live and love in dying bodies.

"This room is terrible, isn't it," she said. "They said we should stay here because it's right across from the hospital."

"Do you want to try to go somewhere else?" I asked.

"No, it's too late, I'm too sick. Let's just go to sleep."

"Claud?"

"What, honey?"

"I'm glad you're here with me."

"I know."

Eventually she dropped off to sleep. I stayed awake for the rest of the night, on watch against all that could harm her and separate us, feeling woeful and lost in this unfamiliar place.

Now we entered, unsuspecting, what I came to call the Decade of Death. Suddenly our work conflicts and domestic problems were not the only forces that battered away at love. The legacies of alcoholism, family ties, sickness, and dying kept pushing us off course, away from each other. It was like trying to survive a riptide. As death began its relentless campaign through my family, I had little energy for Alice or our relationship. The intense focus on my family created tension and resentment between us.

Though she recovered from the illness that had brought us to Philadelphia, menopause and stress began its relentless campaign through Alice's body, and she had less and less energy for me. Ultimately, things couldn't hold together at the center, and we were faced continually with what we both feared most: loss.

First it was my grandmother. Her death came shortly after my vision on the beach in North Carolina.

That August we had celebrated her seventy-ninth birthday. I can remember helping her dress. She'd managed to get out to have her hair done, and she was wearing a stunning rose-colored brushed-suede pantsuit, with a scarf and pin at her neck. I had helped clasp her jewelry and slid the jacket of the suit over her bone-thin frame. She felt too slight, too vulnerable, to move through the world at all. She was in constant pain and spent most of her days severely depressed. Yet she pulled herself together for what would be her last outing, pleased and animated. I held her shoulders once the jacket was on and thought that I could not possibly love anyone more than her. She had always stirred all my compassion, all my affection, all my tenderness. There was no strife between the two of us, no conflict. It was all simple, unconditional love. She had given me most of what I had ever had, both materially and emotionally, in my life. For years I had tried to prepare myself for her death.

"Grandmother," I said, "I don't know how you do it, but you still look beautiful."

"Oh," she said, "I wanted to look nice for tonight. I feel so terrible lately and I get out so little, it always gives me a lift to know that I look nice."

My sisters walked into the room.

Ann said, "Well, Grandmother, you've still got what it takes. You look great."

Therese said, "Yup, I think there's still a man out there for you, Grandmother."

"No, none of that sex stuff," Grandmother said. "Just companionship, that's all." She had been saying this for almost twenty years, since my grandfather's death. There had never been even a hint of any other man in her life.

Alice, who had taken on the role of family photographer, appeared with her camera and took pictures. It was the only role my family permitted her at these gatherings. We would make our usual awkward way to the party, and although everyone was used to seeing us together by now, Alice was never really accepted. So she took all the pictures and was never in one herself.

My grandmother was rarely the object of this much attention. We pinned an orchid to her jacket. Her face tightened a bit, and I could see tears appear at the corner of her eyes. She sniffed and grabbed for a tissue. "Happy birthday, Grandmother," I said.

The next time I was to see my grandmother, it would be on her deathbed. It was two weeks before Christmas, and I was stringing lights on the bushes in front of the house.

From outside I heard the phone ring, and Alice, who was cooking, answered. She called me from the doorway: "Claud, it's Ann on the phone, I think there's a problem."

I picked up the phone. Ann's voice was ominous. She knew how attached I was and how I had been dreading this. "Grandmother is in the hospital. You might want to come, because it doesn't look good."

"What happened? She wasn't sick the last time we talked."

"She went into the hospital for an arteriogram because her

pain had gotten so bad. The doctor told her maybe they could do surgery. The dye or whatever fluid they used backed up in her lungs. She has pneumonia and she's not doing well. She hasn't eaten and is having trouble breathing."

The decorating was never finished that year. We packed quickly and drove the three hours to my family's house.

Alice, who was driving, kept taking her eyes off the road to glance over at me. "Tell me what you're feeling, Claud. You've got to talk."

"I can't. I don't want to be a person who has no grandmother" was all I could say.

When I walked into the hospital, one of my aunts met me as I came off the elevator and cried out, "Thank god you're here. She'll be better now."

I walked into the room. My grandmother's face was puffy and a waxy yellow. When she saw me she smiled and cried at the same time. I hugged her and kissed her and joked, "Grandmother, what are you doing in here?"

"Hi, Susan," Alice said, and handed her a rose from a bush that had still been blooming outside our house. They talked about late-blooming roses, my grandmother, who could not talk well, clearly thinking it was remarkable to be given a garden rose in December. Her supper sat on a tray near her bed. My aunt whispered to me, "She hasn't been able to eat anything."

I turned to my grandmother. "Grandmother, would you like to eat something?"

She nodded yes, and I knew she was so weak I would have to help her.

So I fed my grandmother what turned out to be her last meal. Hamburger and mashed potatoes and some vegetable that I can't remember. She ate well and then tired. People came and went and then, as if by some signal, they all left the room and I was there alone with her. I pulled my chair close to the bed.

She lay there and stared at me with such love in her eyes and with a slight smile, and I didn't know what to do or say. I looked at her, trying to convey my love for her, trying not to know that this would be the last time we would talk in this life. Every Thursday night for years my grandmother had called me, just to stay in touch. What would I do without her caring in my life?

I rubbed her leg and finally I said, "Are you frightened of dying, Grandmother?"

She shook her head no. Weakly, she said, "I'll be happy for the good Lord to take me. I've been ready for a long time." She smiled and waved her hand as if to dismiss her life.

I remember having the sense that she was at peace. All the noise and commotion of the hospital faded from my consciousness in this moment—the slightly sick odor of the room, the oppressive heat, the ugly institutional walls and floors. I remember only yellow walls, her gray hair against the white pillow, and her large eyes looking at me. We stayed this way for a long time, and I don't remember what else I said; it was nothing very significant. Finally the others came back to the room, and eventually I left to go back to my mother's house.

At 2:00 A.M. we were called to the hospital. My grandmother's heart had stopped, and she'd been resuscitated. Alice drove my mother and me to the hospital. We watched from the door of intensive care as they put tube after tube into my grandmother. We watched as she fought the respirator. When she was calmer, we went for five minutes each to see her. She seemed unconscious, but I held her hand and whenever I spoke to her she pressed my hand back.

Now I could not blot out of my awareness the gross contraptions of death. The tubes pouring from her nose and mouth, the respirator pumping in a mechanical, rhythmic time that had nothing to do with my grandmother's life, with her gentleness, her vulnerability. I wanted her to be able to go now. She wanted to, I knew. But as we each took our turns visiting her in whatever state of consciousness she was in, gradually the sun came up and pink streaks appeared on the horizon. It was another day. I felt wonder at how it is that life just goes on, that all over other people were getting up and going to work just as if this were a normal day. For me, for my grandmother, it was the time before death, and it had an out-of-time quality to it that I have come to recognize with each new death I have experienced.

Before long, the uncovered window was filled with light. I wondered how my grandmother felt about seeing another day. She was stable now, whatever stable meant. We left her. She pressed my hand again when I said I was going but would be back and when I said I loved her. It was the last time I would see her. She died one week before Christmas.

In the large cathedral in the center of town, the church where I had spent so much of my adolescent life praying, the priest, a family friend, celebrated a high funeral mass. The choir sang Gounod's "Ave Maria," my grandmother's favorite piece, the one she asked to have played on the stereo each Christmas, the piece that always made her weep because it reminded her of her mother. I had not cried openly yet. Like all other expressions of emotion, this one was difficult for me, too. Father Baker laid the Bible on the lectern. He looked over at all of us sitting in one of the front pews near my grandmother's casket and said in a deep voice full of compassion, "Grief is a small price to pay for love."

These words pierced me. I couldn't hold back the tears now, and I sobbed so hard that Father Baker paused to let me cry. Alice put her arm around me, my aunts offered me tissues, and through the rest of the sermon, which was about love and the fact that if there were not deep love we would not feel grief, I wept because this was precisely what I felt: if I had not loved my grandmother so much, I would not have to be feeling this acute grief, this pain that seemed overwhelming and as if it would never go away. And I knew that he was right, that this love had been a gift, and I knew I would have to pay the price, that I would choose it again, and that that was the bargain, that was life's ledger: love, grief, pain, joy. Never one without the other.

When the mass was over, Father Baker walked with an acolyte bearing the gold cross down the center aisle of the church, sprinkling holy water on my grandmother's casket as he went. The casket was draped in red and covered with a spray of flowers. We walked slowly in procession and the organist played a reprise of "Ave Maria." I watched my mother's bent-over shoulders as my sisters held her arms because my father, for reasons we could not understand, would not bring himself to come inside the church. I felt somehow that I was walking the last mile, and at the same time the beauty of the ritual, of the church, was comforting.

As we filed out of the church, Alice walked beside me, holding me very close. I had two competing images: one was that we were being married and this was our wedding march; the other was that I could see in everyone's eyes—the parents of my high school friends, the social elite of the town—the disapproval of my not being with a man, of my having a woman at my side.

And then the altar boys swung open the doors of the cathedral, the bells of the church began to ring, and the sight that we faced as we reached the church steps was a morning full of brilliant sunlight, a shocking-blue sky, and directly across from the church, on the town green, a huge Christmas tree, hundreds of feet tall, covered with enormous red and green ornaments dancing and bouncing in the sun. It was as if the doors of death had opened to the light, and for a moment I wondered if maybe they had staged this to coincide with all that old biblical mythology about darkness and light, but I could not sustain my cynicism.

This beauty, the words, the music, the joyful image of the holiday full of light and love and so many memories of her were like the last gifts of my grandmother to me. And in that moment I felt at peace because I had some knowledge in my heart that love and beauty are just as real as death—maybe even more.

During this time of loss, the quality of my relationship with Alice swung back and forth like a pendulum. What was very, very good could suddenly become horrid. After my grandmother's death, I told Alvin that I thought Alice had been incredibly supportive, that I thought we were learning to be there for each other in more real ways, and these things were true.

But then there would be fighting. It could be over anything. Sometimes it seemed I could say "the sky is blue" and there would be a fight—irrational, unstoppable, out of control before I ever knew where to look for the beginning of it. I despaired. "Have I fallen out of love?" I would question. "Is our love dying?"

My sense of myself as a therapist was deeply compromised. How could I hope to help anyone else when I was having such seemingly unresolvable difficulties myself?

I began to dream about the past, about Molly, and each time I dreamed of her I would feel nostalgia for that old love that was so much more pure and untried by the demands of real life. Often I had the impulse to contact her. But that was against the rules. I might fantasize about it, but I couldn't do it.

I kept asking Alvin how one could deal with life. I kept talking about anxiety. I wanted to know how he managed; I wanted to know how he would handle loss. I wanted to know why love was there one minute and gone the next.

"Life just has a way of happening to you," he said, "and when it does, you realize that you can handle it. You really don't have a choice."

Then one morning there was a phone call from Alvin. I was startled. He wanted to tell us that his lover had suddenly died. Alvin had it printed in the obituary that his lover was survived by "his long-time companion," and named himself. He came out publicly for the first time in his career. People came from all over the world to be at the memorial service, and they all spoke eloquently of the beauty of the relationship between Alvin and Nathan—how it was impossible to think of one without the other. Alvin read from *Death of a Salesman*—"attention must be paid"—and he had a string quartet play Nathan's favorite selections from Schubert. We were invited to the memorial service. And this was how I learned how Alvin handled life.

"Hi, Dad, how are you doing?"

"Not bad. My throat's pretty sore. That worries me some." My father's voice was raspy. I could feel that it hurt him to talk.

"It's probably just a reaction to the radiation, don't you think?"

"I don't know. I can't ever get to talk to the doctor."

"What about the idea of me getting you an appointment with a doctor in the city at the cancer center?"

"No, I don't want to go through all that. They'll take care of me right here. How's your car running?"

"Fine, Dad. Listen, try not to worry. I'm sure you're doing fine."

"Okay, I'll put your mother on now."

It was two years after my grandmother's death, and my father was dying again. Like many alcoholics, he seemed to have many lives. He would get to the brink of death, as he was when Alice and I met, and then he would rally. At one point, he finally got to the brink of life: he went into a rehab, got sober, and went to AA. It began to seem as if there were a person there after all. I told him in a letter that I loved him. I encouraged him to do what he needed to do for himself, that I supported him. I was proud. I felt waves of gratitude that he could finally have what I knew AA and sobriety had to offer.

Shortly after he stopped drinking, he learned that he was dying.

Cancer of the esophagus is a horrible disease. His was inoperable. Had they been able to do it at all, the surgery would have required terrible disfigurement of his face and neck, and the certain loss of his voice. First they tried radiation to shrink the tumor, and then chemo to kill it. Gradually, he couldn't swallow. He tried to take pills and choked them back up. He tolerated only liquids. My mother spent hours preparing things in the blender, crushing his pills in applesauce.

We watched as they marked up his chest for radiation. For the first year he was strong and noble, went back to work right after each treatment. Even after the chemo, which left him exhausted and nauseated, he rested briefly and then was back on his feet, in his store, eager to be in contact with everyone but his family.

But soon he could not even swallow his own saliva. To be around him was torture because he constantly choked and coughed and filled tissue after tissue with the saliva he could not get down.

And then a new tumor grew in a spot in his neck where they couldn't reach it with all their X rays and scalpels and chemicals. It must have pressed on a nerve, because it caused him excruciating pain. He stopped being able to work or go out. My mother constructed a bed of foam pads for him on the living room floor so that he wouldn't have to be upstairs in his bed alone. He would lie there hour after hour pressing pillows against his neck in various configurations to help ease the pain. He choked. He ate less and less. And he still kept telling us that he'd get well.

My sisters and I would come often to visit. Secretly I believed this was all that kept him alive—having his children, his family around him.

On one of those visits we all sat around talking about the afterlife, and I started to expound on my theories of reincarnation.

"I'm not coming back," my mother yelled from the kitchen. "I've had quite enough, thank you."

"But you might need to," I said, "if you haven't finished whatever growth you came here for. The theory is that people can live hundreds of lives."

"No, that's it, I can't take any more of this, thank you."

I ruminated out loud. "Well, I wonder if I'll have to come back again."

My father looked at me with a dark expression that I could not interpret and said in his raspy voice, "Oh, you will, you will."

And I knew in that moment that for all I tried to be there and give to him and be the loving daughter, this was still his fundamental attitude toward me: something about me was not okay, and I would have to do it over and over again until I learned my lesson, got it right. I never did know what he disliked. Perhaps it was my being gay. But somehow I think it had more to do with my not being the person he needed me to be, the daughter who would give him the unconditional love and attention he craved. I think this was my sin: that I was myself and not his mirror. Somehow I always failed.

I didn't say anything to him. He had been hateful to me at times in my life, had tried to rip the soul right out of me. But could I be angry with him directly? No. I could only be angry with Alice. Only in our fighting did my rage ever come out. How does one feel anger for a dying man?

Finally he could not take in even liquid, so they had to put a tube in his stomach to feed him. For some reason my mother determined that I would be the one to accompany my father in an ambulance to the hospital.

He was as furious as someone in his debilitated condition could be. It was his last raging against death. He didn't want to leave his house. He knew on some primitive level that going to the hospital this time would mean the end.

"They have to do this, Dad, so you can get nourishment," I told him. He looked at me with something close to hatred in his sunken eyes. He choked that horrible rasping choke and spit saliva into a tissue. The ambulance arrived.

At the hospital, he was wheeled to a cubicle in the emergency room and lay there for what seemed like hours with a bright fluorescent light glaring in his eyes. I reached to hold his hand, but he turned his head away and drew his hand underneath the sheet. I didn't know whether to take this as a sign of his shyness with any physical contact between us or as a rejection, his final statement of withdrawal from me, his final act of disapproval and displeasure, his statement of anger that I had brought him here to die.

The next day he was gone. He died alone in his sleep. When they went to insert the stomach tube to do the surgery they found that the cancer had spread throughout his liver so extensively that the anesthesia had no effect. He woke up during the surgery, and, as the doctor told us, "I'm afraid I caused him some pain."

There were no wrenching deathbed scenes of reconciliation with my father. If my grandmother's death had filled me with grief, my father's was like a painful trauma. I grieved for all that had never been, I refelt all the pain there had ever been in our relationship. Throughout the time of his dying, as the tensions grew between me and Alice, I began to learn that there is no way that any of us escapes the defeat of life, the potential for destructiveness; there is no way that we escape the limitations of our humanness and our own personalities.

I told myself that probably my father loved me in his way, as much as he could. And when Alice raged to me about how awful he had been, how awful my family was, I felt compelled to defend them and to resent her for speaking negatively. As the pendulum swung, it was a measure of our distance at this point that, having been so supportive when my grandmother died, this time Alice acted angry at the disruption to our lives.

Alice and I were lying in bed, drowsy. The lights were out, the dog was on the floor at the foot of the bed, and one cat lay at my feet. "Al, I don't want to go to sleep tonight," I said, yawning, in my most childlike voice. "I don't want to leave you. Tell me the names of the wildflowers."

"Okay, honey, come over here."

I slid over in the bed, put my head on her shoulder, and lay in the crook of her arm.

"There is loosestrife, pearly everlasting, lady's slipper, fleabane, and desert paintbrush; bunchberry, beach pea, and vetch; and, let's see . . ."

"Queen Anne's lace," I whispered.

"Good," she said, "that's good, and shooting star and . . ."

"Shooting star?" I said. "C'mon, you're making that up."

"I am not. I'll show you in the wildflower book tomorrow. You love this, don't you?"

"Yes," I said. "It's so amazing to me that somebody gave flowers these wonderful names. It just delights me. Say some more."

"I'm running out."

There was a silence. Alice was running her hand through my hair.

"You know, I really love you, Claud. If anything ever happened to you, well, my life would be over, that's all."

I turned my face to look up at her. "I know that's how it feels. But it wouldn't, Alice. You're more gregarious than me; you would be fine. And nothing's going to happen to me. At least not soon."

"But there's nobody else I can conceive of being with, you know, Claud? I know I'm gregarious, but really I'm a loner and shy, and frankly, you're the person who interests me most. Sometimes you're the only person I feel like being with."

"I know what you mean. Do you think there's something wrong with us?"

"Probably. But who cares."

Drowsiness began to weigh on me. "I have to go to sleep now, Al," I said. My eyes were closing. "I love you." We kissed and drifted off to our own sides of the bed.

And the next day there would be a fight and what was very, very good would suddenly be horrid.

It was Saturday morning.

"What do you want to do today, Claud?"

Already I could feel the tension in me. This was the beginning of the usual conflict.

"Well, I had no special plans. There are some things I want to take care of around here."

"Like what?"

"You know, the garage, all the clutter downstairs, my study. I just want to do some clearing out."

"But it's a beautiful day out. You want to waste it cleaning?"

"What did you have in mind, Alice?"

"I thought we'd go up north to see the leaves. Every fall you promise me we'll do it, and we haven't gotten there yet."

"Well, how about tomorrow?"

"The weather could be bad. And besides, I don't believe you'll really do it. Tomorrow there'll be something else you want to do."

"Okay, Alice." I sighed wearily. "We'll go today and I'll clean tomorrow."

"No, I don't want you to just give in to me, because then I'll pay all day with your distance."

"Alice, we'll go, okay?"

"Are you mad?"

"No, I'm not mad."

"I feel like you're mad."

"No, Alice, I'm just irritated."

"You're irritated at me?"

"No, I'm irritated at the situation."

"You mean you're irritated because I'm asking you for something and you don't really want to do it?"

"No, Alice, I'm irritated because there is no alternative here. I want to make you happy and I want to meet my own needs and I can't do both, so there is a conflict and I'm irritated at life."

"Well, you seem to be mad at me. And I don't want to spend the day with you if you're going to be mad."

"God, Alice, can you just let go of this? We're going to do what you want to do."

"Well, something's not right. You don't have to do it if you don't want to. I can't stand it when you're mad."

I start to shout now. "I'm not mad, but I'm going to get mad if you don't lay off!"

Alice is out of the bed now, pacing around the room like a caged animal.

"You know, you're such a goddamned liar, you don't even see your own dishonesty. You're so fucking concerned about your image, that pride of yours. You're so good, you could never acknowledge being pissed off or that maybe you just want to be selfish and not meet my needs. Didn't you ever hear of the idea of compromise?"

"What is your need to keep this going, Alice?

"You're keeping it going, Claudia, because you just can't acknowledge what's true." Alice was beginning to rage now. Her face was hardening and she was pacing frantically. Her voice was becoming sharper and more hostile.

"Well, maybe you can't acknowledge that you're totally self-involved as usual and can't stand it if I automatically don't just want to do everything you want."

"Oh, aren't you the superior one. Just like your mother—cold, sarcastic, superior. I hate it, I just can't stand it."

"Well, good, then why don't you just get out and leave me alone."

"Poor you, you feel so deprived, so sorry for yourself. It makes me sick, your self-pity."

"Good, Alice, then get out of here and leave me alone." I threw off the covers, charged out of the bed, and started to throw on my clothes.

"That's what you really want, isn't it, Claudia, to be alone, to have me out of your life, because it's too much trouble to have to pay any attention to what I need or want. You're a goddamned bitch and you think you're so giving."

"I've had enough of this, Alice, I'm going out."

"Don't you leave this room." Alice blocked the door.

I screamed at her. "Get out of my way."

"No, don't go." Alice was hysterical now. "I'll calm down, don't leave. If you leave I'll . . ."

"You'll what?" I said, taunting her as I pushed my way out the door. "I don't know why I put up with this. I don't know why I'm even still here."

"That's right, threaten to end the relationship like you always do. You think you love me, huh, well that's the biggest lie. You hate me, that's what's true. Well, I've had it, Claudia, it's over, I'm sick of this."

"Well, I'm sick of your attacking me. I've had it, I can't take any more."

Alice ran downstairs. I retreated to the bathroom, where I collapsed in tears. I felt the hot shame of rejection, and I couldn't understand what had happened. I was frightened by this scene, by the way it got so out of control so quickly. I couldn't follow the process. I didn't know where it came from or how it got to where it went. We had this same fight over and over, as if we were reading from a script. I really didn't think I was mad; I was just in conflict. But maybe I was mad and just didn't know it. But I also thought Alice was demanding in the extreme. I hated her for doing this to us, for getting me this out of control. I hated her for making a mockery of my very sincere wish to make her happy and give her what she wanted. I hated it that it was not okay that I also had my own needs and felt conflict at times. She destroyed any caring for her that I felt by accusing me of not feeling it.

I felt like a wretch. I was reminded of scenes in my bedroom with my father standing in the doorway yelling at me as if he hated me and I couldn't understand why, what he was so angry about. I hadn't done anything; I was this good, model child who had never given him a day's trouble but there he was, yelling, and I couldn't understand what it was about me that he hated. I sobbed the despair of the lost who didn't know why they found themselves so cursed, why they had become so much the object of hatred and cruelty, couldn't figure out what they'd done to deserve it, and could only assume that it was something bad about them, something they couldn't even see.

After a while, my tears stopped. I was spent now, traumatized. I was numb with confusion and felt utterly alone and worthless in the universe. I left the bathroom and went to my study, hoping Alice would leave me alone. I closed the door and stared at the wall full of books, wondering why in the end they didn't help.

After a while there was a knock at my door.

"Claud, can I come in?"

"No, leave me alone."

"Listen, I'm sorry. I don't know how this happened, I . . . I . . . I didn't mean all those things I said. I just got out of control. I'm sorry. Please let me come in."

"I said, go away."

"I know I hurt you. I didn't meant to. I just got frustrated."

Now Alice was crying. She was talking to me from outside the door. "Claud, I just wanted to be with you. I wanted to get out with you, to do something besides fucking work, and I was afraid to ask more directly. I wanted us to do something together. It's such a beautiful day, we haven't been out in so long, can't you understand that, can't you forgive me? Can I come in, please?"

"If you have to." In spite of myself, I felt myself soften.

I knew it was not only my family legacies that spurred these fights. It was for good reason, not just her love for water, that Alice lived halfway across the country from her family. When she screamed at me that I didn't love her, I was just the stand-in for them.

Now Alice walked over to where I was sitting and held me. I cried. I was still feeling the double pain—the pain of us and the pain of me and my father. I took the comfort and I took the apology as if it were him apologizing, which he never did. I craved this from him; I was desperate for him to see how he was hurting me, how I was the child and he was the father. I shouldn't have to understand him; he was supposed to understand me.

It didn't occur to me to apologize to Alice. I smiled at her weakly. She led me downstairs and asked me if I'd like tea, and I said yes, and then we held each other for a while. Until the next time.

I was ten years old, or eleven or twelve. It was the middle of a Saturday night. My sisters and I had been sent to bed, and my parents and my grandmother had stayed up drinking. They smoked cigarettes and talked and laughed, their voices loud and harsh. They sang along with Mitch Miller blasting on the stereo. They screeched "If You Knew Susie Like I Know Susie" (because my grandmother's name was Susan) and sang "Don't Fence Me In" with exaggerated emphasis. They sang "Lucille," my father's favorite song, and they kept singing until they were too drunk to follow the words.

In the quiet after they had finally stopped, I must have fallen asleep. The silence felt strangely heavy now after the brazenness of the noise. I got up to go to the bathroom and noticed there were still lights on. The bathroom door was open, and there was light coming from it. Knowing I was about to see something I didn't want to, I turned into the doorway. There, passed out on the floor of the bathroom, was my grandmother, her head near the toilet, her arms wrapped around herself as she lay in a fetal position, as if she had simply walked in here and fallen asleep. Her nightgown was bunched up around her, exposing more of her than was comfortable for me to see. I heard her breath coming in short, noisy bursts, so I knew she was alive.

This was my grandmother, the person I loved most in my life, the person who made me feel the safest. She was a woman completely without guile and seemingly without anger, who had lived for over thirty years with my alcoholic, abusive grandfather. After he died she sobbed, guilty that she felt so relieved.

It was unusual for her to drink too much, but tonight she had. The horror of seeing her in this degrading position was overwhelming to me. It was worse than the times my father had fallen into the Christmas tree or been sick all over the floor, had been slurred and embarrassingly incoherent and inappropriate. I stood there, silent, afraid to touch her or wake her, and what went through my head was *This will affect me for the rest of my life.* I turned and went back to bed, and whether I slept again or not I don't remember.

Alcoholism played like background music as a theme that shaped the patterns of my life with Alice. If the alcoholics in my life were volatile and angry, withholding and cruel, I was measured and saintly, frantic to give. Though I rarely drank myself, I could be tense and uncomfortable with my own feelings. I was sensitive and shy. I tried too hard to be good and blameless; I worked hard to be loved. I longed for love and contact.

When Alice barged through the wall of silent protection that shielded me by demanding that I respond to her, I was often happy to be pulled from my isolation, elated to be wanted. But in the next breath I might be left bereft because she would open me up, then turn around and leave, push me away, because she was frightened herself.

This was the lasting legacy of my grandmother on the bathroom floor, of the alcoholism that pervaded my life—being disappointed in my hope of love. Love was there one moment and gone the next. And sometimes I couldn't tell the difference.

Then Pat died. Alice and I were on vacation, at a ranch in Arizona. We called the hospital and could hear the life leaving Pat's voice. Alice was strangely out of touch with her grief at the time; it would surface much later. I was angry that she didn't want to cut short our vacation to be with Pat in the hospital. A week later we drove to North Carolina for the memorial service.

The service, held in the little Methodist church there, was simple, moving, and hilarious. We manipulated the pastor into allowing us a musical interlude of "Margaritaville"—a favorite Jimmy Buffett song of Pat's about drinking and chasing women. His somber introduction of it as a song about personal responsibility would have been enough to make Pat roar with laughter. Island people told touching stories of Pat. Jane managed not to cry. Alice read poetry by Margaret Atwood and I read some of Pat's writings.

The next day was piercingly beautiful, with a cloudless blue sky and bright sunshine, Pamlico Sound calm as glass. Pat had wanted her ashes scattered on the sound. We headed out in Gordon's boat, Alice and me and Jane, her son and his girlfriend. Jane carried Pat's ashes in a Ziploc bag.

We read more poetry. We dumped the ashes. The girlfriend threw up over the side of the boat—vomit mixed with the ashes. What would Pat have said? How would she have told this story about death?

The time we'd visited with Marsha and Jeff, we'd gotten to talking about death, Marsha telling the story of her father and her brother, Jeff the story of his grandfather, each of us in turn talking about how we had been affected by loss. Pat had said she'd never forget the day she was standing at the shore and looked up to see three birds—ducks, probably—flying in formation. Suddenly, one of them just fell out of the sky—died, apparently—and fell into the water. One of the other birds circled back briefly, seeming to search for the lost bird, and then simply flew on, rejoining its partner.

"That's how I think about death," she said. "There is the briefest of pauses, and then life goes on."

We said the Serenity prayer and then we went back to the island from the last buoy before the open ocean. It was over. The day seemed less beautiful: the meaning of the moment had gone with Pat's ashes, and what was left was a sense of emptiness and fatigue.

As I grieved for Pat, I knew on some level that I was grieving for Alice; for the love between us that Pat, as our friend, had nurtured; for all that had been rich and beautiful and intensely innocent and creative between us. These deaths of the body couldn't take away love, but what would happen if love itself died? Our love for each other was being stomped out by our very natures, by the stress of our lives together. I cried and cried, pleading with Jane to tell me how to get it back, how to get back to the time when our love for each other worked.

So we went back to Alvin for more therapy. Now things were more serious than red jackets on the floor.

"Alvin, I'm scared," I said.

"We're all scared."

"Alvin, I don't know what's happening to us. These fights are draining us, destroying us. I wonder how much more we can take. I wonder how to stop them. Nothing I try seems to work."

I droned on about my fears, I droned on about Alice and our fights and how I didn't know who was right and who was wrong. Some days he was supportive. He nodded and shook his balding head sympathetically. He was unpredictable. He had a habit of suddenly breaking into a monologue with a slightly sarcastic or ironic comment. "Yes, soooo," he would say, or, "What is it that makes you think this?"

Often he unexpectedly jumped up from his chair and pulled a book from his dusty shelf. He read from Jewish scripture or from his favorite book of poetry.

One day he read from the poetry of Kavafy about the love of two men for each other. We had long conversations about homophobia and the conspiratorial hatred of the straight world for gay people. He told us, "In the suburbs, the outskirts, the city there are thousands of gay men and women living together, living good, ordinary, unnotable lives. Nobody pays attention to them, because what the straight world wants to hold up as an example are those of us they can point to and say, 'Look how crazy, how different, how sick.' This is not who we are; this is not who you are."

Alvin worked hard to help us with the cycles of anger and

depression that pounded away at our connection. To Alice he said, "I know how deeply you love her and how deeply she loves you, but if you're not careful you can kill that love." He told us stories, fables, fairy tales, anything to get us out of our rigid patterns of seeing and interacting with each other. Of Alice he said to me, "She's very frightened." I fought back, saying, "But, Alvin, that doesn't justify her behavior."

Alvin would shout, as Alice and I left the office after a particularly abusive battle, "Don't kill each other," and I sometimes felt that, realist that he was, he knew we had to make the most of the positives and learn to minimize the very real negative and painful aspects of our interaction. I learned to accept our limitations, that life had handed us a very difficult deck to deal with. For a while I would feel compassion for both of us, I would forgive us both our hostility and our rough edges, and we would go on. Because basically we loved each other deeply.

But all love contains the seeds of its own destruction. What is alive is also dying by small degrees. I thought to myself, What will really decide our fate is not how we love but how we hate, how we deal with anger, how we come to terms with the wild core of darkness in ourselves and not allow it to overwhelm.

I did not have the heart to leave Alice, though I really thought I should. Being a lesbian, I had paid too high a price to be with her. There was too much that I savored, too much that I feared. How would I create a life centered on myself? It was important not to leave; it was important to say to the world, "You're wrong, this love can last as well as any other, we can do it, we know about love as well as any of you, and maybe we even know better." Making it work was a matter of pride.

And we were fighters, the two of us, determined and willful. And if any two people were going to slay the dragons, we were. Claudia and Alice, Camille and Elizabeth, the two of us, indomitable, inseparable, marching against the onslaughts of life and of our own natures, determined to preserve this love that dare not speak its name.

12.
The Other Woman

I waited for Cass inside the doorway of the restaurant where we had planned to meet for a pre-Christmas lunch. It was a cold and blustery day. Cass was late, but my irritation didn't last long. She burst into the restaurant in a draft of cold air, her face glowing with the cold, her eyes sparkling. She was wearing a full-length fur coat. The word "stunning" kept going through my mind—she looked stunning. I hung up my coat and then found myself very gallantly helping her off with hers. The waiter seated us at a table in the back room that looked out on a patio dotted with white lights. We were in one of those nooks that heighten a sense of intimacy. I ordered a glass of wine; Cass ordered mineral water. We sat facing each other across the table.

"So," she said, "I'm so glad we planned this."

"Yes, so am I," I said.

We both looked away, as if to take in the ambiance of the restaurant. It was one of those elegant little downstairs places in the basement of a city brownstone, with deep mahogany moldings and an intimate bar. Thick red carpeting muffled the sound of clanking dinner plates and cutlery, and tables with proper white linen cloths and green linen napkins were arranged in small alcoves and nooks of rooms. A wall of glass doors and windows opened out onto the patio. Inside, the decor was festive. There were large, elegant vases filled with dried Christmas-flower arrangements with lights strung through them. Small velvet Christmas trees with red bows sat on each table, along with a flickering candle in an elegant glass holder. The walls were covered with heavily framed paintings lit with small portrait lights from beneath. This was vintage city atmosphere, romantic, festive, like another, magical world.

We turned back to each other. Cass was smiling, acting as if nothing could make her happier than to be here in this place having Christmas lunch with me. She wore black. Her skin was smooth and creamy. She had large blue eyes and short, well-styled hair that was colored blond. As usual, she was dressed stylishly, adorned with expensive jewelry. Her husband was a successful architect in the city.

"You look great today," I said, understating my ardor. "I've never seen you wear that coat before. Have you had it long?"

"Oh, Adam gave it to me a while ago. I like to wear it when it's really cold; it keeps me so warm."

I, of course, believed she had worn it as a seductive gesture, knowing full well just how attractive she looked in it.

We glanced at the menu, smiling at each other conspiratorially. We always joked about how much we each loved food and how much we both needed to diet.

"This is a special occasion, though, right?" she said. "So we'll just have whatever we want."

"Of course, whatever we want," I said.

Cass put her menu aside. "How are you, Claudia?" She looked directly into my eyes, intently, as if no one else in the world were this important, as if the answer meant everything to her. We had been friends for a long while, as had she and Alice. She knew how tenuous things were with us. She had been solicitous and clearly took my side.

"Well, I'm okay. This is such a busy time, and we have our usual fighting and tension."

"Oh, I'm sorry," Cass replied.

"How do you manage to get through the holidays, Cass? Do you and Adam fight?"

"Oh, not really. Because I take care of everything, I just do whatever has to be done, he leaves me alone. I do some of the shopping, and I have a personal shopper who takes care of quite a bit of it for me."

"Cass, tell me something. How do you handle it when you're mad?"

"Well, I'm usually very quiet. I just withdraw."

"So if you're mad at Adam, how do you both get over it?"

"Usually he has to make some move toward me to apologize. Eventually it gets over with."

"Sometimes my anger frightens me," I said. "I'm so angry now I think it has begun to kill my feelings for Alice. I try and try to tell her, but it doesn't seem to help."

"It's so hard for me to think of you being angry," Cass said. "You have never seemed anything but perfectly controlled to me."

"That's an illusion, Cass. I can be very uncontrolled."

Now there was an abrupt shift in the tone of the conversation.

"How uncontrolled?" she asked. "Like, would you ever have an affair?"

"I always thought that would be out of the question, but now I'm not so sure. I think I'm capable of it, if it were the right person."

"You know, I really love talking to you," she said. "Tell me how many people you've loved in your life." So we talked about Mike Carey, about David, about Alice, and I told her the story of Molly, that I thought about her often, wondered what had happened to her, what she had done with her life, "I think I'll look her up someday," I said.

"With Alice, it's sad, because I loved her so deeply, so fully, and so much has happened to destroy that feeling, I think I can never love her quite so much as I did, and she can't accept that she has pushed me away." As I was talking I felt a tremendous weight come over me about Alice, an anger that what I once felt I no longer felt, that I had been robbed of the ability to feel loving, except now here at the table with Cass. I felt alive and present and I knew I shouldn't.

Cass rested her chin in her hands. She looked at me softly, a smile playing at the corners of her lips, a soft smile, what seemed almost a look of love. I'd had a few sips of wine by now, and the air was filled with the fragrances of flowers and candles and good food. I looked at her in the half-light and I felt myself slipping, thinking, I shouldn't be here having this conversation with her, feeling this way for her. I should be here with Alice, feeling this for Alice. But I'm not. I felt as if I had been stabbed. I felt desire and arousal. I felt as if I had slipped into a trance.

"Cass," I said, "I think we're put in this life to learn how to love. That there really isn't too much of it to go around, and that we're challenged to realize how important it is. I think we have to learn how to give it and how to take it. I've felt this ever since I was very young. There's a favorite quote of mine by William Blake that goes, 'We are put on earth for a little space that we may learn to bear the beams of love.' I think I saw this realization happening for you with your father, while he was dying. You were so loving to him."

Cass talked, but not as openly. I accepted her need to fashion her image with me, her need to selectively tell me about herself. There had not been quite so much passion in her relationships, she told me, except for one man, a priest. There it was again, the persistence of infatuation with priests.

Now we had both slipped into a trance. We talked looking directly into each other's eyes, we kept talking about love, about our relationships, and I think that unless I was very mistaken, Cass was as unsettled as I. The waiters hovered trying to get our attention without intruding, deep in conversation as we were. When it came time to order dessert, Cass suggested we share a chocolate mousse. We ate it together from the one dish, carefully orchestrating the dipping of our spoons into the creamy darkness of the glass, watching each other, laughing about how much we loved sweets, both savoring the rich, forbidden taste of the chocolate, sharing in a way that, to me, was highly intimate.

By the time the waiter brought the bill, I was unable to add it up. I fumbled for my wallet. I struggled with the numbers; Cass tried to add them and she was just as distracted. We laughed and left something on the table, and as we rose to leave, the waiter nodded at the two of us with some knowing look and said, "Good morning, ladies," though it was the middle of the afternoon.

In the coatroom, I helped Cass on with her fur. We walked outside into the sharp cold of the afternoon, and she stood facing me. Something about the cold softened her face even more; her eyes began to tear a bit. She looked at me as if she might want to cry. She pulled a city guide from her bag and suggested that we spend the afternoon together, do something in the city. But I said I must get back, though everything in me wanted to stay with her, never leave. She handed me my Christmas gift—she had opened mine at the table—and we turned and walked in the direction of my car. At the corner we turned to embrace each other, and it may have been only my imagination but I think not, that her lips grazed mine in a furtive kiss, and I drove back home knowing I had fallen in love, feeling unutterable sadness that this was as far as it would ever go. It was improbable—impossible. One day we were friends, and the next I was in love.

My consciousness was now split between the two banks of the river. On one lay the city and a fantasy of love made up of moments that were the merest suggestions—the soft elegance of a fur coat; the inflection of a voice, a look, a glance; a conversation that could mean one or many things or nothing at all. On the other bank was home and the painful conflicts born of years of working at love.

I remained in a daze that entire holiday. I felt desperate. I felt overwhelming guilt toward Alice, knowing it was not fair to her. This was the first time that my feelings for her had been seriously challenged. I felt despair about what it all meant. But like a moth drawn to the flame that will eventually kill it, I was unable to stay away.

As soon as I could, I called Cass.

"Hi," I said. "I need to talk to you."

"Is anything wrong?"

"I . . . lunch last week. Something happened for me, Cass. I started to have feelings for you that are disturbing. I want to be open with you. I don't want to be seductive or inappropriate in any way. I can't keep talking with you about Alice. It isn't right."

"Lunch for me was, well, very magical, but not the same, I don't think. Why would you be so upset? We have a passionate friendship, that's all."

"But, Cass, you're straight and I'm gay. It's different. I feel like we've been getting much closer lately. I just need you to know that this is happening, so that if I seem to be pulling back, you won't take it the wrong way."

"I understand, I think. Is there any way I can help?"

"Just be honest with me, Cass. And don't reject me because of this."

"Well, I certainly wouldn't do that. I love you."

But I knew that something had changed between Cass and me, that more was happening than she acknowledged. I felt that she was becoming more seductive with me. She talked often about how much our friendship meant to her. I could not get her out of my mind. I dreamed about her, longed to talk to her, and I tried to understand what was happening to me in all the analytical ways I knew. Some days I filtered this predicament through the lens of my psychological knowledge, and some days I thought of it as a spiritual crisis. Either way, it haunted me. There was no easy solution to the pull of Cass.

Finally, knowing I had to be honest because she would pick up on it anyway, I talked to Alice, who was upset but nevertheless tried to help.

"Just be careful," she warned me. "She'll hurt you."

She didn't ask me to stop having contact with Cass. It would have been awkward. We were part of a close-knit group of friends of whom Cass was the center. Alice vacillated between a vicious jealousy and a sincere desire to be helpful to me. The jealousy made things worse, and when she tried to help I was grateful. But try as I might—therapy, talks with friends, reading books—nothing helped. I was lost, obsessed with this woman. The fact that she was heterosexual made no difference. There was something between us that I felt to be tinged with a passionate eroticism.

Jeff and Marsha joined us as always that year to help us decorate the Christmas tree. We sat down together to a pre-Christmas brunch. Whenever Alice left the room, I tried to talk to Jeff about Cass.

"It's not fair to Alice," I said, "to have this feeling. Our issues are one thing, but they don't justify this."

Jeff listened, but there wasn't much he could say that I hadn't already told myself.

The days just before Christmas brought with them the usual tensions and conflicts about family and money. Alice and I had added an addition to the house, a large room ringed with cottage windows and a French door looking out onto a brick patio. It opened out from the kitchen. We called it the great room. It had a woodstove in one corner. We had designed it ourselves, and to me it was like a small-scale version of my dream house. It had a spare, Shaker quality to it. We furnished it with a dining room table, an antique hutch and dry sink, and some comfortable chairs placed near the woodstove. We put our Christmas tree here and filled the room with greens and red Christmas linens, and every time I walked in there I felt happy.

But two days before Christmas, I walked in the door from yet another shopping trip loaded down with packages that still had to be wrapped. There were hours of fussing with the house and cooking ahead of me. Alice was stretched out in a chair by the woodstove peacefully listening to music on the stereo, watching the tree lights, thoroughly enjoying herself. I felt a cold, icy rage take hold of me, but I kept it to myself. When, I thought, do I ever get a chance to simply sit and enjoy? Why am I the one running frantically to take care of the preparations for her family's visit? Why am I making Christmas happen while Alice sits and enjoys it? Alice noticed my hostile, sharp movements through the house, and by the time she finally started to get angry back because I wouldn't tell her what was wrong, I exploded, screaming, "I'm sick of doing all the work to make it possible for you to have what I want."

There it was, out—I had said something that thoroughly offended my principles and my sense of myself.

Alice got up from the couch, threw her magazine across the room, and screamed, "I can't help it if you have to buy everybody ten different gifts, if you have to do everything perfectly, if you have to make a complete production of this. Why do you have to rob me of what little enjoyment I get? I don't have to do everything the way you do it. If you don't want to do so much work, then don't do it!"

"It's your family who's coming!" I screamed. "I don't think you'd be very happy if there were no decorations and no dinner."

I felt both righteous indignation and intense guilt. But this was part of the growing disenchantment between us. I was becoming someone I didn't like, someone frustrated, bitter, and envious, a martyr. I had loved Alice almost desperately, but I had also always taken on more than my share of the work for us both, and I had begun to resent it. Yet part of me knew this night's outburst was really all about Cass. Now Alice was furious with the uproar I had created, and I was being punished for my betrayal.

In the face of all the stress that dominated our work lives and our families and our life with each other, the solution Alice and I had settled on was to move. We thought we might live in Maine. We reasoned that it was the structure of our lives that needed to change. We were too driven by work and by economic stress. We both wanted more time to write, to do more creative work. We wanted not to sit for hours in traffic; we wanted to be somewhere where we could enjoy being outdoors without running into crowds. We wanted more beauty in our lives, a simpler lifestyle. What could be better than moving to Maine? we thought. Or were we desperately trying to relocate our relationship to a place where we had felt closer in the past, where we thought we might be in love again?

13.
The Great Migration

Alice and I checked in to the Baxter House Bed and Breakfast, in the middle of the small Maine town that would soon become our home. Just before our arrival on this February day, there had been a major snowstorm. When we hit the Maine turnpike on the other side of the Kittery bridge that morning, we were greeted by a world of pristine white, the evergreens massing against the snow like the tufts of a quilt on a winter bed. The sky was cloudless, a brilliant turquoise blue.

It was perhaps unfortunate that we arrived the day after a snowfall, because we were confronted by a winter idyll. Children were skating on the town green; the sitting room of the bed and breakfast was warmed by a crackling fire; the air was crisp and enlivening. The whole scene was like a Currier & Ives print. We were charmed. Winter, we thought—no problem. We promised ourselves that we'd take up cross-country skiing. We told ourselves the beauty would sustain us. We didn't think about enduring the whole winter, the mud season that must be forded before there was any sign of spring, the dark, damp, gray days that are often more persistent than the sunny, clear ones, the days that diminish any motivation to do anything and make you wish you could just stay in bed with the covers pulled over your head.

Alice, her usual gregarious self, had become fast friends with the house cat within a half hour of our arrival and had already struck up a running conversation with the owner of the inn.

"Are you from Maine?" she asked her. "How long have you owned the inn?"

"No, we moved here from Florida, actually," Dot told us. "Used to come here on vacation, and fell in love with it. So many people have that experience. You wouldn't believe how many of the guests who stay here with us end up coming back to live."

"Well, we may be two more of those," Alice replied, grinning.

"Really?" Dot said. "What do you two do?"

"We do therapy, we teach, and we write," Alice said proudly.

I was always struck by the way Alice talked so openly of our life together, as if she had no concern that people should know we were a couple. Within an hour we knew much of the history of the innkeepers and the saga of their buying and renovating the inn. And they knew half our life story. Dot told us about two women who had moved here three years earlier who would be able to tell us what it was like to pull up stakes and make a life change like the one we were considering.

So we walked down the main street of town to a little shop called People and Pets. On the sign over the front door was a painting of the face of a grinning girl holding a dog. The wrought-iron brace that held the sign was a large sewing needle with another dog sitting on top of it. The shop featured needlework supplies and gifts for pampered pets. Sitting in the window was a large Maine coon cat wearing a red baseball cap. He was named Pete Rose, after the owner's favorite baseball player. As we opened the door, the ringing of the bell set two small dogs to yapping frantically, and we heard a woman's voice telling them to be quiet.

"Hi, can I help you?"

"Hi," Alice said. "We're staying down the street at the bed and breakfast, and the innkeeper told us to look you up. We're thinking of moving here, and she said you'd be happy to talk to us about what it's been like for you."

"Well, sure." It came out sounding like "shoeah"—a definite

Massachusetts accent. "My name is Betsey." She offered her hand and there were hearty handshakes all around. Her partner, Barb, walked down from the back of the store.

"These two ladies are thinking of moving here, and Dot sent them down to talk to us, Barb."

"Oh, isn't that great!"

Barb was more reserved but equally friendly. Betsey was clearly the more outgoing of the two. She wore a sweatshirt emblazoned with Mickey Mouse, Mickey earrings, jeans, and Maine hunting shoes.

"How long have you been here? We live down south, outside the city, and our life is getting out of control. We need a change. Actually, I want to move here for the beauty," Alice said.

"Well, I know what you mean there," Betsey replied.

In their past lives they had been professors of dental hygiene at major universities. Good friends who met at professional meetings and kept in touch through their work, they began to vacation together and would take long, leisurely treks through Maine in an RV. Just as Dot had said, like many who vacation here, they finally gave in to the pull of the place and decided that they wanted to live here permanently. When the time was right and the stresses of their professional lives were no longer worth the wear and tear on their bodies and souls, they decided to throw in their lots with each other and move. They bought a building and followed their dream of being shop owners. Barb had always loved needlepoint and Betsey was an animal lover; hence the mixture of pets and people.

"Why don't you join us later for dinner at the restaurant next door?" Barb said. "We'll convince you to pack up and come."

Barb and Betsey were so friendly, so welcoming, that we felt this move was somehow meant to be. After dinner we walked back through the town, admiring the Norman Rockwell quaintness of the green surrounded by centuries-old captains' houses and the tall spire of the Congregational church at one end.

"I think it's time for us to make this decision," Alice said to me. "We've been ambivalent long enough, don't you think?"

I felt a pang of fear. I had pushed for this move, and now I was overcome with a sense of loss. How could I leave our home, my friends, Cass?

"Well, I think we have to make a decision, yes, but . . ."

"No buts, Claud. Let's agree that we'll make up our minds before we leave here."

Back at the bed and breakfast, there was a message from my mother to call her. I looked at Alice, who said, "Oh no." Just weeks ago, my mother had had surgery for uterine cancer. We thought they had gotten it all. After the surgery, she had spent several days lying inert with radium implants inside her body. I thought to myself, What next? I was almost afraid to dial her number.

"Hi. Mom?"

"Claudia?"

"Yes, it's me. Are you okay?"

"I don't think so." Her voice was weak and ironic. She wasn't saying anything, waiting for me to ask the right questions.

"What's wrong?"

"They've found another spot."

"Oh no. Where?"

"In my esophagus. I have to have surgery."

"Oh, god, this is terrible," was all I could say.

The surgery she needed would be very extensive. She was terrified and depressed. I turned to Alice, who looked at me with despair, anger, and irritation. She managed to say something like "You must feel terrible." Now, on the verge of making a major life decision of my own, of trying to create a life that would be more congruent for myself—hopefully for the two of us—I would probably have to face my mother's dying. But I knew this new development didn't change the need to make a decision. Too much of our lives and attention had been focused on the dying of my family, and it was not fair to Alice. I had to make up my mind.

I slept very little that night. We were in a room with twin beds at the front of the inn. My body began to take on the posture of rigid anxiety that would entrap it for many months to come. I felt waves of fear. I listened to the occasional traffic on the main street outside, to the click of the electric space heater. Adrenaline shot through me, keeping me in a state of such agitation that I began to wonder what could possibly calm me. The fear was not just about Maine and moving. Added to it now was a kind of primal separation anxiety in the face of my mother's impending death. I knew this cancer to be ruthless, and I could see that her body was invaded by it, almost as if she could not sustain life any longer because her life had been too damaging. I had read extensively about this cancer. I knew its course; I knew the odds. I'd been through it before.

My mother used to tell us that she hadn't been able to get too attached to any of us because she was sure that if she did, we would be taken away. In her mind, god was ruthless and punishing, and attachment meant only pain. The subtle message of my childhood was that I should stay with her always, that I needed to take care of her. This was my tie to her—that she needed me, even if she gave me little. So to be separate, to live my own life, was an act of great disloyalty. To have chosen a relationship with a woman was treason. To be myself was to be in conflict, and it was sometimes simply untenable. And now I was faced with a major act of separation at a time when she would need me most. How much was I going to be there, and how much was I going to live my own life? And which relationship where I was needed would I give the most to, her or Alice?

In spite of my mother's illness, in spite of my serious concerns over my relationship with Alice, by morning I knew I would agree to the move. I would do the thing that was to be done. Having suggested this move, having raised Alice's hopes, I couldn't now say no. I had grave misgivings, but I felt I had to do it anyway. Something had to change or Alice and I wouldn't last.

By the end of that trip, we had contacted a realtor and begun to look at houses. By spring, we had found one. It was a saltbox with four bedrooms, two parlors, a large kitchen, and a small dining area. There were a lot of rooms, but they were small and had a chopped-up feeling to them. But the two-parlor setup would make it possible to see clients in the house. We would stagger our hours and share the one consultation room. That would help accomplish our goal of saving money.

It was the outside of the house that sold us. It was ringed with gardens, and behind the house was a wooded, rocky area that was the remains of an old quarry. Stones with the original cut marks in them created a natural sculpture garden. We were surrounded by pine trees and granite. It was dramatic and caught our imaginations. We would now live on two and a half acres on a country road with sheep grazing in a nearby field, with cross-country ski trails within walking distance, with a pond down the road where Alice could fish. No more neighbors ten feet away.

We began to close up our practice, sell our house, and detach ourselves from our lives. As always when there was a major project to work on, Alice and I functioned well together. We had a goal now; we were a team again. We spent our days fantasizing about how wonderful it would be to live in Maine, the new things that we'd do, the new people we'd meet.

"Are you sure you still love me?" she'd ask. "Because I don't want to make this move with you if you don't."

"My feelings for you are different now than they used to be, but I'm committed to this relationship, yes."

I wasn't really sure anymore what was true. Was I lying to Alice? I tried to put my ambivalence out of my head. But every night I had trouble falling asleep, or I woke with a start in the middle of the night and couldn't get back to sleep.

I arrived at the hospital early on the morning of my mother's surgery to be with her before she went up. She was tense. There were deep creases in her face. She kept plucking at her covers anxiously.

"I know you'll be fine, Mom," I told her. "Who knows? Maybe you'll have an out-of-body experience."

She laughed.

"Tell you what," I said. "Try visualizing a scene that makes you happy and calm. See yourself somewhere you'd like to be."

"Well," she said, looking off into the distance, "I see a young girl in a dress, and she's running through a big field of yellow flowers."

"Daffodils?" I asked.

"Yes, I think so. Why?" She looked puzzled.

"Don't you remember the poem you gave me when I was young, the Wordsworth?"

"Oh, yes," she said, smiling. "But this young girl is running, she's so happy. Maybe she's me when I was a child. My happiest times were at my grandmother's farm. The field is so full of yellow."

My mother had never felt safe or adequate as an adult. Life had been too much for her, and now, when it was most demanding and frightening, she had only her childhood images to hold on to.

I took her hand. "That's a wonderful image; hold on to it. I love you, you know."

I remembered the times as a child when I had been sick and in the hospital and she had not come, when she had abandoned me to my own terror and loneliness. Now I was the mother and I would not abandon her. I wanted her to know that I had survived this pain without hating her, without holding it against her. But I don't think she felt this. Later, she would let me know that it was not enough, because I would not leave my life to be with her as she died. I remembered with an ironic clarity the talk Mike Carey gave so many years ago about the conflict between the mother and the daughter over this same issue. I remembered his saying, "There are two people to be considered here."

During the eight-hour surgery, the surgeons removed most of her esophagus and pulled her stomach up into her chest and her intestines up into where her stomach should have been. To look at her, you would never know anything about her had changed. The surgery was a masterpiece of reconstructive work. I went to intensive care just after they brought her back from the recovery room. She was awake, talking but groggy. It felt like such a relief to be standing by her, talking to her after the long, tense hours of waiting. She said her chest hurt. Then, suddenly, the heart monitor started to beep, nurses came running, the doctor pushed his way into the cubicle. My mother asked what was happening, but she was too sedated to be alarmed. Her heart had gone into fibrillation. I was watching it happen on the monitor, the rapid-fire jumping of the green line on the screen. They pushed me out into the waiting room. I kept trying to send her mental messages that I was there because I knew her fear of being alone. They pulled her through, but considering what she went through in the two years longer that she lived, I had to wonder if it was worth it.

April. It was my birthday and Cass's, and our group of friends convened in the city for dinner to celebrate. One of the four looked at me and Alice and said, "Okay. Tell us what's going on. Are you two moving to Maine?"

We shook our heads yes. Cass burst into tears. I took this as further evidence that she was in love with me, though she might not know it. I couldn't bear Cass's tears—they melted me, made me want to seize her and comfort her with tender embraces. But I was across the table from her, and all I could do was look at her with pain in my eyes, with longing and love.

She gave me jewelry for my birthday, beautiful cultured pearls and a pin to match. During this time, my relationship with Cass grew even more intense. We sat in various restaurants over lunch and I talked about my feelings for her and she talked about hers for me.

"Are you hurt that we're moving?" I asked.

"I was at first," she said, "but I've come to accept it now. We'll have to work at staying in touch." She paused. "There's something I need to know. You aren't leaving because of me, are you?"

"No, not really. We're leaving for a lot of reasons. My feelings for you made it very difficult for me to make the decision. But in some ways maybe it's for the best. It's hard with Alice's jealousy."

I looked at her shyly, embarrassed. "Do you think we'll ever be together, Cass?" It was the first time I had so directly alluded to the logical outcome of what we had been saying to each other.

"I'm committed to Adam. Aren't you to Alice?"

"Yes," I responded. But part of me wasn't sure that this was true.

There would be playful references to our being together. Over one lunch, we decorated a house together in our imaginations. And then Cass would say, "I love you very much, but I'm a heterosexual woman." There would be a hesitation and another "But . . . ," and the sentence would trail off, leaving me hanging. We behaved together as if we were two fond friends, but we spoke as if we were something more. I thought, She knows this is more than simple friendship for me, and I felt convinced it was more than that for her. But she had all the control, and I felt as if I were being played for a fool. She had the privileged, safe position of the heterosexual woman who loves a lesbian. I wondered, Why do I do this to myself? as if I had some choice over what to feel and how deeply to feel it. Was it shame at being gay that I loved straight, unavailable woman? Was it misplaced grief about my mother, misplaced grief about Alice?

When we finally moved it was November, just before Thanksgiving. We joked that we'd hired a mover with an orange truck to keep from being shot at during hunting season. We packed all our valuables, the two cats, and the dog into the car and drove to Maine to stay in a motel for the night before the closing. I was so anxious that as usual I couldn't sleep, and I finally resorted to soaking in a hot tub to try to calm myself.

The day the furniture arrived, Betsey and Barb came with it, bearing pizza and soda, and then they helped us unpack the kitchen.

For two or three weeks life was a great new adventure. Three days after the move, Jeff and Marsha arrived to spend Thanksgiving with us. We put them on the pull-out couch in the consultation room. "Infuse it with your healing energy," we told them. They had accepted our decision to leave with a kind of sad resignation. "I don't like it," Jeff had said, "but we'll do everything we can to support you."

Once they left, we set out to explore the town. We drove down the long fingers of land that skirted the ocean, exploring frozen coves, being engulfed by dense thickets of pine trees and other evergreens. I could hardly believe that I lived here, that the pervasive beauty of nature was now to be part of my daily life. Driving through one of the small towns just outside our own, we saw signs advertising a craft fair. We stopped to visit a pottery shop and struck up a conversation with the two women potters, who turned out to be lesbians, transplants from New York.

"We heard that two women were moving into town—you must be them," they said. "There's a big lesbian potluck tomorrow night. Why don't you come?" After years of having no lesbian community to connect with, this invitation seemed like a homecoming.

We shopped for computers to begin work on a new book project. And one raw wintry day, we drove to the end of the peninsula to stare out at the ocean as it spit cold blasts of spray onto the rocks. We talked about our hopes for change.

"I want our relationship to deepen. I want us to be closer," Alice said.

"You know, it's funny," I said to her. "When we first thought about moving, I had this strange sense that I was coming here to confront some hidden truth about myself. It's a little frightening. Who knows what that may be?"

"I want us to write a good book, I want this move to put us more in touch with our creativity," Alice said.

"Yes, and I want us to make good friends. I want us to be more loving to one another."

"We could have a very good life, Claud. We've done this thing now, and there is so much potential. Having done this, we could do anything. Sometimes when I think about what we've done, it's a little overwhelming to me."

"Leave it to us," I said, "to create major uproar for ourselves."

Then, in December, we went back "home" for the holidays. We visited Cass, who answered the door sporting a new short haircut and wearing a bodysuit so suggestive and finely etched to the contours of her body that I was all but vaporized by lust. She sat next to me on the couch. I found myself looking right down an effectively designed opening in her suit that revealed the soft, milky-white cleavage between her breasts, and I wondered why exactly she would need to be so seductively dressed for dessert on Christmas day. Each time I thought I had put my feelings for her in perspective, there was this kind of reminder that I could be so easily pulled back into her orbit. I hated my own desire.

In the post-holiday letdown, the pain of what we had done and of all the conflict that I'd been riddled with for months suddenly hit full force. In the depths of the winter now, surrounded by the towering pine trees that circled the house, feeling hemmed in by them and by the deep freeze of ice and snow that seemed to mute all energy and motivation, I began to sink into a kind of despair that I hadn't known since my college days and the deeply ill-fitting confines of my married life. I was ready to go back home now, but there wasn't one any longer.

Finally Alice succumbed to despair, too, and this frightened me, because I had always depended on her to have the energy to keep us going, to make things happen. We developed what we called the alternate-day syndrome—each day one or the other of us would wake feeling happy and optimistic, and the next day there was the recurrent despair. How could we have done this to ourselves, where was home, what ever made us think this change was possible? These were the questions that haunted us. We were certain we had made a cataclysmic mistake. There was gray icy day after gray icy day. In the past, we had always been in Maine during the summer, when there was lush green and brilliantly clear blue water slamming against the rocky coast. It was all romance and ease. Living here now felt like a marriage instead of an affair.

I withdrew inward. Early mornings found me lying in bed reading spiritual texts, writing in my journal, trying to get some hold on my life. This was a source of constant irritation to Alice, who liked to be up early, who wanted me to be out walking with her, who needed contact, who chattered at me or lay on the bed waiting, hovering, wanting me to be available to talk.

After having had little contact in the course of our professional days, we now lived and worked twenty-four hours a day under the same roof. We were thrust at each other constantly, with all our despair and irritation and hard edges.

Suddenly, I had no patience for Alice any longer. "Leave me alone!" I kept screaming at her. We'd be working on the book. She'd hand me a section that she'd written, and I'd throw it back at her, saying, "This is lousy. Do it again. It doesn't make any sense."

"You think you're the great writer. Well, I was writing for years before you ever thought of it!" she'd scream.

What began to pour out of me was my long-repressed anger and bitterness with Alice. Anger for all the hurts, for all the rages and fighting, for all the times I had felt constricted by the relationship, had felt like the one who did more, who had become the oppressed wife. Anger at the ways I felt my self submerged by her personality, by the ways I had allowed myself to be passive and submissive. Anger at being less important in the relationship, at being so much the background person while she was always the visible, entitled one. Anger at the slightest, most minor of frustrations in our daily interaction. Anger, anger, anger, raw and cold and oppressive.

This was at a time when she needed me more, when her expectation had been that we'd be closer.

"Why won't you ever do anything with me? Why are you so angry at me all of the time? I thought we'd do things together, I thought we would take walks every day. You act like you don't want me anywhere near you," Alice said.

"Alice," I would scream, "I can't stand the way you're at me all the time. We have to learn to be more separate. I'm trying to change my life here. Change your own and stop bothering me. I don't know that I want to let you in again, Alice, I don't want to be vulnerable, I don't want to be hurt anymore. I feel exploited, like you haven't respected me, like I have to do all the giving. You're never satisfied. You never just accept me as I am."

"You're talking about the past, that's all in the past," she screamed back.

"Well, I can't just pretend it didn't happen. Get out of my face!"

I embarked on a program of self-improvement. I formed a lesbian support group. Alice's anxiety about being abandoned was now at such a fever pitch that all she could do was try to control me. We had fight after fight, rage upon rage.

I longed for Cass, who called on occasion but never enough, who knew what we were going through, who seemed genuinely concerned about me, who told me that she was keeping her distance to try to cause less strain on my relationship with Alice.

I was faced with truths about myself that became almost unbearable. I was an infidel; I wanted another woman. I treated the person I had loved most with a kind of scorn and hatred. I felt selfish, unable to love, as if my whole life had been based on a lie that I was loving. I questioned everything now; I was back in the throes of an adolescent indentity crisis. What is it that I want in life? I asked myself. And will I stay and make this relationship work with Alice, or will I go? Can I go? Is there a life without this woman who has been so central to my life for so long? Am I anything without her? What is it that I've called love, and where did it go?

There was no drawing on our alter egos now, no Camille or Elizabeth to get us through the rough spots. Things were too raw, too real for our humor to relieve us. We stopped being able to write the scripts.

Frantically, I called Alvin. We agreed to have sessions on the telephone.

"Alvin, I'm just not sure I love her any longer."

"Then tell me, what is it that you do feel?"

We'd be in the middle of a conversation, twenty minutes into a session, and suddenly Alvin would say, "Well, that's all, we have to get off now," and he'd abruptly hang up. He seemed vague and distracted.

Finally I said, "Alvin, we have to come down there to see you."

He gave me a date and a time. We made the seven-hour drive back to the city and sat waiting for Alvin in the waiting room, comforted by the familiarity of its shabby furnishings. Ten minutes passed, fifteen, a half hour. Finally I got up and knocked softly on his door. He wasn't there. His office mate said he hadn't seen him.

Something was wrong. Alvin had always been a little forgetful, but this was completely unlike him.

When I finally reached him on the phone, he was stunned by his own forgetfulness. "Oh, I'm so, so sorry," he said. "I don't know how this could have happened."

"Alvin, I'm confused," I said. "The last time we talked, you hung up in the middle of the session. Had you been planning to talk for the full hour?"

"I don't remember that," he said. "I can't imagine why I would have done that. But please, Claudia, don't think it had anything to do with you. I really don't know why I would have done such a thing."

We made another pilgrimage to the city, and this time Alvin was there. He said, "I have something that's difficult to tell you. The doctors feel certain I have Alzheimer's disease."

14.
Anyway

Matt's therapy room was a large, carpeted cavern of space in the basement of his house. There were a couple of swivel chairs, a leather desk chair that he usually sat in, and lots of blankets, pillows, and puppets, toys that intrigued and distracted me. Alice and I traveled two and a half hours to get here, and we stayed two or three hours, or as long as it took to work on the particular pain of the day.

"It's always been a very hard relationship," I said to him. "Sometimes it's very good, and other times it's very bad. We have conflict about everything, and we seem less and less able to talk. Alice gets angry and I shut down. I feel that we've never been separate enough. I stop myself from doing things that I know might make her anxious or angry. For years I've been saying I was going to leave, but I don't really want to—I want to resolve some of these problems. I want to make a decision once and for all about whether to stay or go. I want to feel better about myself and to stop being so depressed all the time. I'd like us to be closer, but I think I've given up too much of myself to try to make that possible."

"Matt," Alice said, "she's not telling you about the emotional affair she's having with a woman back home. Before we moved to Maine she told me it was over. We get here and she's totally distant from me, angry all the time. She lied to me. I got here expecting that we'd be closer, and in fact we're more distant. She won't even take a walk with me. All she does is work."

"Cass is not the real issue," I said, defensive. "I haven't done anything wrong. I've worked very hard to put it behind me. The issue is you and me."

Deftly, Matt maneuvered us away from this potential runaway train and commented about how little we seemed to recognize the impact of the many stresses external to our relationship right now. Relieved at the interruption of what could have become one of our typical fights, I talked about my mother and the anxiety of her approaching death. We talked about the move to Maine and the pain of the adjustment. We talked about the loss of Alvin, and I wondered wryly if my entire history, the whole continuity of my life, was lost with Alvin's mind, since he had been recording it for years. There was no longer an outside witness to tell me who I was.

The pain of Alvin's loss was profound for both of us. I suffered for him, wondering how this man of such great intellect and wisdom tolerated living with the knowledge that his mind was leaving him in small pieces. When we talked, he told stories of forgetting his way to the office, of walking in front of cars. Finally, a caretaker was hired for him. Over time, we simply lost touch.

Matt was heterosexual. In my lesbian support group, my choice to see him was viewed as politically incorrect. But I knew him to be a good therapist, and he worked often with lesbian couples. I made a decision to trust him because I was desperate, though for a long time I would test him and call him on every breach of feminist principle. I was not totally at ease with him, and neither was he with me.

But it took me very little time to realize his capacity for empathy, his surefootedness with feeling, and his willingness to examine his own reactions. And I knew he worked a great deal with children, and so I trusted him to understand the part of me that was still a child.

Alice was anxious at first, her voice loud, insistent, intrusive. Then one day Matt simply moved his chair near her and sat looking warmly and calmly into her eyes, and immediately she quieted and to my surprise burst into tears. It's not that I hadn't known this vulnerability in Alice—it was part of what I fell in love with. It was just that I'd had no access to it for as long as I could remember. It was so layered over with tension and stress, constant activity, defensive talking and demanding, that I had all but forgotten that it was there.

When Alice cried, I, to my own amazement, cried, deep, racking sobs. This was so unusual for me that I was disarmed and began to feel frightened by my openness with Matt. There was a lot at stake here: I had never been this vulnerable with a man, not even Alvin, and my fear of rejection was at times unbearable.

I would fight with Matt and rage at him, doing everything possible to keep him at a distance. Some deeply layered system of defense had been shifted by him, like the movement of tectonic plates that would later result in an earthquake. The therapy began to teach me that I didn't have to be so afraid.

And the therapy began to reconnect me—slowly, painfully, minimally at first—to Alice. Sometimes these sessions were the only experience we had of being in touch with each other, of really talking. Once every other week, or once every month, as often as we could manage to see Matt, I could feel empathy for Alice, could feel in contact with the softer parts of her, and I felt heard by her.

We made slow, sometimes agonizing progress. I told Matt this therapy sometimes felt like having surgery without anesthesia.

Matt asked me to take some action that would dramatize how I felt about myself. With no hesitation, I went to a corner of the large room and curled into a ball and pulled a blanket over me. I was hiding, frightened, trying to make myself safe and invisible to the world. I was crouched, cowering.

Matt said, "How does it feel in there?"

I was silent.

"Hello, are you there, is anybody there?" he called.

Slowly, I poked my head out. I was like a child playing a game of hide-and-seek. But this withdrawal into myself, into a safe corner, had been a necessary protection. It was a reflection of the invisibility I had felt all my life: stay hidden, do not emerge; people will hurt me, will be angry that I exist.

I told Matt how anxious I was all of the time. "I can't sleep," I said. "I'm always exhausted."

"What do you think is making you the most anxious?" he asked.

"I think it's my mother's dying. I'm frightened that I can't handle this. I don't know how to resolve the issues around her care. Can I do it? How will it feel to be an orphan?"

We sat in chairs facing each other, and Matt held out a blanket that he had rolled into a thin, twisted rope. He told me to take one end and he held the other, and then he said, "This is your mother." I laughed, but he was serious. He began slowly, imperceptibly to pull the blanket away, and immediately I clutched it, grabbed it, pulled it back, tried with all the power I had to keep it from slipping from my grasp.

"Wow," he said, "you really want to hold on." He pulled harder. Finally, after struggling, I didn't know what more to do. Matt was pulling as gently but determinedly as me. Slowly I loosened my grasp. My mother was going to die, and when the blanket was finally out of my grasp I felt that emptiness and space that surrounds one in the time after death. Matt watched me. I felt tears gathering, but this time I didn't cry—it was too dangerous. I felt as if I might never stop, as if I might collapse into a drowning mass of tears from which I'd never emerge because this loss would be about all loss, about all the times I'd felt abandoned, alone, afraid. I was faced with annihilation and profound, unquenchable grief.

At home that night I went to my study and, sitting cross-legged in a chair, cried deep, racking sobs for what seemed like hours, the grief coming in waves. Alice left me alone, until finally she became concerned. She came in and sat in front of me and called to me gently, "Claud, are you all right?" I was in some very distant place outside of myself, and I felt great relief that she had come to call me back. She covered me with a blanket and led me downstairs, where she gave me tea and asked me to talk. I did, and I felt better and grateful to her for being there.

A trip back to our old home early in the spring stirred the obsession with Cass again. In spite of all the work I had been doing in therapy, I still longed for her constantly. I hadn't said very much about this to Matt or to Alice. I kept thinking that I was handling it, that it was coming into perspective for me. But that April, just after Cass's return from a trip to the Mideast—where she had bought me a silver filigree bracelet for my birthday—her mother died unexpectedly. Alice and I went to see her. I went into her bedroom to find her; she was all softness and tears as I held her briefly. She looked into my eyes and said, "It's hard, it's so hard." We both had very difficult mothers, and I perfectly understood what she felt.

Cass wanted us all to go to a nearby park to be outdoors. It was a gloriously sunny day. We sat on a bench looking out over fields full of flowering bushes.

"I'd like the two of you to meditate with me for a while. Would that be okay?"

We joined hands and sat quietly for a long time. Cass cried softly and I tried to pray for her mother, but lines of poetry kept going through my head and my heart felt as if it were about to break open.

Back in Maine, I called Matt and told him I wanted to come for a session on my own. As I was about to leave, Alice said, "What's this about, anyway? What do you have to say to Matt that you can't say with me there?"

"I want time to talk about some of my own issues. It's private."

"Private or a secret? Is this about Cass? Are you still preoccupied with her? I told you that I wouldn't tolerate dishonesty from you. Has she still been in your head all this time and you haven't told me? I want to know, because I can't live with this any longer. I can't bear this lying that you do. I have to know, and I want to know now."

And we are off into one of our typical raging battles, me yelling that she has no right to demand that I tell her everything, that this is something I'm dealing with, she yelling that she is going to leave me.

I went to Matt knowing I must either resolve this obsession or act on it in some way. In Matt's basement I took out a letter that I had written to Cass. In it I told her that the more I tried to deny my feelings for her, the more troubling and intense they became. I told her that if she could give up her attachment to her image of herself as exclusively heterosexual, I was at the point of being willing to risk my relationship with Alice to be with her. Indirectly, I was proposing an affair.

Instead of mailing the letter, I decided to bring it to my therapy session. I asked Matt to read it. He studied it a long time. Then he looked up at me and asked, "Have you mailed this?"

"No. I want help with this, Matt; I've been struggling with it for over two years now. I can't go on like this. Either I have to act on it or end it. I want to try to work it through, and nothing has helped. It's not fair to Alice. I don't talk about it much with her because I think it would only be hurtful."

Matt sat quietly, looking very thoughtful. "I guess I wonder how you let yourself get into this. I mean, were these feelings reciprocated? What did you think, knowing she was married? Or were there games being played?"

Matt conveyed great understanding of my feeling for Cass and he never trivialized the fact that I felt that I loved her deeply. He seemed to have a deep respect for the very human dilemma of falling in love with one person while being committed to another.

"Would you be willing for us to work on this?" he asked.

"Yes, I was hoping you would suggest it."

I was relieved that he was taking this seriously, that I was finally able to let him know the depth of my feeling and my torment about it, that maybe we could get to the bottom of it, resolve things one way or the other.

I told Matt that I was drawn to Cass's attractiveness, her liveliness, her warmth, her humor. How she could be responsive and nurturing, that there was a vulnerability to her, a softness that I missed in Alice. I told him about what I experienced as confusing, subtle, seductive messages; what seemed invitations to intimacy that went nowhere, that left me hanging; the way I felt that Cass always had to be in control of our contact; the way that every time I tried to get some distance she seemed to pursue me more, while at other times she kept her distance, was unreachable.

He said, "Let's try something. You be Cass. I'll ask questions and you answer as if you were her."

He began to question Cass almost as if she were a child. "Tell me about yourself, Cass. What's your family like?"

I as Cass began to talk like her. I poured out all that I knew of her background, of the trauma of her family life, the grief at learning her father was gay, the difficulties with her mother.

"How did you handle this?" he asked.

"Well, I just tried to become part of other people's families," I heard myself say.

I watched myself begin to act flattering. I started pretending that Matt was someone whose attention I wanted and that I was being deliberately manipulative to get it, to get him to like me. I said things I knew would have the desired effect. I knew that if I wanted to, I could charm and flatter him enough to get what I wanted, which was to be special, the only important one. And at once I felt the emptiness and the fear that this behavior covered.

To an outsider, Alice and I seemed to have a deep and inpenetrable bond, and it occurred to me that Cass might have envied what Alice and I had, that maybe she wanted to get in. And at the same time, I knew that part of myself wanted this same power, but I had never been able to allow myself to so blatantly act in a way that would get it. Maybe Cass was some part of me that I could not be. I envied her capacity to get what she needed from people, this love and attention. Did I want her, or did I want to be like her? Was what I called love really only envy?

As our session ended, I wasn't even conscious that I was aware of all this. In my mind I was still protesting, "I love her anyway." But some profound shift had taken place in me. Acting the part of Cass had totally turned around my view of her and myself. I saw that I was infatuated with her as an escape from emptiness, that I lived with the hope that a relationship would do for me what only I could do for myself: face me, face my aloneness on the planet, face who and what I was and accept it—accept that I was complete enough as I was. This facing of myself meant accepting the truth of my love for and need of women. Maybe I had loved Cass *because* she was straight—because she had all the social approval I was excluded from. Maybe I envied the status she had as a heterosexual woman with all the privileges of being with a successful man.

And maybe all heterosexual women envy in lesbians the freedom of not being tied to a man. Maybe they envy the emotional intensity that can exist between two women. Maybe straight women like to dally with unwitting lesbians like me, pretending to have what they will never pay the price for.

How long, I wondered, would I be in this closet? How long would I be a lesbian who could pretend to myself on some level that I had never really left the straight world?

I drove the two and a half hours back home, agitated and preoccupied, wondering what the fallout from this session would be. I had the clear sense that I had changed in some way that wasn't apparent. For the first time I felt some relief from the torment of Cass; for the first time I felt that, as much as I loved Alvin, with Matt I was involved in a therapeutic process that was really working.

The next day I was to leave for the West Coast to do a five-day, one-city-a-day media tour. I knew things were tenuous between Alice and me. Just before I left, still upset about Cass, Alice said to me angrily, "And to think I had planned to have flowers sent to you in L.A.!"

I looked at her and said quietly, "Send them anyway."

At the airport, for the first time, I looked at Alice, aware of the pain and destruction I had caused. I said to her, "I'm sorry," and walked onto the plane not sure what shape my life would be in when I walked back off.

The media tour was a blur. I was numb. In Denver, my first stop, I took the letter to Cass from my purse, ripped it up, and threw it in the wastebasket. The strains of "I Left My Heart in San Francisco" ran through my head, and I cursed the brain that was always feeding me ironic song lyrics or other commentary on my emotional states. But that's what it felt like—leaving my heart in a wastebasket in Denver.

In L.A., the flowers from Alice arrived—yellow roses, my favorite. The card said "Anyway." I walked to a nearby mall. In Portland, Oregon, I had lost a Swiss watch hanging on a chain I had borrowed from Alice. I had given it to her as a gift for her fortieth birthday, as we were traveling through Europe. Another loss, another pain I had caused her, I thought. How symbolic. I went to a watch shop and bought her one that resembled the lost one as closely as possible. On the back I had engraved, "To Alice—anyway," with the date. I sent it Federal Express with a note telling her that I knew what hurt I had caused her and that I wanted to try to recover what we had had, that I was committed to it. I walked back from the mall thinking about how I felt essentially unloved, and that for all of it, Cass was the only one who made me feel cared for right now.

But I wanted to try again with Alice. Love, infatuation, I told myself, was not the answer. Anyway, I said to myself. Love me anyway. Let's try again anyway, even though you're hurt and I'm hurt. Let's work at it anyway. It's important, I thought; we've been together for a lot of years. My pride in who we were together, in the image to the lesbian world of stable coupleness, won't let me let go. My pride in the notion of commitment, of doing what's hard, of growing up, being mature; my sense that it is important to be realistic; my need for stability, continuity, won't let me let go. Let's work at it anyway.

Alice later told me that at precisely the moment the Federal Express package arrived, she had been on the phone with Jane telling her that she was clear that she could survive on her own and that it was quite likely she would leave me. The watch and the note melted her resolve.

Like the many remissions of my mother's cancer, this was only a reprieve.

For a long time after my session with Matt I did not call Cass. And I felt relieved. I found myself focusing on Alice for the first time in a very long while. The fantasies began to recede; I felt as if I'd gotten my mind back—it was not owned anymore by constant thoughts of her. Then, one day, as Alice and I were on our way out to go hiking, the phone rang and it was Cass.

"Hi," I said.

"Hi," she said. "How are you? Is everything okay there?"

"Yes," I said, "fine."

There was a hesitation. I knew she wondered why I hadn't been in touch.

"Cass," I said, "I know we haven't talked in a while. I've

been giving our relationship a lot of thought. I think what I want right now is to have a little distance. I need time to sort some things out."

"Okay," she said, "I understand. Take as much time as you need. Is there anything I could do to help?"

"Well," I said, "you could be more clear with me, Cass. You know my feelings, and I think you've been acting very seductive. I don't know where I stand with you, and I've got to get back to focusing on my relationship with Alice."

"Claudia, I've said this before. I love you very much, I will always love you, that won't change. But I'm a heterosexual woman." There was a hesitation. "There's more I would say if it weren't for Alice."

Facing this cryptic double message yet one more time, I was finally angry.

"Well, what does that mean, Cass?"

She fumbled for an answer.

"Look," I said, "I don't want to hurt you, and I don't want to hurt Alice. I need some time to work this through once and for all. I'm sorry."

"It's all right. Take whatever time you need. I'll do anything I can to help."

I got off the phone. This was the last time I was to talk with Cass. Five months later, just before the holidays, I called her. Things with Alice were much better. We had heard from other friends that Cass had been very sick. I deluded myself into thinking I could handle talking with her again. Her husband answered, and I thought I detected a snort of disbelief when I asked him to have Cass call me.

She never did. Two days before Christmas I got a note from her. It was abrupt and cold, written on fine, personalized stationery. In it, she told me not to call her. Because she was in a period of intensive meditation, she needed to let go of any relationships that were conflictual. She wished me and Alice well.

I remembered our talk about how she handled anger. I didn't know whether she was hurt or mad. But I knew I wouldn't be the one to try to reconnect.

This was the last Christmas my mother would be alive. We all knew it. She was too ill to go out, so we gathered in her small apartment. She was only a specter now; she had lost most of her flesh, her hair and her teeth. Her bones protruded so much that it was painful for her to lie in certain positions.

Weeks earlier, Therese had taken the children to decorate her apartment and set up a small artificial tree. We piled the presents around it now. My three nieces sat surrounding her on the couch. She was dressed in layers, her head wrapped in a turban against the relentless cold that came not from outside but from within her body.

Ann and Alice and I and Therese and her husband sat wherever we could find a space in the small room. The girls were excited in spite of the somber mood.

"Open this first, Grandma," my youngest niece shouted, and they all competed to thrust their gifts into her lap.

After we had finished opening all the packages under the tree, my mother pointed to three carefully wrapped boxes sitting on a shelf across the room.

"Alice, hand me those," she commanded.

There was a gift for each of us, Ann, Therese, and me. With the help of neighbors, she had managed to get out to shop. My gift was a solid-gold chain, Ann's a sapphire ring and matching earrings, and Therese's a gold choker with matching earrings. My mother had never given us such extravagant gifts. We looked up at her, completely surprised.

"I wanted to give you something to remember me by, in case I'm not here next year."

In one breath she talked about not being around next year and in another made plans for the coming months.

As she slipped from life, she got angrier. Finally, in March, she was admitted to the hospital. She was still getting chemo, and she contracted an infection that her body could not fight. By now the cancer had spread to what was left of her stomach. She had a large tumor there, and it was no longer an option to operate. Now the pain became so unbearable for her that they began to administer morphine. I went to the hospital. Alice was with me. She had come to say what she knew would be her final good-byes.

This was the day my mother was to make her last stand against my lifestyle. She was irritable and nasty. "And you," she said, glaring at me bitterly, "I don't like the way you live your life." She was sitting on the edge of the bed, slightly bent over, her robe clasped shut around her.

"What don't you like?" I demanded, angry now myself.

She was unused to my fighting back, so she backtracked. "Well, what are you doing to save for retirement? You spend too much money."

But I knew the issue was not money. My mother was going to die and I had not pleased her: I was queer, and she hated it. This was the personality of her drinking—angry, bitter, attacking. By the end, just before she died, she would become lighter, more luminous, sweeter. She said to me, "It will be hard to put up with Alice, but I want to come and spend two weeks with you in Maine. You are the one I have always had the most in common with."

All that day, she kept asking me to affirm that her life had had meaning, that something she had done for us had made a difference. She looked at me and said, "Were there any good times?" I had the sense that she was asking my forgiveness. I told her she had done the best she could—that there had been some good times, that she gave us some important things. She was so frail and vulnerable. How could my anger at her coexist with compassion for her pain, sadness at the emptiness of her life? And with the wish that the drain on us of her life would be over?

These questions, this self-evaluation, came in the brief times when she did not have the television on. My mother had lived most of her life staring at the television. Since my father's death, she had had it on almost twenty-four hours a day for company. She had become addicted to the Shopping Channel. When I asked her why she watched it so much, she said, "Because there are nice people talking to you, and I feel like I'm not so alone."

It became wrenching to see her in pain. I sat in the hospital room uneasy because I didn't know what to say to her or what I could do. I fought not to be drawn into the antics going on on the TV. Regis Philbin was having billiard balls knocked from his mouth. Geraldo did a show on women who visit male prostitutes. I didn't want to be distracted by this absurdity from the reality that my mother was dying.

The doctors told us that it could be another six months, but they sent Mother home, at her request, and she was dead within ten days. She died alone, an aide sitting nearby in a chair, early in the morning, lying on the couch with the television on. Ann had been due to arrive there in a few hours; I had been planning to come back in a couple of days. She didn't wait. Ann, always the bearer of the news of death, called me. "I had a plant all ready to take to her," she said, sobbing. Therese and her husband went to the apartment and sat there quietly with her body stretched out on the couch. Like everyone in my family, my mother had chosen, I suppose, to die alone. It was a measure of our isolation from one another. At least that's the story I tell myself about it.

She died three days before my birthday, and it was on my birthday that we buried her. Ann said to me, "Maybe this was her gift to you—freedom to live your life now without guilt, without the drain of her needs."

In spite of her rejection of me, in spite of all the hard times I had with her, I grieved. And I felt guilt, because I had wanted so much to have been there for her at the end.

I guess I loved her anyway.

15.
Moving Violations

It was an October afternoon a few months after my mother's death. The sun was full in the sky, the temperature pleasantly warm and pleasantly cool at the same time. I had finished my work for the day and decided the dog and I would go for a drive.

Fall in Maine can be hypnotically beautiful. It is a haze of redness and yellowness, of hay being rolled in the fields, of children playing soccer against a backdrop of saltwater farmland and stands of evergreens in the distance.

The day seemed no different from any other. I had been writing. Alice and I were close to being finished with our second book, but the work was difficult and slow. That morning we'd learned that a teaching contract had been canceled. Money would be tight for a few months. I was feeling frustrated and morose, sorry for myself. Life seemed hard and unrewarding. No matter how much I worked, I never achieved what I thought I wanted, even though I was never entirely clear what that was. This was a familiar mood of mine—I called it "Claudia's lament."

I drove to a soccer field on the other side of town, past farms and cows grazing lazily in the fields. I walked the dog a bit, watched the children playing soccer, and got back into the car to drive home and make dinner. One part of me lamented while the other felt elated at the beauty of the day. I scanned the fields and trees in the distance. I thought of my mother. I thought briefly about Cass. I ruminated about myself and my shortcomings. I mused about sin and reparation and forgiveness. Why my old Catholic preoccupations with sin and guilt were haunting me this day, I'll never quite understand. Maybe it was an antidote, a punishment of myself for my self-pity, for my wanting something for myself.

I drove up to the intersection near my home, one of my favorite spots in town. It was a country road bordered by broad, textured fields and a white barn in the distance with a clock tower. I loved the openness of this spot, the peacefulness of it, the sense of vastness and of roads running off into an unknown distance.

I was thinking about dinner and about the intense colors of the foliage when I pulled away from the stop sign and into the intersection. The sun was just beginning to set, and light caught the tops of the trees. I know I had looked both ways. But suddenly, coming from the right, there was a car in front of me. In that split second, I couldn't comprehend where it had come from and why I hadn't seen it. I felt an impact, a jolt, and I heard the sound of metal being ripped apart. I had grazed the back bumper of the car as it passed, and I sat in the middle of the road now, my foot on the brake. I saw a bumper fly, and when I turned to look, a huge gray Wagoneer was careening down the road. I watched, horrified, as it flipped over end to end, twice, then landed on one side of the road, then bounced to the other. I saw objects flying through the air, and I didn't know that one of them was a body.

By the time the sun went down that day, the dusty, blood-rose streaks of that sunset in her face as she drove west, the woman driving the other car was dead. And my life was irrevocably changed.

I remember watching it as if it were in slow motion, as if it wasn't really happening. My mind felt heavy and blank, bewildered. What was impossible to connect was how the minor impact I had felt could cause this pandemonium of a car flying around as if it were weightless. The intersection was eerily empty of all other traffic except for two bicyclists and a jogger, also traveling west, none of whom had seen what happened. When all the motion and the noise finally stopped, I was jolted into a panic by the silence. It finally reached my awareness that something very serious had happened. I pulled out of the intersection and jumped out of my car, and without even looking to see if there was other traffic, I ran to her. I expected smoke, fire, a mangled, bloody body. The Wagoneer was lying on its roof. I thought I would have to help extricate people, but when I got there all was calm inside the car. The radio was playing. The windshield was gone, and there was no one there. I thought with horror that someone might be trapped underneath. I wondered if there were any children in the car. I couldn't figure out where the people were. Finally I ran around to the back of the car, and then I saw her lying some distance away in the field. Oh, I thought, the field is soft, it will have cushioned her fall. People had started to pull up. I yelled for them to call an ambulance. I knew I had to go to her, to be there, but I didn't know what I could do.

She was lying on her side near the edge of the road, her head facing southwest. I seem to remember that she tried to turn toward me, to see me as I ran to her from behind the car. Her eyes were wide open, and her breathing was labored. She was moaning in an almost rhythmic way, as if speaking a language only she could understand. It was as if she wanted to say something but couldn't open her mouth or get her lips to move. I covered her with my jacket because I remembered it was important to keep an injured person warm. I wanted to be able to do something, after all, because from what I could tell at this moment, I had somehow done this to her. In my mind I was saying, Take a good look at this, Claudia, because you are responsible. I was punishing myself, taking it all on, knowing I was no good.

I tried to comfort her, told her it would be all right, that the ambulance was coming. I lightly rested my hand on her hip. I wanted to comfort but not cause her more pain. Her lips were tightly drawn, and there was a piece of grass between them. Had she landed on her face and rolled over? Her body looked broken. She didn't move; her arm was twisted at a strange angle to the rest of her body. There was no blood; there were no cuts. I thought I saw a small bruise beginning to form just beneath her right ear. She had pierced ears and wore earrings. She was wearing a wool sweater, khaki pants, and boot-type shoes. She was small and thin, with strawberry-blond hair. She looked younger than she turned out to be. As she lay there, her face looked steely and cold. I had the sense that had she been able to speak she would have been yelling at me, enraged. I could only imagine how damaged her body must be. I felt unutterable pain and despair for her, for what I thought I had caused.

People ran up and asked what had happened. But I couldn't remember how it was we managed to collide. I know I did not see her; all I remembered was motion, a sense of moving slowly across the road and suddenly running into something that I didn't know was there.

The ambulance pulled up after unbearable moments in which doctors on their way home from work stopped, ran to her body, and said things like, "Well, she's breathing," or, "Yes, there's brain damage, but I can't help." The police arrived. The ambulance driver sauntered over and asked her if she could hear him. She was still moaning rhythmically and didn't say anything. He acted as if there were nothing urgent to be done. He stood there slowly pulling on his rubber gloves. The police started shouting for everybody to get away. I stood and walked over to the officer who seemed to be in charge. "I was driving the other car."

For a time the woman lay there alone in the field with everyone appearing to be busy with everything else. It seemed to take them a long time to get her into the ambulance, and when they left there were no sirens. I wondered if she were already dead.

The police called Alice. When she came I was huddled in my car, parked now by the side of the road, crying over the steering wheel. She ran up to me and asked if I was all right. She grabbed me and held me. She was unusually calm. "I'm not hurt," I told her, "but I think I just killed somebody." One of the neighbors was standing there. She overheard this and said, "Don't say that. She's going to be all right, you'll see."

"But her life will never be the same," I said.

Alice turned to me and said fiercely, "Yes, and neither will yours."

The police told me to go home. But later that night they called me to come to the hospital emergency room so they could test my blood for alcohol. There was nothing in my blood. But that was only the beginning of the interminable questions.

"I know, ma'am, that this is very hard for you, but we need some information for our report. Could you tell me, as nearly as you can remember it, what happened? Did anything unusual happen today? What work do you do? Could you tell me what you had for lunch today? Did you get a good night's sleep last night? Exactly what time did you go to bed? Where were you going? Why were you going there?" Every last-minute detail of my day was questioned—not once, but, in the days to come, several times. As if there were something particularly relevant to be found. As if it had not been just a completely ordinary day in a completely ordinary life. As if it had not been just an accident.

Shall I tell you how I wanted to kill myself? How there seemed to be no real reason to go on living, that I knew I did not deserve to go on living? Shall I tell you how it crossed my mind that the woman I had killed was probably an upstanding heterosexual wife and mother, and that she was probably much more valuable in the world than I, the middle-aged lesbian? That the only way I could get through the night was to sit on the floor in my study and write and write in my black composition book? That I was unendingly cold, shivering for days, as if I were going through a withdrawal from normal life? That I sat in the bathroom with my head in my hands, overcome by the horror of what had happened, thinking why, why, why, and not knowing whether I would be sick or pass out, and not knowing how I could possibly bear one more moment of life? That I was numb and could not eat? That all of my life was now open to question, that there were questions of meaning and reason and random terror and my own value on the planet? That I thought incessantly of her husband, of her family, of how I would be feeling if this had happened to Alice, how I would be in despair and overwhelmed by grief? How I could not walk into town without fearing that people were watching me, that everyone knew who I was? That people would call and I was incapable of talking, that my mind would not work, that everything seemed to be collapsing around me? That in the weeks afterward when I could go out, I would hear a concert or walk in the woods and cry because I had deprived her of this?

One friend, a Buddhist, came to be with us and said, "Let's set a place for her at the dinner table, because she is here anyway." And I knew that her presence would not be exorcised very soon, and so I left that place setting for days, until it was possible for me to put it away.

Alice said, "You're going to need a lawyer."

I looked at her numbly. "Do you think someone is going to make trouble about this? The insurance company will take care of it, won't it?" My usual naiveté and my numbness protected me at first.

But this was a small town. Friends who had friends who knew the family sent warnings that, indeed, I should get a lawyer. By the next morning, Alice had found me one. We went to see him, and he prepared me for what could be. He was a decent, straightforward, good man and I trusted him. I could not have imagined what would ensue.

For a while, things were calm. In any case, nothing so prosaic as a lawsuit would affect me for a while: I was still struggling to find a reason to be alive.

I was now faced with fundamental existential decisions in a way that I had never been before, and if I was to stay alive, I had to construct answers for myself. My first response was to go to church. Betsey took me, and Alice went with us. By now everyone in town knew of the accident. When he greeted me that morning, the pastor of Betsey's church knew why I was there, and on the spot he reconstructed his sermon to make it about forgiveness.

Alice took over negotiating life for me. She simply took care of me—brought me tea, covered me up when I was cold, put me into the car and drove me where I had to go, made phone calls for me to my family and friends, called a minister friend, who came to the house to talk to me. For weeks she drove me places because I couldn't drive myself, and when I jumped at every passing car and froze with anxiety she was patient, understanding that this was a reaction to the trauma.

Alice insisted I go to the hospital and see a doctor, even though I wasn't hurt.

The doctor walked in, looked at me, and said, "How can I help?"

"I'm not physically hurt," I said. "It's more psychological. I just don't know what to do with my sense that I'm responsible for this woman losing her life. Just check my heart, because it has irregular beats. Just make sure my heart is okay."

He listened to my heart, and while he did I thought of the irony of my concerns. Of course it was my heart that was hurt: this was a pain of the soul, of the part of me that thought of myself as a caring person who wouldn't intentionally hurt anyone. My heart hurt; my heart screamed with pain.

"There's nothing I can do for you physically. And about the emotional pain, all I can do is share with you what I did the first time a patient died because of my own mistake. I went home and I stayed awake all night and I thought about what was important in life. And it forced me to totally realign my values. I learned to put my family and my relationships at the center. I began to know that caring was what was important in life."

Those words stayed with me, and for the next few days, as I experienced help and support and love pouring in from everyone in my life, I began to realize that I was realigning my own values. I could not help doing it; this experience was forcing me to know things I hadn't known before. One evening shortly after the accident, I looked at Alice in the midst of my evolving reconstruction of my life, and said, "I know now that I will never leave you."

"What do you mean?" she said, a little nervously.

"It's resolved for me, all that we've struggled with. I can't describe what I know now. I just know that our relationship is what's most important, that connection to people is all that really gets you through, that commitment means everything. The crazy stuff we fight about doesn't matter. What matters is our bond with one another—that you're here for me now, that I be there for you. I know now that all the rest is not important."

There was this knowledge and the other, "terrible knowledge" of death—the sense of knowing something others didn't know, of having gone into the underworld and seen death firsthand and come back to tell about it; the sense of having done something very few other people had ever done; the knowledge of what it was like to be, as one book I read called it, an "accidental killer."

Alice watched this transformation happen in me and was glad of it. The loving part of her had always supported me in my growth, but the angry part had attacked me for my weaknesses, had been uncomfortable with my vulnerability. Things would change now, we both knew it, but I couldn't have known how. For all of my emerging faith in life, there would be more of its difficulties to face. This was not the end of the lesson.

In the aftermath of the funeral and the dying down of the publicity about the accident, there was silence—just as there had been after the pandemonium of her car flying and crashing down the road. I slowly pulled myself from numbness and took care of what had to be taken care of. I was nervous in the silence, almost wishing that if something were going to happen, it would happen soon. I began to think that I could actually feel the energy of the family's anger in the air around me. I walked through my days with the knowledge that I was hated by a whole group of people who didn't even know me. How familiar that was—how like being a social outcast, anonymously judged and reviled for one's very existence, for the concept of who I might be.

It was later in the fall now. We had turned back the clocks; the days were dark. The early-winter gloom settled in. One night one of our former neighbors from back home called. Pete wanted to know if anything was wrong, because a detective had been going around our old neighborhood asking questions about us—about our life together, about our business, about our house. I was appalled. At first I didn't even realize that this was connected to the accident. But when Pete had asked what this was about, the detective had said, "I don't really know. Something about assets."

And then I knew. In the silence after the accident, as I had struggled to deal with its emotional and spiritual impact, the family had been wondering how much money I had, wondering who I was and how vulnerable I was.

I called my lawyer, and he said, "Oh no."

"Is this legal?" I asked.

He hedged. The bottom line was that there was nothing to be done about it—nothing, that is, if I wanted to avoid creating protracted legal wrangling. I did. I hung up. And from that moment, Alice and I began to live in a state of chronic anxiety, waiting for the next blow to fall.

Six weeks after the accident, the police arrived with a summons. I had to answer it. It charged me with failure to yield, a moving violation. There was a stop sign in the intersection, and she had had the right of way. This fact alone, whether I had stopped or not, made me responsible and at fault. It was frightening but, as the lawyer said, under the circumstances it was the most innocuous charge to have leveled against me. It was good, he said.

Then, the day after Thanksgiving, a certified letter arrived. It was a notice of intention to sue me for damages. The widowed husband was claiming I should pay him almost one million dollars for "willfully" causing the death of his wife.

Alice looked at the letter and then looked at me and said, "We're going to lose everything."

"Alice, this doesn't involve you," I said, defensive.

"You think they won't come after me?"

"How can they? It's not like we're married. This is one of those situations where not having legal rights works to our benefit. They can't have it both ways. They can't refuse us the right to marry and then claim we have a legal connection when it suits their purposes."

"Do you want to bet?" she said.

Now I walked through the days chronically frightened, not believing this could be happening to me. I had few assets. I lived the life of someone trying to do creative work. I had a retirement account, some small savings, a little money from my mother's just-settled estate. That was all. And the house that Alice and I shared. But my insurance policy was very inadequate. This man was not to be content with what my insurance would pay. He wanted as much money as he could get.

Some days later, the lawyer forwarded a fifteen-page document that the husband had asked him to send me. It was essentially a biography of the deceased. It described her childhood, her accomplishments in high school, her marriage, her children, her community life and involvements. It came complete with childhood photos and pictures of her with her family. It talked about her centrality in the lives of her family, how she and her husband would curl up on the couch, affectionate, loving, how they were passionate lovers, how the husband's life would never be the same, how they had said good-bye that day on the deck of their lovely home looking out over the cove after she had spent the day gardening, how she had never returned. It included an itemized accounting of the value of each and every task she was responsible for around the home, the value of her role as bookkeeper in her husband's business; it quantified everything right down to her polishing the furniture and providing the children with emotional support. I called it the "family values" argument. It seemed designed to make me feel guilt and to somehow suggest that his wife had been a better woman than I.

The district attorney was urged by the family to review the case. The family was determined that criminal charges should be filed against me. Reporters from the local newspapers called asking sinuous and inflammatory questions, which I refused to answer. People told me they heard on the local radio station that I was being investigated by the district attorney.

My lawyer met with theirs to try to begin to talk about a settlement. His strategy was that if they persisted in a suit, he would put me into bankruptcy, effectively preventing them from getting anything beyond my insurance. When he called me later that day after the meeting, I could hear the upset in his voice.

"I have to tell you," he said, "that things did not go well. I have not, in all my years at this work, ever heard another lawyer so emotionally overinvolved with a case."

What her lawyer had said, ominously, was, "Everything this woman has, we want. There are a lot of people in this community who are very angry, and if your client goes into bankruptcy to try to avoid paying for this, this community will become even more outraged. If you put her into bankruptcy, it's our intention to go after her partner's assets and to force the sale of the house."

It didn't take me long to realize what was at stake. This was a small, conservative community. I believed they would go after Alice's assets and that a judge or a jury would side with this native and powerful Maine family against a lesbian outsider. My lawyer had already advised Alice to get counsel, and she wasn't even a part of this suit. She was vulnerable by association. And I didn't want her assets touched. It was bad enough that my life was being ripped apart, that she had had to go through all of this with me, that she was being so affected by my troubles. For all of my bravado and my determination not to closet myself and slink away in shame, I didn't want to make this a test case about lesbian rights and discrimination. Someone had died. I didn't want my life tied up, possibly for years, fighting a painful battle in a small town where the odds were against me. I wanted to put my energy back into living my life, to fighting other, more productive battles. I thought, It's only money, it could be worse. I thought of the many people who had lost more. All of my life I had struggled with not having enough money, with wanting more, with my greediness for life, for experiences, for things. Now it seemed I was being taught another lesson, about putting the value of money in its proper perspective. It was not worth giving up my energy, my focus, my partner's well-being.

Now I needed to figure out how I would come up with the money. After legal fees, after withdrawing a significant portion of my retirement money, I still needed thousands. The only way to get them was to remortgage the house. Alice came upstairs to my study and I told her, "I'll find a way to pay you back. I'll work harder, make more income; I'll pay it off in chunks as much as I can at a time."

She said, "We're married. I'm taking this burden on with you." As always, part of her was generous and loving; but secretly, another part was furiously angry.

My lawyers helped set up the refinancing. In two weeks we had a new mortgage on the house, defeating the original purpose of our move to Maine, which was to keep our expenses low. I paid to be freed from the torment that had gone on for more than six months.

The great irony, of course, was that while Alice could be so affected by a suit against me, had she or I been the one killed in an accident, neither of us would have had the right to sue for damages done to the other. We had no status together under the law.

I decided not to indulge in bitter regret but to get on with my life—the life that I now understood quite differently. While not a day went by that I didn't think of the other woman, while I lived with a chronic sorrow, I began to wake up happy, having realized the preciousness of the life that I had. I was determined to savor the good as much as I could, to create as much good as I was able, and to accept the bad as a necessary part, but not the whole, of the story. After all, I did not design the plan, if that's what it is, so what made me think I should have any say about it? What made me think I had the right to do anything other than accept the good with the bad and stay alive until I was dead?

16.
Accidents of the Heart

It was early May. The lawsuit had been settled two weeks earlier. I had my life back. I was going off for the weekend to Therese's because my niece, Emily, was making her first Holy Communion. There would be a family party. Emily was my godchild. My brother-in-law had had to do some very fancy footwork to get the priest to agree to this, given my outlaw status in the Church. I gave Emily the gold cross that my grandmother had given to me when I was a child. To do this gave me a sense of continuity, of passing something on, of being a part of a family. Alice stayed home.

I showed up at my sister's feeling happy and connected, free to really enjoy myself in a way that was new. It was unusual for Alice and me to be separate. But I felt I could move about in the world now without the sense that it would threaten our relationship. I felt more myself.

I went to the rehearsal with Therese the Friday afternoon before the Communion mass and was amused when one of the little girls raised her hand and asked, "But, Father, why do the boys always go first?" Father struggled to give a little homily reflecting the Church's new consciousness of the role of women, and, to his credit, he changed the order of things and had the boys and girls alternate going up to the rail for the host.

Emily beamed as she stood with her class looking out from the altar, where her teacher had gathered them to sing. It was so natural for her to enjoy attention. She had two adoring parents and a host of aunts and uncles and grandparents who doted on all the children in the family. This was a child who had no question that she was loved. I felt tears come to my eyes because I knew that my sisters and I had each overcome some of the damage of our own childhoods, and these children would not suffer directly the pain of alcoholism.

On Friday night, Alice called. I heard some distance in her voice that I couldn't place. She said that she was feeling elated to have a weekend to herself, to do what she felt like doing. That was fine with me.

But by the end of the weekend, there was a sound in her voice that alarmed me. She told me what a wonderful time she'd had. I got the feeling she wasn't really looking forward to my coming home. I tracked her down at a friend's house the night before I was due to arrive back, and there was an edge, a distance to our conversation that was so palpable, I deliberately stayed away until later that day to give her more time to herself.

When I got home she was sitting in the backyard in the May sun. She didn't race out to greet me as she usually did. I walked out the French doors into the yard and she looked up and said, "You're late."

"Yes, you sounded so happy to be without me, I thought I'd give you more time to yourself."

"Is this a game?" she asked.

"No. I think something's wrong. What is it?"

"Nothing's wrong, and yes, I did enjoy myself. Do you realize it's been over a year since I've had any time to myself? It felt freeing to me not to have to be focused on you, that's all."

"Well, I'm glad. I had a good time, too."

"Good" was her retort.

"What did you do all weekend?" I asked.

"Why don't you tell me what you did. How is your family?"

It went back and forth like this, the tension palpable between us. I had no clue what this was about, but finally the story leaked out.

"I took a long walk with Donna," she explained.

Donna was a friend who dropped in occasionally. She often helped us with computer problems. Alice had more contact with her than I did. I really knew very little about her.

"We talked a lot. I got to know her better. It's the first time since I've been in Maine that I've felt at all connected to someone on less than a superficial level. It was nice to get to know her better. I realize we have a lot in common. She's really a very interesting person. She's very straight, though."

I knew that Donna was married, but I didn't know why Alice was telling me this, and I didn't find it comforting.

"Could I ask you something?" she said.

"Yes, of course," I responded.

"How did things happen with you and Cass? Were you confused about what your feelings meant at first? Did you tell yourself right away that you were in love with her, or did you think of it as a deeper level of friendship?"

"Where is this coming from?" I asked. "Are you feeling attracted to Donna?"

"Well, I felt very close to her. It's hard to sort these things out, and it's so unusual for me to feel strongly about someone so quickly."

I now knew that something serious was going on here and that I had better handle it well. I put aside my anxiety and told Alice how it had been for me with Cass. We talked a while. I could tell she was conflicted, disturbed.

"It sounds like something really meaningful is happening with you two. Why don't you just see where it goes. Maybe you're finally going to make a good friend here." Of course, I assumed her commitment to me, her intention not to let it go further than friendship.

"Yes," she said, "I think that's what could happen. Thank you, Claud, for talking with me about it."

I went upstairs to unpack, but before much came out of the suitcase I collapsed on the bed in tears. What kept going through my head was "I have lost Alice." It was a devastating, empty feeling, unimaginable, and I tried to talk myself out of it. But I knew in the way one knows such things, completely intuitively. I just knew.

That spring, as the days lengthened and Maine became full of lupine, wildflowers, and the breathtaking seascapes of summer, we talked incessantly about Donna. Alice was changing. She felt that she needed something different in her life, that she wanted to get back to writing plays, that now that all the crises in my life were over she wanted time to pay attention to herself. She and Donna spent long hours working at the computer on various projects. I thought how ironic it was that I was now on the other side of the same pain I had caused Alice. I could experience the great good fortune to live out two sides of a karmic lesson in the same lifetime. I decided to exercise tolerance.

We took a long, leisurely vacation that summer in a cabin on a lake in the north woods of Maine. Each morning Alice went out on the lake in the rented boat and fished just in sight of the cabin. The dog and I stayed on the porch, where we could watch her, I with my coffee and computer, working on a new project. It was idyllic, like the vacations we took together in the beginning at the cottage on the bay.

We sat on the porch at night in the glow of the small lamp, reading and painting. And we listened to the loon, to the silence, or to the lapping of the lake in the night; watched the moon begin to cast long fingers of light across the water; just soaked in the kind of primordial peace of being in a remote place.

But underneath, Alice's inner life was anything but peaceful. By late fall, it was clear that things with Donna were more intense than ever. We worked with Matt and tried valiantly to deal with this new intrusion, to get past the more destructive interactions that it caused. I kept trying to be patient, to control my own jealousy, to stanch the fear that flowed out of me like lifeblood from my veins. By Christmas, I threatened to leave for the holiday if Alice couldn't be more civil to me. I told her I didn't want Donna in the house. We became silent adversaries in our own home.

Over the years Alice and I had developed certain rituals together that spoke to a sense of the continuity of our life, to all that we shared. Going to Maine each year, visiting the same spots, sitting under the same trees was one. At Christmas we'd make a pilgrimage to her old, red house to cut holly and greens. Jumping in the car to take a ride to the ocean, to sightsee and look at foliage in the middle of the week, were activities we could count on to punctuate the rhythm of our days, to reconnect us to each other.

It was our spring ritual to take a trip to a flower show. We loved to see flowers together, to talk about them, to sit planning Alice's garden. I dreamed of flowers, and Alice planted them and made them grow. It was a ritual to visit the gardens of any city we traveled to. We had been captivated together reading about the white English garden of Vita Sackville-West; I had made Alice promise me that someday we would have such a garden, a field full of white. We tried to list the names of every white flower we could think of that might possibly grow in the short, cool growing season of Maine.

As the dreariness of winter began to lift, we'd pile into the car to make our pilgrimage to some armory, where there'd be vast arrays of flowers elegantly displayed; huge, enchanting indoor gardens.

This year, Alice told me, she'd be going to the flower show with Donna.

That was the death knell. I tried to fight. We were still seeing Matt, pretending that we were working on our relationship.

"Alice," I pleaded, "this is *our* ritual, something we've always done together. I've tried to give you a lot of space to work out whatever you need to with this woman, but I'm asking you: I want you to go with me, not with her."

Alice looked at me with rage. "No. This is important to me, and I don't want to go with you. Donna never asks directly for anything. It was a big step for her even to ask. I don't want to say no to her."

"But wait a minute, who's your priority here, me or her? Are you committed to our relationship at all at this point or not? What *do* you want, Alice?"

She looked at me for a long while and finally said, "If I'm honest, I want to separate. My feelings for you have changed. I don't want to have to caretake you anymore. I feel like I'm fighting for my life."

For the second time in two years, I felt as if I couldn't keep on living. The pain was too unbearable, the disbelief overwhelming. I had never thought this would happen. In all the times I had threatened to leave, I had never expected that Alice would. I cried for most of the weekend. I spent hours on the phone with June, the friend who had, years ago, been so blunt in helping me to be serious about my writing.

She challenged me. "Well, what's it going to be. Are you going to kill yourself or not?"

"No," I told her, "no, it just feels like I can't take any more, like it's all been too much."

"Can you see that there are good reasons why you have wanted to end the relationship, how it could just as easily have been you?"

"Yes," I said, "yes, if I'm honest. I just don't think I would ever have done it. I had decided not to."

"Yes," she told me, "but things have been very bad for you too, and you know that and have to acknowledge that if you're to get through this."

"Yes, I know, you're right. But how does one rebuild a life? I don't want to be without her."

There is nothing like divorce to bring out the worst in people. There is bitterness, there is recrimination, there is distrust; there is the growing, overwhelming reality of suddenly hating the sight of someone you have lived with and loved, someone with whom you have shared the most minor and the deepest intimacies of your life. There are the moments of grief when you talk calmly and intently, more openly and sanely than you ever did when you were together, when you think, If only we could have done this then. When you are tempted to make love for one last time, when you remember how bad the last time was and wish you had known then that it would be the last. When you remember every single detail of every good time that you've ever had and feel totally overcome with nostalgia, longing for the past, grief, disbelief that you could be going through this. There is numbness, and for me the same coldness in my body as after the accident. For days I simply went to bed whenever I didn't have to function. I felt the life-energy just drained out of me. I couldn't comprehend what was happening to me.

For weeks I spent as much time as I could away from the house and tried to avoid the knowledge that I would have to move out. Because of the accident I was in debt to Alice. I would have to turn the house over to her. The loss of the house, of the space I had made a haven for myself, for us, was almost as devastating as the loss of Alice.

And every once in a while I thought, Maybe this is just temporary, maybe we can get back together. Maybe she'll change her mind, see the error of her ways, realize this was just an unfortunate phase she's going through. But suddenly I realized that the love wasn't there anymore in any recognizable way. What was left was hurt and rejection and guilt and a terrible sense of failure, and somehow a wish it had never happened at all because then I wouldn't be feeling this pain. I thought, There was my accident in a car, and Alice's accident of the heart. I collided with one woman and she collided with another.

I found myself driving alone now down the Maine turnpike to see Matt. I listened to all those songs on the radio that talk of unrequited, damaged, lost, forsaken love, Barbra Streisand singing "You Don't Send Me Flowers," crying, shaking my head with the irony of this, of my listening to love songs written for men and women, racing to see my male, heterosexual therapist about the demise of my lesbian relationship. He had worked as hard as anyone to help us to stay together. But when he listened to the stories of divorce bitterness going on between us, he looked at me and said, uncomfortable and fumbling for words because I know he wanted to tell me what to do and stopped himself, "Do you think you are avoiding moving out?"

In retrospect, it is amazing to me that I didn't fight more, didn't refuse to end it, didn't plead with Alice not to do this. Always I had said to her, joking with mock drama, "If you ever betray me, I will kill—you or her or both. I will fight and scratch out her eyes and come after you." But this was just a fantasy of myself, it was

Camille talking. At the first hint of rejection, I was gone. If I was not wanted, I would go, accepting the sentence as if I expected it all along.

By the end of May, I had bought a small house. I could not bear the thought of going back to apartment living. So I begged and borrowed and scraped together what money I could. I looked at the house one morning and bought it that afternoon. It had a porch, a lovely secluded and wooded backyard, room for a study, and space for an office. It was cosmetically in horrible shape, but perfect for my needs, because I needed a project to keep me busy. Betsey and Barb and another friend helped me paint it and clean it, and by the end of the summer I had managed to renovate it simply and economically, and I kept feeling that this was my refuge and that it was what helped me get through.

Just as, eighteen years earlier, there had been no wedding, there was no external symbol of divorce. One day we were together and the next we were not. We wrote up an agreement, the ground rules for separating our lives, something the lawyer called a "termination agreement." We fought over it; we met over the lawyer's conference table; we signed it. And that was it. I took off the gold signet ring Alice had given me the first year we were together and it sits in a drawer, a reminder of what was.

Gone was the relationship I had felt would always be. Gone was my pride at our having made it work. Gone was all the richness of experience and relationship, of work and dreams we had shared. Gone was the person I thought of as my family, my teacher, my soul mate, and my nemesis. Gone was Elizabeth, the alter ego, the fiery woman of my dreams.

I did not succumb to bitterness. I did not think, They're right, gay relationships can't work. I thought, We had it better. We had more passion than most people I know; we had problems as deep as those that most people experience. We did not break up because we are gay; we broke up because we are people—people who know what it feels like to suffer and to love.

In my imagination, Elizabeth lamented. "Camille, come back," she said. "With you I can be anything, with you my life is right. I made a mistake, Camille, come back. I need you, I have always needed you, I will try not to push you away, come back, Camille, I didn't mean it, it isn't true. I was the boy crying wolf. Camille, you were the best thing that's ever happened to me and I was confused, I didn't mean a thing that I said."

Camille was sad—a sadness that reached deep into the marrow of her bones and into the inaccessible strands of her veins. Camille wondered what it was that happened to love, or what love was in the first place. But one thing she did know: life had taken its toll. When the face of passion cracks, when grief finally drowns you in its liquid, burning flow, there is no going back.

17.
Full Circle

One summer night, sitting on the floor of the study in my new house, I decided to open Pandora's box—the cache of "love letters" I had been saving to read in my old age. It was an eclectic collection. There were the few treasured letters from Mike Carey; the notes, penned in small, almost indecipherable script from K. There were cards of congratulations for my wedding and birthdays, the rare letter from my parents, letters from old college professors, one from Helen Scott at the time of my eighth-grade graduation. There was a special selection of of David's letters I had saved, a few desultory notes from other women, letters from Linda, my college roommates, and other good friends. But mostly there were letters from Molly—long, newsy letters and some short, intense ones. I pulled from its envelope the card that she had sent just after I had moved in with Alice.

"The very real possibility of never seeing you is distressing and difficult to accept. If you have terms and conditions, at least tell me—-I've listened to your silence for too long."

I decided to find out what had happened to Molly. I was curious. As I read more of her letters, there was kindled in me a memory of my love for her, the way it had changed me, forever given me a passion against which to compare others. In the many times I had thought about her over the years, I had always told myself that someday I would track her down, find out how her life had turned out. I wanted to know if she had found the love she wanted, had had the children she wanted. Sometimes I wondered if she was even still alive. I wondered if she was still with her husband or had remarried or perhaps found herself with another woman. I was curious and I wanted to apologize for having been hurtful to her.

I couldn't imagine how I'd find her. It crossed my mind that I might need to hire a detective. She could be anywhere now, so many years later. As a start, I called directory assistance in the town her last note was mailed from and ask for a listing for her husband, Phil. To my amazement, instead of the anticipated "I'm sorry, ma'am, we have no one listed by that name," I heard, "Hold one moment, please," and as I scrambled to find a pen, the computer robot announced the number. Now what? I thought. Maybe it's a different family, a different man with the same name. Maybe Molly's not with him anymore. Mustering much more bravado than is typical of me, I dialed the number. A young girl answered.

"Hello, is Molly there?" I asked.

"Yes, she's here, who's calling, please?" the young girl said.

"It's just a friend. I'll call her back." I hung up. Could this be a daughter? I wondered. I wasn't ready for an instant reunion on the phone. So I wrote a letter. Always my undoing, letters, because in writing I say things I would never risk in person. But I was circumspect.

Dear Molly,

Imagine my surprise when I called your house and a child who must be your daughter answered. It's me, Claud. I'm writing because my relationship with Alice has ended and there's no longer any reason not to be in touch. I have thought about you often and about the painful way I cut you out of my life. I'm very sorry about that—it must have been hurtful and I will understand if you just take this letter and throw it in the garbage. But I'm terribly curious about how things have gone for you, how your life has worked out, and would love to hear from you if you have the impulse to write.

I made some very general comments about me and what I had been doing. I had no sense of how this would affect Molly, but some part of me knew that she'd respond.

I mailed the letter and left for ten days on vacation with my sister Ann and my niece Tracy. When I returned, I found a letter.

Dear Claudia,

I am not angry.

It has been a very long time since we've been in touch, and I wonder just a little if we would even know each other anymore. But we knew each other once, and knew each other well, and out of respect for that I respond to your reaching out. No, that's too contrived. The truth of the matter is that I have never stopped missing you.

I'm glad to hear of your successes, but saddened by the troubles you've had. I suppose life is just like that, little comfort, I know.

I live with Phil and our two daughters in a turn of the century "fixer-upper." My oldest daughter was born in 1979 and the younger (the voice you heard on the phone) in 1983. Pregnancy and childbirth were wonderfully exhilarating for me—motherhood is a mixed bag of the proverbial joys and sorrows, my marriage alternates also, mostly, I regret to say, because I always seem to have one foot out the door—and though I've never left, it's taken its toll and things at the moment are shaky and I'm as close to terrified as I've ever been in my life.

To answer your question, I guess I didn't get what I wanted, not fully anyway. Full-time jobs, home ownership and far-from-placid children consume most of our time and energy and we both feel that life should be more fun.

A friend of mine thought that your contacting me was wonderful, that it would bring us "closure." Are you surprised that I've spoken of you? I don't know that I want closure—but the apology sure was welcome. Your last letter to me was devastating—it's one I could not keep. I respected your wishes and stayed out of your life—though I, every few months, would dial your number and hope for the comfort of just hearing your voice.

So I stayed out of your life, but your letters were read over and over. And when the phone rang a few days ago, I thought perhaps it had been you. I'm glad it was.

I am feeling rather tenuous about Phil now, though I'm hopeful that he and I can get through this period and on to a new phase of life together. I love him deeply and want a life with him. But there's part of me that's only for you, and always has been.

Maybe now, after all these years, you and I can finally find where we fit each other. I will call you very soon.

Thank you, Claud, for still caring.

When I first heard her voice on the phone, there was an immediate shock of recognition. It plunged me right back into the pain of having lost her. I had worked hard during those years of being married to distance myself from her, to become irritated with her way of toying with my feelings, with her continually challenging me about why I needed another degree and whether or not I was really gay. Molly had seemed content so long as I was there somewhere within the perimeters of her life, but she seemed too frightened to show up for any more committed involvement. I had never really forgiven her for leaving me at the height of my feeling for her to stare out my dormitory window alone, feeling as if my soul had been ripped out of me.

Ever since, I had cursed the capacity of women to betray their feelings for one another to flee to the safe harbor of heterosexuality, my obsession for Cass notwithstanding. I often think that what defines many straight women is not so much their sexual preference as it is their cowardice. I had the anger of the righteous about straight women and yet I was attracted to them always.

Molly and I talked on the phone, tentatively at first. I was wary. I knew that I was vulnerable, and I didn't want to get caught up in any marital problems of hers. I would protect myself at all costs. I was prepared, because I knew her power over me; I knew how much I had loved her. I also knew that if she wanted me back in her life in some way as a friend, I would not reject her again. I was wiser now about deep connection, and I knew it to be too valuable and too rare to waste.

"The timing of your letter was a rare coincidence, Claud. Two weeks before it arrived, Phil told me he wanted a divorce. I've been pleading with him to change his mind. We go back and forth. I've been trying to make the changes he wants. I don't know what will happen."

I said, "I'm so sorry, Molly. Do whatever you have to. Divorce is a terrible thing. It's the worst pain I've ever been through, even worse than the accident I told you about."

"Where do you see your life headed now, Claud?"

"I have no idea. One thing is for certain—I am staying far away from anyone who has in any way had any problem with alcohol. I think by now I should have learned my lesson."

"You know, I always knew we would be back in touch someday," she said. "I have never had the same kind of closeness I felt with you with anyone else."

I kept hearing the seductive pull of Molly's protests about my specialness to her, but I was not about to think it meant anything, anything at all. I had been down this road too often, hearing more than was meant in the declarations of affection for me from other women. It felt good to be in touch with her again, but I was careful to think of it as just that—being back in touch, no more, no less. I got on with the work of rebuilding my life.

A couple of months later, Molly decided she wanted to come to Maine for a visit. At the Bangor airport, I found my way down to the arrival gate for commuter flights. I watched as a plane taxied in. No one was announcing what flight this was, and if it was Molly's, it was a few minutes early. Before I could find anyone to ask, passengers started pouring off the plane and walking from the tarmac to the gate. I saw Molly moving slowly toward the terminal. I raced out onto the landing area to meet her, propelled by an excitement that felt out of control and rare to me. She was wearing a soft, flowing white blouse, dangly earrings of silver and turquoise, jeans and sandals. It was Molly, there was no question.

It's amazing how one holds the memories of other times and

places in one's body. It was all the same—the same feeling, the same intensity. We looked at each other, then held each other for a long while, the tears trailing down Molly's face, making her mascara run, as they always had. She looked the same to me, only older, the creases in her face showing the stress of all the years, but she was the same Molly and I felt that I could not keep from touching her. I rested my arm lightly on her shoulder as we walked through the airport. "You're very much a woman now, aren't you?" she said to me.

"Yes"—I nodded—"I am."

Once in the car, we kissed and hugged, and then drove the thirty miles home, feeling awkward and shy with each other. When we arrived, she took herself on a tour of my house, as if to get some sense of who I really was. I had made dinner; it was ready to be heated and eaten. But we were too nervous to eat. We sat on the floor and talked and talked, and we couldn't seem to stop long enough to focus on anything else.

When I went to offer her a glass of wine, she hesitated and said, "I don't drink anymore."

"Okay, that's fine," I said.

"That's why I came—to talk to you about it," she said. And she started to cry.

"What is it, Molly?" I asked, melting at her tears, as I always had.

"I needed to tell you about my drinking. I couldn't keep it from you any longer; it felt too dishonest. After we talked that first time and you told me how much you had been affected by the alcoholism in your family, that you knew you needed to keep your life free of people who were involved with alcohol, I knew if I wanted you in my life that I would have to stop. I knew anyway, have known for a long time that I had to stop. But after we talked a couple of months ago, I did. And I just wanted you to know this. I feel so ashamed. It's been bad, Claud, it's been very bad. It may be why my marriage is ending. But I think Phil has a problem, too. He drinks too much and he hasn't stopped. And I want to change. I'm stronger now. I want to get my life back."

What came from my lips was "Oh, Molly." I wanted to cry, I wanted to hold her and comfort her, I wanted to tell her how wrenching it was for me to hear her say these things. I wanted to know why it was that all the people I had cared most for in my life had been nearly destroyed by this drug. I still wanted to know why, even though I knew this territory almost better than any other in my life. I'd had years of writing books about it, of teaching other people about it, of watching miracles and tragedies, of helping people with it. But I still wanted to know why, and there just wasn't any answer that made sense—not any sense to my heart, which had been broken too often by the reality of addiction.

Molly sat with the tears running down her face. She was on her own journey, at the crossroads of middle age. Alcohol had been a major player in her story. I remembered that I had suspected it in those days when we socialized as two heterosexual couples. But I didn't know anything then. She had asked me once, "Do you think I could be an alcoholic?" and I had said, "I don't know, Molly. I don't know what an alcoholic is."

The next day, we went for a hike. She put on shorts and a T-shirt and sneakers. She was still attractive, thinner than when I had seen her last. She still had wonderful hair, colored now, but still that same thick, dark mop, straight, fine, and elegantly styled. Her eyes, though clouded from the drinking, still looked wide and bright, and she had not lost that impish, chipmunk look that I had so loved when we were young.

We piled into the car. I was aware of how different our lives had been. It was a weekend, and in my life with Alice the priority had always been this—to be outdoors, away from the house, hiking, boating, anything but staying around to care for our home. To me this was what one did on weekends. To Molly, who had been raising children in suburbia while working a forty-hour week, to hike on the weekend was a rare treat that came in the midst of ferrying children, doing the laundry, cleaning the house, and doing the shopping that couldn't get done during the week.

I packed sandwiches and drinks, and we found a trail that ended on a spectacular beach where there were generally few, if any, people. We sat on a log and ate our lunch, looking at the islands in the distance—but not before Molly had run to the water's edge. She had not lost her love of running. I watched her from a distance and took pictures of her as she ran back toward me.

I realized that I knew her and I didn't. Years of intimacy with another person had insulated me from knowing other people very well. I didn't know the cues yet—I had to guess at the meaning of silences; I misinterpreted things at times; she was like a vast, uncharted land with strange new markings that had evolved since my last visit.

As we hiked back to the car, Molly said, "Claud, I really hesitated about coming up here to see you."

"Why? Did it cause problems for you with Phil?"

"It wasn't that."

"What was it, then?"

"I was afraid I'd want to make love to you."

"Well," I stuttered, "we shouldn't do anything like that. You're still married, after all. It wouldn't be right."

"Yes," she said. "I just want you to know I still have those feelings."

I walked along, now silent, not knowing what to say. I thought back to the long, sensual nights in our room in the dorm with the green lightbulb in the lamp and the soft jazz playing on the stereo to cover the sounds of our lovemaking. I remembered the way Molly touched me, so softly, and I thought, You're a middle-aged woman who is overweight and has just gone through three years of trauma and knows better, so forget it. It was not that the thought of our being intimate hadn't crossed my mind. But I muttered to myself about rebound reactions and transitional relationships and thought, Never again. Mostly I told myself, You're a therapist and you know better, and you're not going to get in the middle of whatever is going on in this family, and that's all there is to it.

But I stopped on the trail and pulled Molly to me. We looked at each other for a long while and I said, "Molly, we can't make love. Not now, not until you know what will be with Phil, maybe not ever."

"We won't," she said.

Before we got to the bottom of the trail, I decided I needed to know how she really felt about my lesbianism, and so I asked, cagily, how she would feel if her children were gay.

"I don't know," she said, "but I would feel a lot worse if they were alcoholics or did something to harm themselves or someone else. Why do you ask me this?"

"Because I can always tell what people really feel about homosexuals by their reaction to the possibility that their child might be one."

"So this is a test?"

"Yes, in a way it is."

"You know I love you, Claud."

And we left it at that.

We did not make love that weekend, but we may as well have. We were close in the ways we had always been—close physically, holding and being affectionate with each other, close emotionally, close out walking, close inside watching videos of her children. I read her poetry and she read my journals, because in our own ways each of us has held the need to write to be central to our well-being. And there was the tenderness we had always felt for each other, the softening, the gentleness of truly caring, of touching carefully, without any hint of distance or anger. There was the easiness and the hint of play.

In the night while she slept, I woke up and went to sit in the living room and thought, What the hell are you doing to yourself, stirring this whole thing up? Because I knew I was in trouble again, still, with this woman, and it made no sense in any logical way given the timing, given the constraints, given our pasts. But in my heart there were no barriers. There was a familiarity, a comfort, a sense of myself that bridged my youthful intensity and my middle-aged maturity. Do I really have anything to lose by caring for her? I wondered. Or am I doomed to repeat the mistakes of the past? Or is the mistake that we were ever separated in the first place?

But right now I was determined to maintain my position of noninvolvement. I sent her off with copies of my books and chapters, with admonitions about staying sober, with all my love and respect for her strength in finally coming to terms with her alcoholism. And I said, "It's important that you work it out with Phil. You care for him; you have children. Go back and make it work, and I'll still be in your life." I remembered my self-sacrificing gesture of years ago, telling her that I could not be her friend if she kept sleeping with the other woman, and thought it ironic. This time it wasn't a question of righteous self-sacrifice. This was the right thing to do. I knew better now. There were other lives involved, and I really wanted only what was best for her. I just loved her in that way.

When she left, we had no idea when we might see each other again. She had no idea whether she still had a marriage to work on, and I still had my own life to sort out, to put back on a track in which I could salvage it from the common trauma of living.

I watched her walk down the gateway to the plane and then stood staring out the window until long after the plane had taxied away. I thought I saw her waving from the window, but the face was indistinct and I told myself it was just my imagination. I couldn't bring myself to leave the airport. This is what it means to be human, I thought, to be so attached to someone that their going makes you weep. Finally I turned and went to my car, crying all the way home and for hours after I got back because the house was so silent and empty without her and I had rediscovered her and she was gone again. I thought it odd that, in some inexplicable way, I felt more bereft now than I had at the loss of Alice.

I made my way as best I could those first few months. I surrounded myself with people; I worked. I looked around me and I was fine, really, if lonely a great deal. I was like someone who'd fallen off a horse—I kept checking to see if I was in one piece.

I flew out to Santa Fe to help a friend uproot her life in middle age. We were like Thelma and Louise riding off to the Northwest. Our week's drive up through Colorado, Utah, and Oregon into Washington State and then to Seattle was healing, a metaphor for the journey inward that we both needed to make. I flew back from Seattle to take up my new life again, surprised that I could travel without Alice and enjoy it.

In the next weeks, letters and phone calls between Molly and me become a staple of each day. And so did frustration. I knew I wanted her again, but it seemed it wasn't to be. Was this the closure we would reach, I thought? A final ending, a final letting go, a final working ourselves into a friendship?

But over time, Phil made it clear that the marriage was over. And one day I heard myself blurt out to Molly on the phone, "If you want me, you can have me."

A letter came back.

> *Dear Claud,*
>
> *I'm sure that I want you. I'm sure that not having you would be devastating to me. I'm sure that I love you in the deepest sense of loving—and I need you so very much. I'm forty-five years old and I'm finally trying to be true to myself. My love for you has sustained me, the thought that someday I would see you again has always been present. And now that we have renewed a real, tangible relationship, the reality of you is ever so much stronger and compelling than the memory.*
>
> *This is full circle, Claud. All those loose ends. The suspension of desire and devotion, the unbearable absence of you in my life—give me permission to love you wholly, continually, in the real world, make this my real life. I do not want my love for you to stay harbored in my heart—I want it out of hiding. Loving you is a basic, primary need for me—like breathing and eating and sleeping. There will be no peace, no rest if there is no you.*

I thought, this time for different reasons, how true all those love songs on the radio were. Meant as they were for the straight of heart, they still somehow applied. Now there was Melissa Etheridge singing, "Yes I Am," capturing the essence of my passion for Molly. I determined that I was crazy and told myself and all my friends how crazy I was about her, as if my passion were suspect.

"I'm holding you, always," I wrote to her, "as much as one finite body can hold another one and as long as one infinite spirit can be connected to another. I'm holding you with a tenderness that is beyond all reason, with a passion that is overwhelming me. I am excited by the sound of your voice, by the sound of your name, by your telephone number, by your picture, by your handwriting, by the names of your children and the thought of you at your desk at work. I love who you are, I want who you are. I love you in some timeless way. You're with me all the time now."

The truth and the depth of these feelings were real, even if the mundane realities of the lives we construct betray them. Even if feelings, like life, have edges, and will change and transform themselves and sometimes die.

Sometimes what bothers me most about life is that it doesn't seem an adequate container for passion. There is never far enough to go, never enough that you can do with feeling. Maybe if I were more heroic, more ascetic, more involved in some cause, I would see this limitation differently. But it's just that when I've watched the beauty of something happen around me, when I've deeply loved someone, there's always been the frustration of feeling there was nowhere to go with it, not enough to do with it. Life doesn't seem big enough. So I just write it down.

And somehow I am aware, as I was even as the young girl meditating in the chapel asking questions about the inscrutable presence of god, that there is more than meets the eye here, that life really is a spiritual path, because it takes us to an awareness that there is simply more than we *can* know, than we can ever understand.

They say everything happens for a reason. I don't know about this. Do accidents happen for a reason? Is the timing of my reconnection with Molly just an interesting coincidence? Or was it somehow preordained? Have I worked on understanding addiction for twenty years only to be able to use my understanding to help my first lover overcome hers? Life is ironic if nothing else. And it is mysterious above all.

So here in middle age I am back where I started, still taking field notes on the landscape of love. What have I learned? That as imperfect as it may be, for all that it eludes us, love is all there is. Love for the turn of a phrase, love for a dark night sky, love for a strain of music, love for one person, many, all people, for friends, for one woman, for nieces and sisters and parents, love for the process of it all, even for the pain. Love for the name of a wildflower. It's all stronger than hate. There is no weakness in love. It's all wildness and it shimmers with light.

Mysteries of the Sea

Mysteries *of* the Sea

How Divers Explore the Ocean Depths

By Marianne Morrison

NATIONAL GEOGRAPHIC

Washington D.C.

One of the world's largest nonprofit scientific and educational organizations, the National Geographic Society was founded in 1888 "for the increase and diffusion of geographic knowledge." Fulfilling this mission, the Society educates and inspires millions every day through its magazines, books, television programs, videos, maps and atlases, research grants, the National Geographic Bee, teacher workshops, and innovative classroom materials. The Society is supported through membership dues, charitable gifts, and income from the sale of its educational products. This support is vital to National Geographic's mission to increase global understanding and promote conservation of our planet through exploration, research, and education.

For more information, please call
1-800-NGS-LINE (647-5463) or write to the following address:
National Geographic Society
1145 17th Street N.W.
Washington, D.C. 20036-4688
U.S.A.

For information about special discounts for bulk purchases, please contact
National Geographic Books Special Sales at ngspecsales@ngs.org

Visit the Society's Web site: www.nationalgeographic.com

Text revised from *Divers of the Deep Sea* in the National Geographic Windows on Literacy program from National Geographic School Publishing, © 2002 National Geographic Society

Published by National Geographic Society.
Washington, D.C. 20036

Design by Project Design Company

Printed in the United States

Library of Congress Cataloging-in-Publication Data

Morrison, Marianne.
Mysteries of the sea : how divers explore the ocean depths / by Marianne Morrison.
p. cm. -- (National Geographic science chapters)
Includes bibliographical references and index.
ISBN-13: 978-0-7922-5954-1 (library binding)
ISBN-10: 0-7922-5954-8 (library binding)
1. Underwater exploration. 2. Deep diving. I. Title. II. Series.
GC65.M65 2006
551.46--dc22

2006016323

Photo Credits

Front Cover: © Darryl Torckler/ Stone/ Getty Images; Spine: © Georgette Douwma/ Digital Vision/ Getty Images; Endpaper: © Georgette Douwma/ Digital Vision/ Getty Images; 2-3: © Emory Kristof/ National Geographic Image Collection; 6: © Getty Images; 10: © Naval Historical Foundation; 13 (bottom): © Hulton Archive/ Getty Images; 14: © Bates Littlhales/ National Geographic Image Collection; 15: © Luis Marden/ National Geographic Image Collection; 16: © NOAA; 17: © Darlyne Murowski/ National Geographic Image Collection; 18-19, 19 (bottom): © NOAA; 21 (top): © Al Giddings Images; 21 (bottom): © Wolcott Henry/ National Geographic Image Collection; 22: © Wildlife Conservation Society; 24: © William Beebe/ National Geographic Image Collection; 25: © Peter David/ Taxi/ Getty Images; 26: © Getty Images; 28, 29, 30: © NOAA; 31: © Ralph White/ Corbis; 33 (top): © Woods Hole Institute; 33 (left): Emory Kristof/ National Geographic Image Collection; 33 (right): © APL/ Corbis; 8-9: Illustrations by Levent Efe, CMI; All Other Illustrations by Dimitrios Prokopis.

Contents

ittle about many
mazing creatures
ve beneath the sea.

The Oceans

People have explored most of the land on Earth. They've climbed the highest mountains, hiked the deepest forests, and traveled to both Poles. But if you think we've explored most of Earth, think again.

Earth is covered by about three times more water than land. And most of that water has never been explored. We know a lot about the surface, or top, of the ocean. But what lies below the surface?

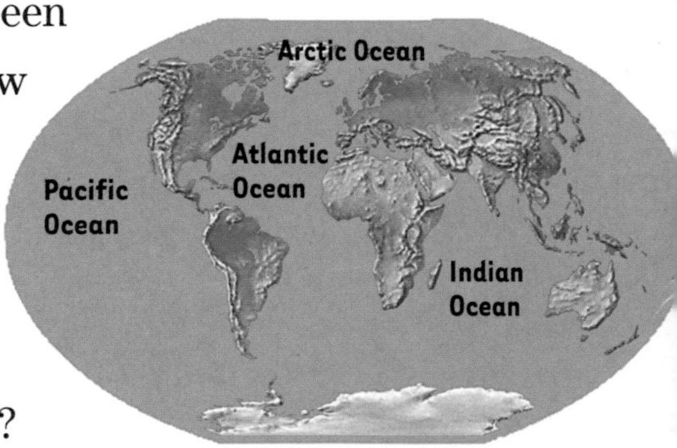

The Four Zones of the Ocean

The ocean is divided into four zones. The amount of light and the depth of the water change from zone to zone.

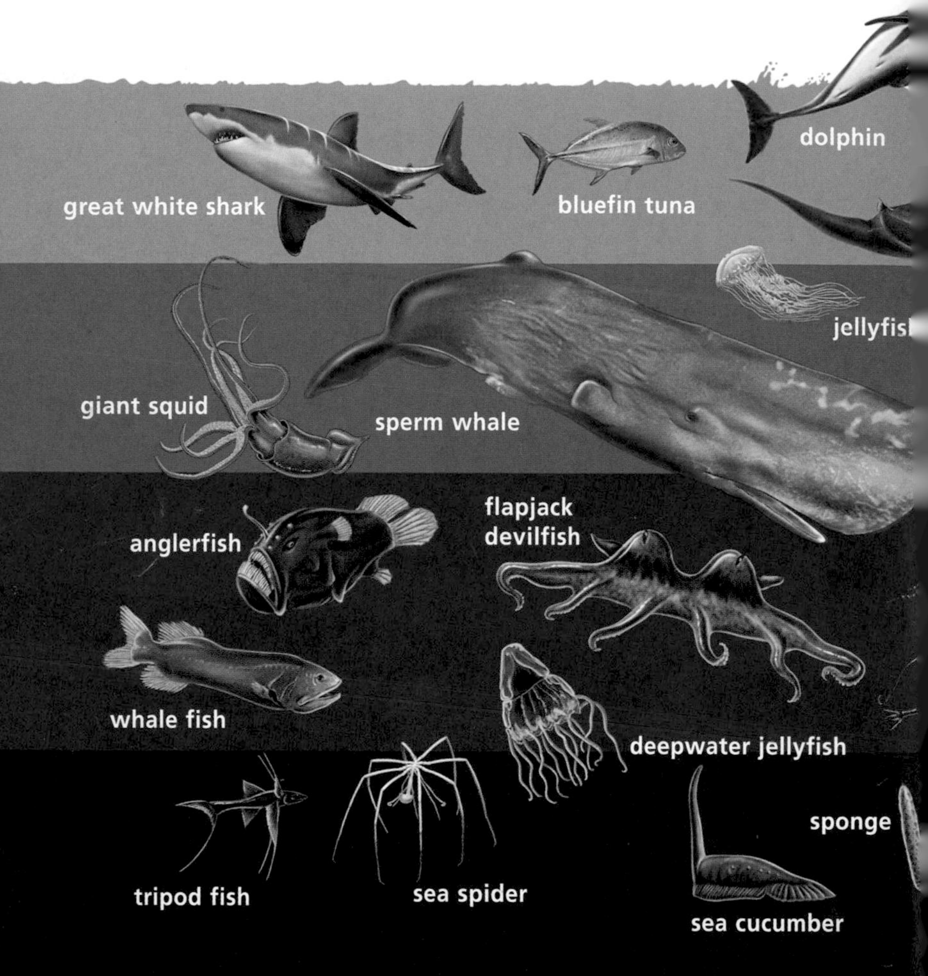

Note: Creatures and zones are not drawn to scale.

The Sunlight Zone is near the ocean's surface. It receives the most light and has the most plants and animals.

In the Twilight Zone, the light is very dim. At this depth, it is darker and colder. There are not as many plants and animals.

siphonophore

In the Midnight Zone, there is no light. It is completely dark and very cold. Strange creatures live at this depth.

gulper eel

angler shrimp
larvae

The Trench Zone is the deepest part of the ocean. The deepest part of this zone is almost 7 miles (11 km) deep.

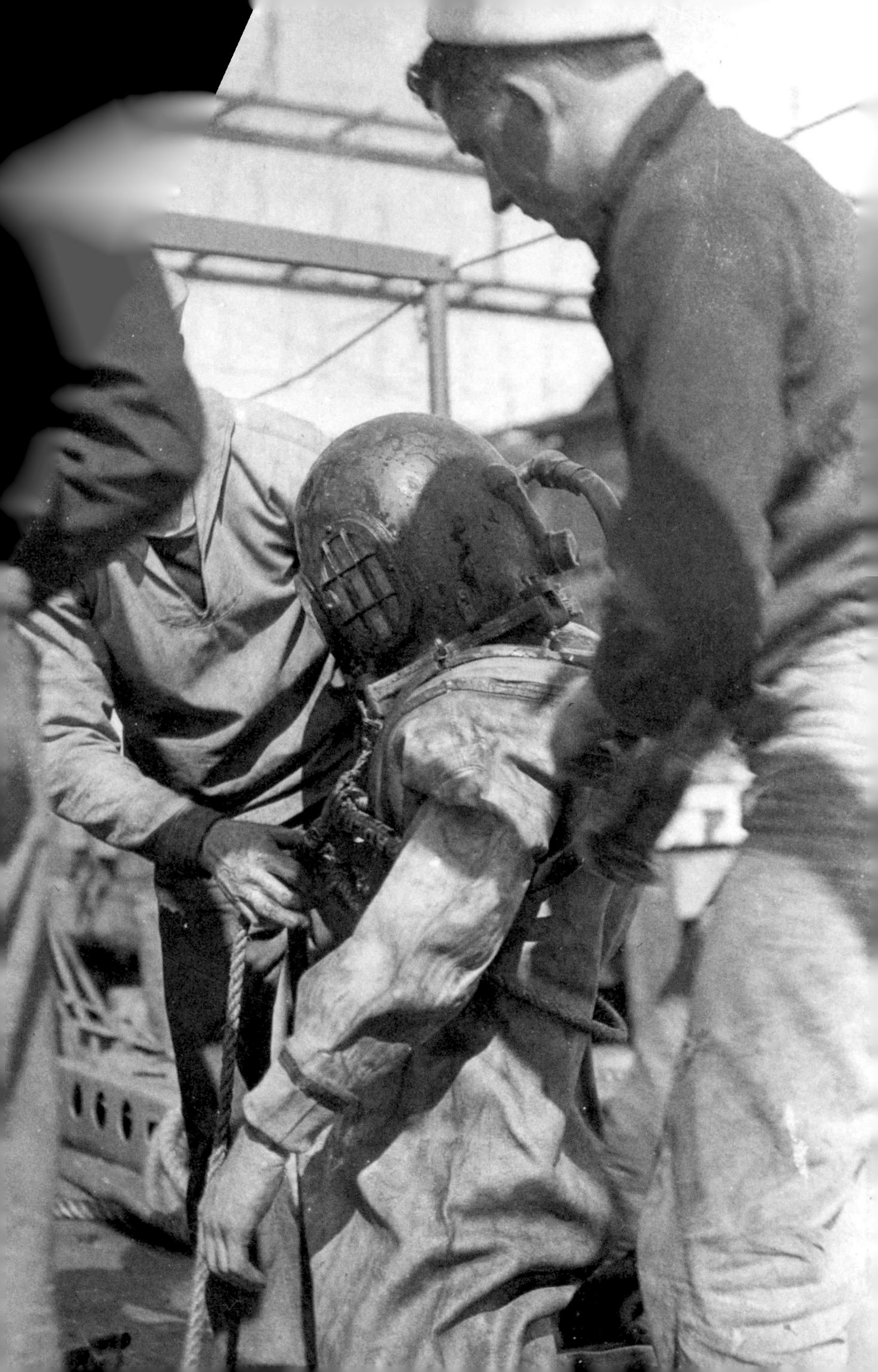

Chapter 1

Divers Go Deeper

The Diving Helmet

People have always wanted to explore below the surface of the ocean. The earliest divers held their breath and went as deep as they could go before needing more air. That wasn't very deep.

Then the diving helmet was invented in 1839. It was copper and very heavy. The helmet was attached to a heavy diving suit. An air hose from the surface brought air to the diver. A diver could go 230 feet (70 m) below the surface wearing a diving helmet.

A Navy diver suits up for a dive in 1914.

Beneath the Sea

-gean Sea, off the coast of Greece
May 1869

-kes 30 minutes for the diver to put . his diving gear. The heavy helmet is finally bolted to his suit. The air hose is attached. Weights are put on his chest and his back. His boots also have lead weights on the bottoms.

The diver is helped into the water. The weights help him sink. Air pumps into his helmet as he goes down.

He looks through the faceplate in his helmet. A parrotfish swims up to get a better look at him. A school of squid seems to hang in the water.

Finally, he is 230 feet (70 m) below the surface. A ray rises from the sandy bottom. The diver starts to walk slowly towards the rocky ledge where sponges grow. He begins to collect the sponges that he will sell.

◀ Divers collect sponges like these from the ocean floor.

▼ A diver wearing a diving helmet and heavy suit prepares to dive.

Aqua-Lung

Divers could go deeper with the diving helmet, but it did not allow them to move around freely. They dreamed of swimming like fish. In 1943, Jacques Cousteau made this dream come true. He invented the Aqua-Lung. This tank allowed the diver to breathe air and move about freely underwater. It was the start of scuba diving. Scuba stands for "self-contained underwater breathing apparatus."

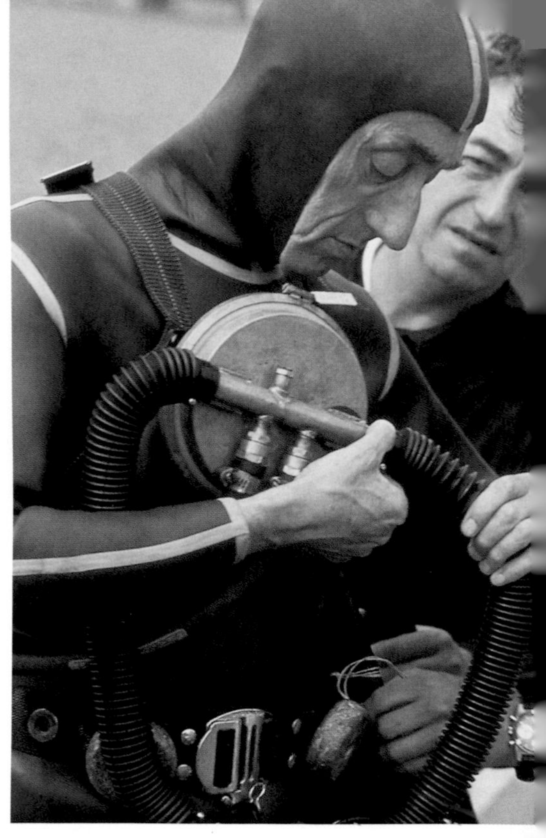

Jacques Cousteau prepares to dive. Divers have gone as deep as 210 feet (64 m) using the Aqua-Lung.

Beneath the Sea

Diver: **Jacques Cousteau**
Place: **Mediterranean Sea, off the coast of France**
Date: **June 1943**

Cousteau straps the heavy tanks of air on his back. He puts on his diving mask and fins. With 50 pounds (23 kg) on his back, he waddles into the sea.

He looks down and sees a canyon far below. He kicks his fins and starts down. He glides through the water like a fish. Then he lets the air out of his lungs. He watches the bubbles rise. Next he takes a deep breath. It works! He can breathe underwater.

Cousteau's dream has come true. He can swim freely. There are no ropes, hoses, or heavy helmet to slow him down. He rolls over. He does a somersault. He even stands upside down on one finger.

Using the Aqua-Lung enables a diver to swim with the fishes.

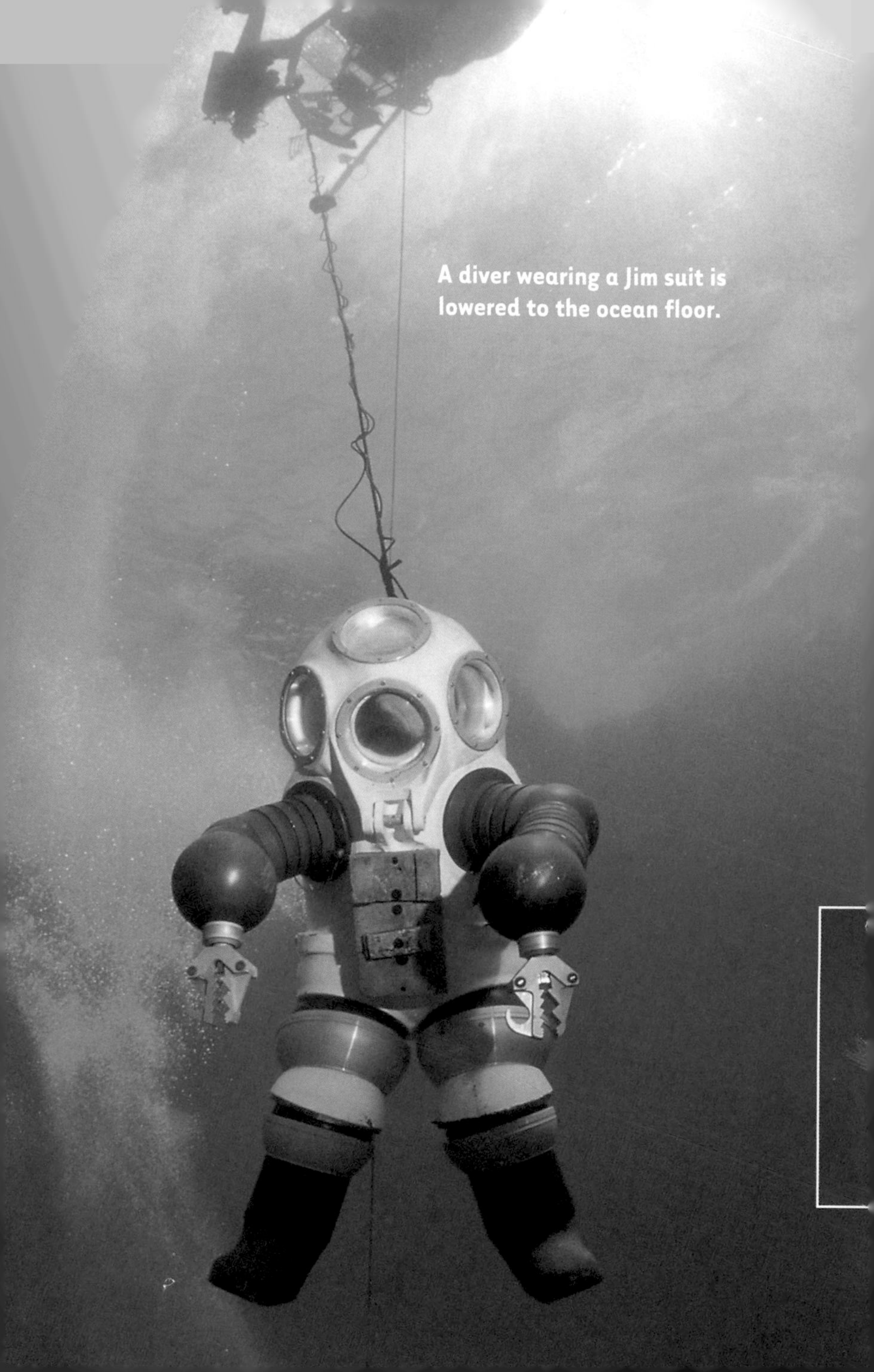

A diver wearing a Jim suit is lowered to the ocean floor.

The Jim Suit

Divers wanted to go much deeper a
be able to move around freely. This was
problem. The deeper you go, the colder it
gets. You start to feel as if you are being crushed because of water pressure. Water pressure is the weight of water. The more water above you, the more weight presses on you.

The Jim suit was invented to let divers roam freely in very deep water. It is named for the first man who used it, Jim Jarratt. The Jim suit is a heavy metal suit. It looks like a spacesuit. It protects the diver from the cold and the water pressure.

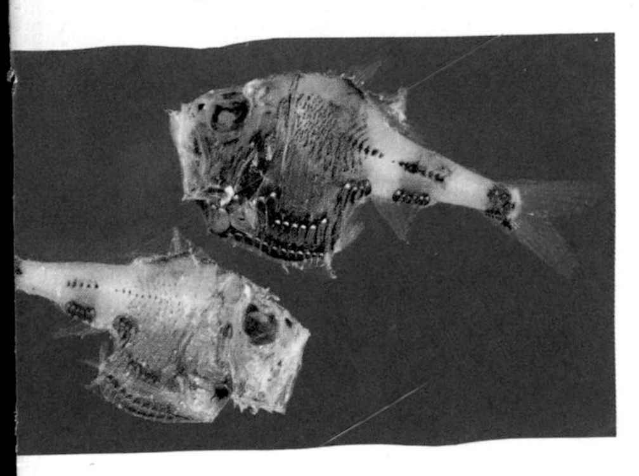

Odd fish, such as these hatchetfish, live deep within the ocean.

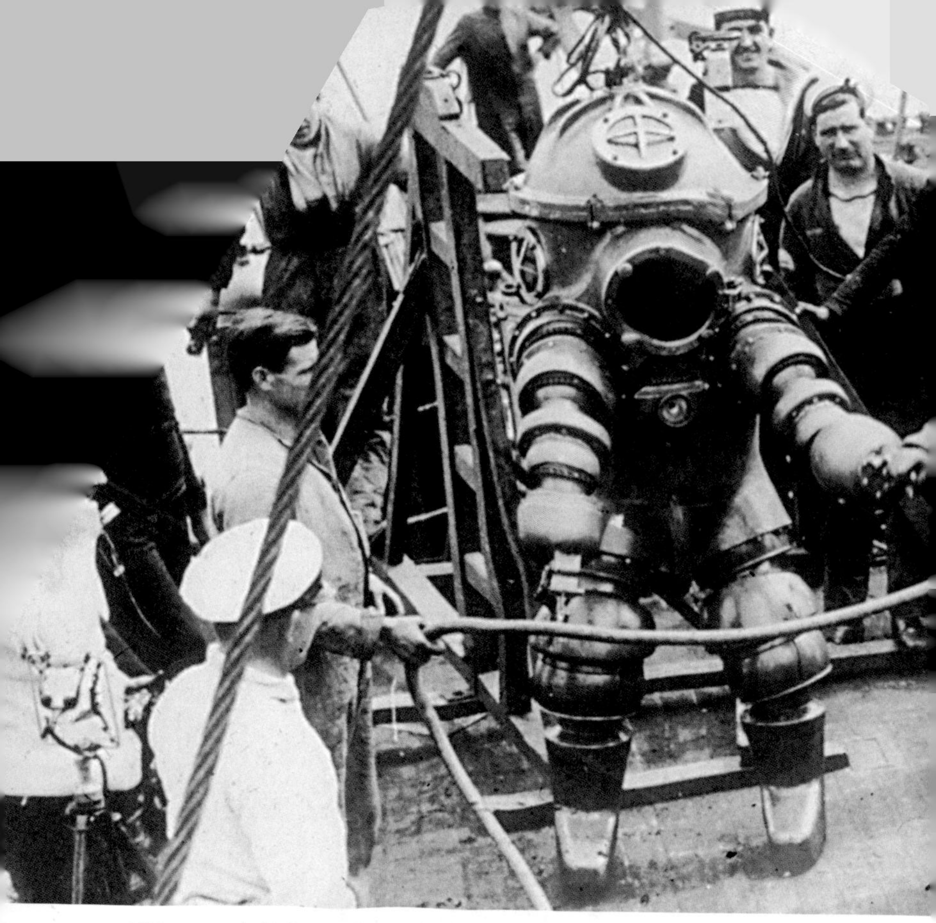

This metal diving suit was used in 1937 to explore a shipwreck. Its use led to the creation of the Jim suit.

Attached to the Jim suit's arms are two metal claws for lifting things. Inside, the diver can breathe air that is cleaned and recycled. For most dives in the Jim suit, the diver is lowered on a rope from the surface.

Some Jim suits have thrusters that help the diver move around.

Beneath the Sea

Diver: **Sylvia Earle**
Place: **Pacific Ocean, off the coast of Hawaii**
Date: **October 19, 1979**

Everything around her is blue as she begins her dive. Earle is strapped to a small submarine. As she goes deeper, the water changes from blue to gray and finally black. She feels a soft thump as the submarine touches the bottom.

Finally, they stop at 1,250 feet (381 m). The pilot releases the strap holding her onto the submarine. She is free to explore the deep.

A small circle of light from the sub shows an amazing and wonderful world. A dozen bright red crabs with long legs sway on a red sea fan. A lantern fish swims by with lights glowing on its side. Earle looks away from the light and sees sparks of living light. Tiny fish light up as they brush against her. She explores strange coral that glows in the dark.

After two and a half hours on the ocean floor, Earle heads back to the surface.

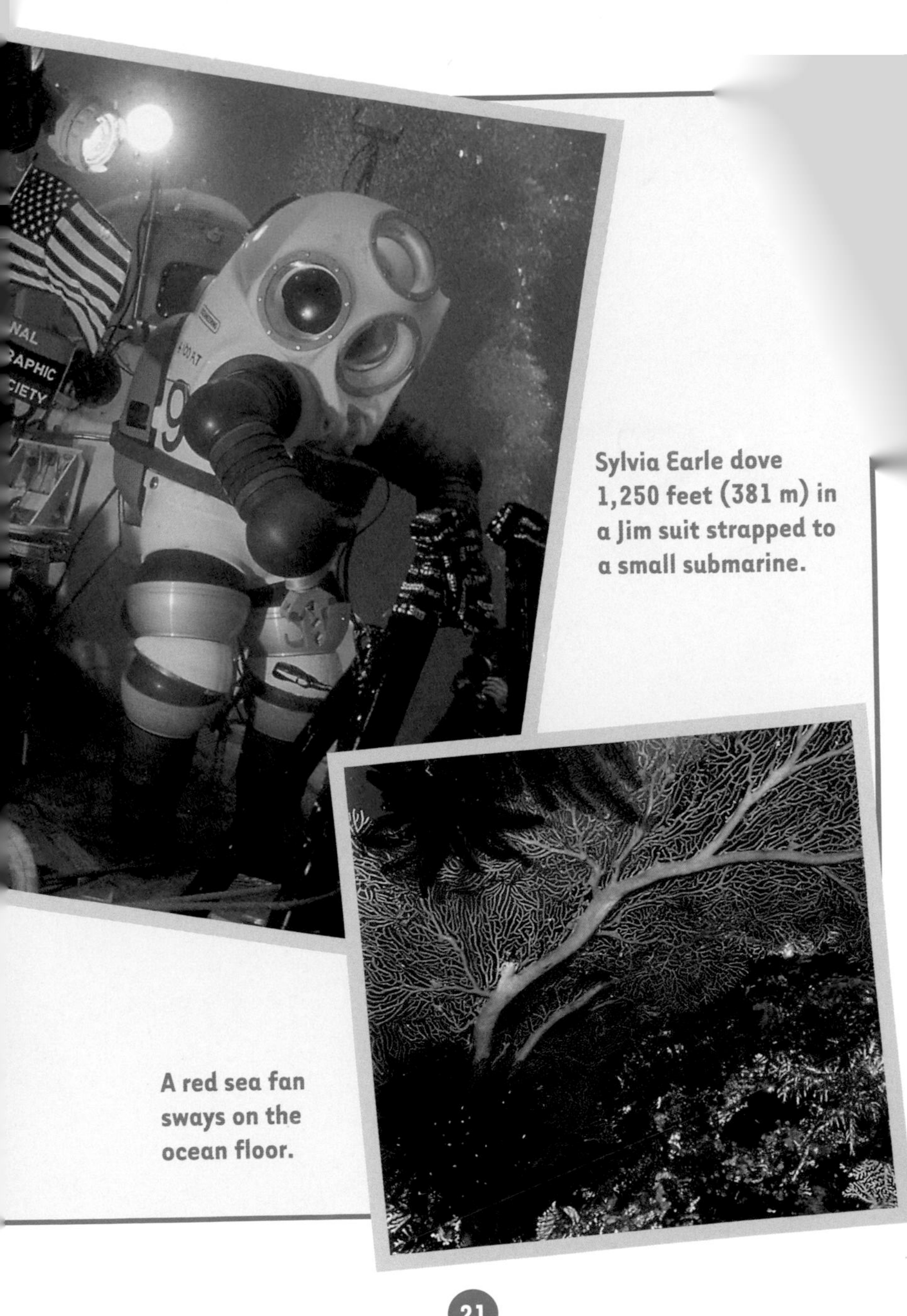

Sylvia Earle dove 1,250 feet (381 m) in a Jim suit strapped to a small submarine.

A red sea fan sways on the ocean floor.

m Beebe sits on
of his invention,
bathysphere.

Chapter 2

Diving Ships Go Deeper

The Bathysphere

Parts of the ocean are almost 7 miles (11 km) deep. People needed to invent diving ships in order to dive that deep. To make these deep dives possible, William Beebe and Otis Barton invented the bathysphere.

This strange round chamber on a wire cable was like an elevator to the deep. It could go up and down, but it couldn't move sideways. The bathysphere looked like a giant eye. The divers inside recorded every animal that passed before its round window, or porthole.

Barton were the first to enter
. the ocean where there is no light
ıy the light from a small bulb inside
ɪhysphere helped them see the
zing things of the Midnight Zone.

William Beebe and Otis Barton dove 3,028 feet (924 m) in the bathysphere.

Beneath the Sea

Diver: **William Beebe and Otis Barton**
Place: **Atlantic Ocean, off the coast of Bermuda**
Date: **August 15, 1934**

Beebe squeezes head first through the small opening to get inside. Once inside he makes room for Barton. There's not much room. They untangle their legs and get ready. Then the heavy door is bolted shut.

They begin to go down. The deeper they go, the darker it gets. It also gets colder, much colder. Then they start to see the strange creatures of the deep. An anglerfish swims by. As they go deeper, several hatchetfish swim through the beam of light from their little light bulb.

Finally, they enter the Midnight Zone of the ocean. This is a world of complete and total darkness. They reach a depth of 3,028 feet (924 m). They stay there for only three minutes. They have just enough air for the trip to the surface.

Anglerfish live in the Midnight Zone.

...e Bathyscaph

To help divers go even deeper, a diving ship called a bathyscaph was invented. It could move up and down but could not move around easily.

In 1960, Jacques Piccard and Don Walsh used a bathyscaph named the *Trieste* to dive almost 7 miles (11 km) down. They explored the Trench Zone, the deepest known part of the ocean.

No person has ever returned to this depth. These two men still hold the record for the deepest dive.

Jacques Piccard and Don Walsh dove to the bottom of the ocean in the *Trieste.*

Beneath the Sea

Diver: **Jacques Piccard and Don Walsh**
Place: **Pacific Ocean, off the coast of Guam**
Date: **January 23, 1960**

Huge waves pound the *Trieste* as Piccard and Walsh climb on board. Then, at 8:23 in the morning, they begin their dive. Three hours later they are 27,000 feet (8,235 m) deep and still going down. They go deeper and deeper.

As they near the bottom, fear comes over them. What if the ocean bottom is a thick ooze? The ship could get stuck. No one could save them. They would freeze to death in this cold, black world.

Finally, they reach the bottom. They do not get stuck. They are 35,800 feet (10,919 m) deep. This is almost 7 miles (11 km) down. Piccard looks out. He sees a flatfish with two round eyes swimming away. Life exists this deep!

They spend only 20 minutes on the bottom before they begin to go up. After more than eight and half hours, the dive is over. They reach the surface again.

...les

...ubmersible is like a small submarine. ...e in the water, a submersible can move ...ound. It also has lights that help divers see underwater. An explorer can stay underwater in it for about ten hours.

Today, divers use many different machines to explore the deep. Some submersibles have robots attached to them. The crew inside the submersible can send the robot into small places to take pictures.

A moray eel swims next to a reef.

Submersibles like this one allow divers to explore underwater for long periods of time.

In 1986, Robert Ballard led a team to explore the *Titanic*. This famous ship sank in 1912 and was over 2 miles (3 km) deep when found. Ballard went down in the submersible named *Alvin*. Attached to *Alvin* was the robot named *Jason Junior*, or *JJ*.

This submersible named *Alvin* dove 12,460 feet (3,800 m) to explore the *Titanic.*

A robotic arm retrieves a leaded glass window from the shipwrecked *Titanic.*

Beneath the Sea

ver: Robert Ballard
Place: Atlantic Ocean, off the coast of Newfoundland
Date: July 1, 1986

It takes more than two hours to get down to the *Titanic*. This is the third dive to the *Titanic* in the little submersible *Alvin*. But this is the first time Ballard and his team will use the robot *JJ* to explore the inside of the ship.

They reach the deck of the ship. Slowly they steer *Alvin* inside. They go down the main staircase of the ship. Then they park *Alvin* and send *JJ* out into the ship. They guide the robot down into the ship. They see the grand clock on the landing of the staircase. Then they see a beautiful light hanging from the ceiling by its cord.

The team makes ten more dives after this one. They see an amazing collection of things from the ship. They see the dinner plates, beds, sinks, bathtubs, doorknobs, and windows that were once part of this great ship. They are the first explorers to find and explore this famous sunken ship.

explores parts of the *Titanic* that *Alvin* can't reach.

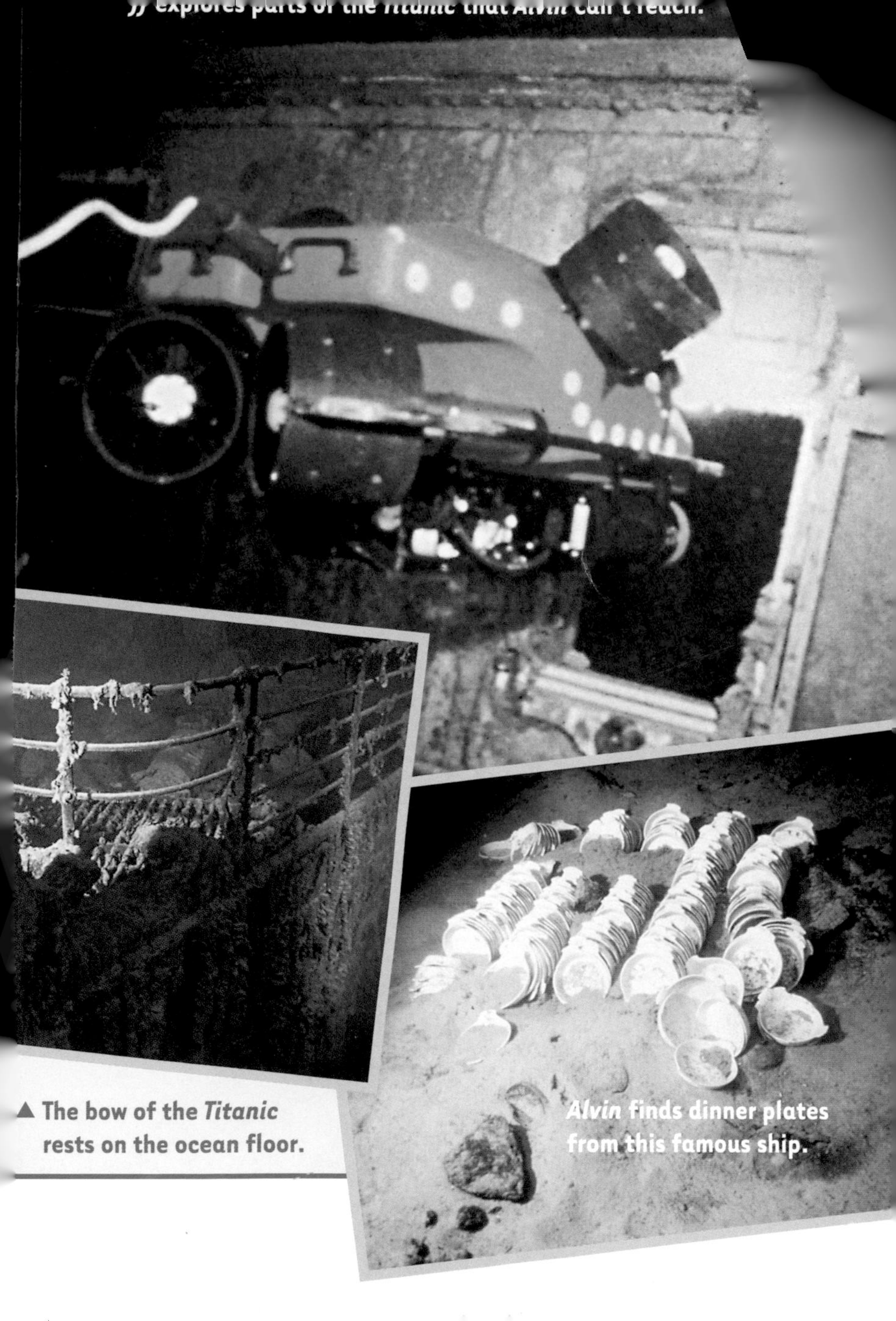

▲ The bow of the *Titanic* rests on the ocean floor.

Alvin finds dinner plates from this famous ship.

A History of Deep Sea Dives

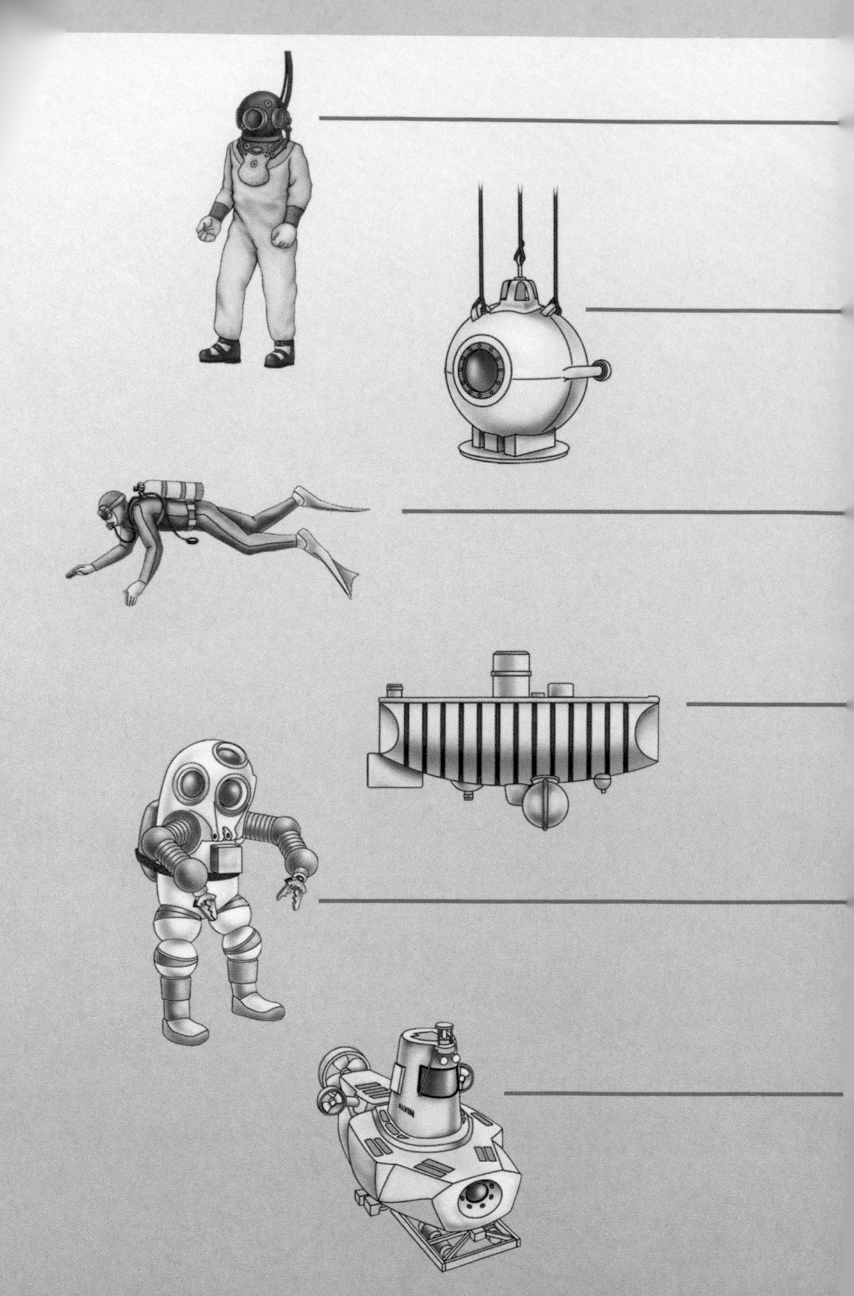

Diving Helmet:
230 feet (70 m). Augustus Siebe invented the closed diving helmet in 1839.

Bathysphere:
3,028 feet (924 m). William Beebe and Otis Barton reach the Midnight Zone in 1934.

Aqua-Lung:
210 feet (64 m). Jacques Cousteau makes the first dive with an Aqua-Lung in 1943.

Bathyscaph:
35,800 feet (10,919 m). Jacques Piccard and Don Walsh reach ocean bottom in 1960.

Jim Suit:
1,250 feet (381 m). Sylvia Earle completes the deepest solo dive in a Jim suit in 1979.

Submersible:
12,460 feet (3,800 m). Robert Ballard explores the *Titanic* using *Alvin* in 1986.

How to Write an A+ Report

1. Choose a topic.

- Find something that interests you.
- Make sure it is not too big or too small.

2. Find sources.

- Ask your librarian for help.
- Use many different sources: books, magazine articles, and websites.

3. Gather information.

- Take notes. Write down the big ideas and interesting details.
- Use your own words.

4. Organize information.

- Sort your notes into groups that make sense.

- Make an outline. Put your groups of notes in the order you want to write your report.

5. Write your report.

- Write an introduction that tells what the report is about.
- Use your outline and notes as you write to make sure you say everything you want to say in the order you want to say it.
- Write an ending that tells about your report.
- Write a title.

6. Revise and edit your report.

- Read your report to make sure it makes sense.
- Read it again to check spelling, punctuation, and grammar.

7. Hand in your report!

Glossary

Aqua-Lung	an underwater breathing machine that enables a diver to swim freely
bathyscaph	a diving ship designed for deep-sea exploration
bathysphere	a round diving ship that could only go straight up and down
depth	how deep something is in the water
diving helmet	copper helmet with an air hose that brings fresh air from the surface to the diver
Jim suit	self-contained, deep water diving suit for a single diver
recycled	to be reused
submersible	a small underwater craft used for deep-sea research
water pressure	the weight of water

Further Reading

• Books •

Earle, Sylvia A. *Dive! My Adventures in the Deep Frontier.* Washington, DC: National Geographic Society, 1999. Ages 9-12, 64 pages.

Earle, Sylvia A. *National Geographic Atlas of the Ocean: The Deep Frontier.* Washington, DC: National Geographic Society, 2001. Adult, 192 pages.

Matsen, Brad. *The Incredible Record Setting Deep-Sea Dive of the Bathysphere.* Berkeley Heights, NJ: Enslow Publishers, 2004. Ages 10-14, 48 pages.

Matsen, Brad. *The Incredible Quest to Find the Titanic.* Berkeley Heights, NJ: Enslow Publishers, 2003. Ages 10-14, 48 pages.

Submarine (Eyewitness Books). New York, NY: DK Children, 2003. Ages 9-12, 64 pages.

• Websites •

British Broadcasting Company
http://www.bbc.co.uk/nature/blueplanet/blue/master.shtml

The Jason Project
http://www.jasonproject.org/

National Geographic Society
http://www.nationalgeographic.com/seas/

Public Broadcasting System
http://www.pbs.org/wgbh/nova/abyss/

Science News for Kids
http://www.sciencenewsforkids.org/articles/20041110/Feature1.asp

University of Delaware: Mission to the Abyss
http://www.ocean.udel.edu/extreme2002/

Woods Hole Oceanographic Institution
http://www.whoi.edu/k-12/

Index